5/11

"You're cut from the same cloth as your brother—selfish to the core!"

He felt her accusation as keenly as a knife to the chest. Leaning his face close to hers, he whispered, "Rest assured I am nothing like my brother. I would have no problem consummating my marriage. More specifically, I would have no problem bedding you."

If possible, her eyes grew even bigger, green saucers in her pale face. She went as still as stone beneath him. "How do you know Edmund never consummated our marriage?"

He ignored the question, but instead ran a finger along her jaw and down the column of her throat. Her breathing hitched, and he stopped at the throbbing pulse on the side of her neck. "It's an easy enough matter to prove. Maybe that's what you need, hmm? A man in your bed to rob you of your rebelliousness? You could use a little taming."

SOPHIE JORDAN

Once Upon A Wedding Night

AVON BOOKS

An Imprint of HarperCollinsPublishers

This is a work of fiction. Names, characters, places, and incidents are products of the author's imagination or are used fictitiously and are not to be construed as real. Any resemblance to actual events, locales, organizations, or persons, living or dead, is entirely coincidental.

AVON BOOKS
An Imprint of HarperCollins*Publishers*
10 East 53rd Street
New York, New York 10022-5299

Printed in the U.S.A.

For my parents,
Eugene and Marilyn Michels—
Dad, for showing me
what it means to persevere.
Mom, for instilling your love of books
in me at an early age.
I love you both.

And for Jared—
You're the inspiration
behind every hero I dream up.

Acknowledgments

Many thanks to those who read and critiqued this book in its various and dubious stages: Tera, Leslie, Ane, and Christy. Tera, your savvy (or second sight?) helped get me here; Leslie, you made sure my scenes had the requisite "sizzle"—this book wouldn't be what it is without the "cabinettes." And thank you to Ane, my first writing friend, your enthusiasm feeds my soul. Thank you, Carlye, for being so mule-headed. You never stopped nagging me to write and sell a book—even when I begged you to. Thank you to my mother-in-law, Rosanne, for countless hours of baby-sitting. To my fellow writers at West Houston Romance Writers of America, thank you for your support and encouragement. Not so long ago, I walked through your doors a stranger, having no idea I would find a haven among you. And thank you to my agent, Maura Kye-Casella, who called at precisely the right time in my life and said all the things I most needed to hear, and to my editor, May Chen, for believing in this book.

Chapter 1

Oh what a tangled web we weave,
When we first practise to deceive.

Sir Walter Scott, "Marmion"

England, 1835

"**I**t cannot be true." Lady Meredith Brookshire paced her drawing room, fisting the missive only just delivered into a crumpled ball.

"Might I see the letter?" her aunt asked, flicking her wrist in the air impatiently. "Before it is destroyed?"

Meredith blinked at the ball of parchment in

her hand and quickly passed it to her aunt as if it were a deadly serpent. It might as well have been for the death knell it rang in her heart.

They had found him. The *new* Lord Brookshire. The missive did not indicate where they had located him, but he would surely descend upon them soon. Like a vulture scenting its next meal.

So much for the solicitors' assurances that he was dead, she mused wryly. Despite those assurances, they had put forth a search for him anyway. Blasted solicitors. Must they follow the letter of the law precisely?

Her aunt smoothed the crinkles out of the parchment, her expression growing perplexed as she scanned the message. "But, dearest, isn't he dead?"

Meredith continued to pace, rubbing the base of her palm against her forehead to ward off her impending headache. "Unless a ghost is about to descend upon us, Nicholas Caulfield is alive and well and intends to claim his inheritance." She halted her pacing steps as the ugly significance of Nicholas Caulfield's pending arrival washed over her. Ruin. Destitution. Doom settled like a heavy stone in her chest.

Surely he would rid the premises of his half brother's widow and her few clinging relatives. Then what? They had no other family to take them in. And Edmund had not provided for her beyond his death. Not that she would have expected him to for all the care and thought he extended her over the years. Still, she had not anticipated her husband expiring so young. He had only been thirty-five, and robust by all appearances, rare though the sight of him might have been.

Her hands balled into fists at her sides. "Blast Edmund! Do not husbands set up jointures for their wives?"

"Do not curse, dearest, and do not speak ill of the dead," Aunt Eleanor reproved with a chiding tsk. "Especially since he no doubt suffers in the throes of hell as we speak."

A smile tugged her lips at her aunt's uncharacteristic spite. Aunt Eleanor's nostrils quivered with disdain. "After all he put you through, the Almighty is not going to take a kindly view of him as he stands at Judgment."

"He did not put me through anything." The lie tripped off Meredith's tongue with practiced ease. "He wasn't cruel or abusive. He was just—" She paused, groping for the appropriate word. Arriving at it, she shrugged and uttered, "—absent."

"For seven years," Aunt Eleanor reminded hotly, her indignation on Meredith's behalf both familiar and tedious.

"I was quite content with the arrangement." Again, the fib fell smoothly. *Content?* Lonely was more accurate. "Many wives would appreciate being rid of their husband's oppressive yoke."

"Well, then he has put *me* through much suffering. Look at these dreadful frocks. I hate to speak uncharitably of the dead, even his rotten soul, but he's getting the last word if we wear these ghastly gowns." Aunt Eleanor plucked at the heavily starched black paramatta of her mourning dress. "I cannot wear black for an entire year. *And certainly not for him.* I haven't a turban to match."

Meredith looked down at her dress and frowned. Her aunt was correct. Nothing could complement such atrocious gowns, matching turban or no.

Aunt Eleanor's gaze slid over her in distaste. "You look like a ghost. Completely washed out."

Meredith sighed and touched her cheek wistfully, knowing—with exception of a spattering of unfortunate freckles—her skin was white as milk. A black gown had little to do with her resembling a ghost.

"We're not in Town. This is Attingham," Aunt Eleanor continued. "Who will comment if we only mourn for, say . . . three months?" She shrugged one thin shoulder. "Everyone knew you had a disagreeable marriage. No one would blame us for the slight breach."

"My marriage was perfectly agreeable." Meredith leveled a stern look on her aunt, annoyed by her allegation that *everyone knew.* If everyone knew, it was because her aunt's complaints had reached all of Attingham.

"Posh! He embarrassingly neglected you."

"Only *you* were embarrassed," Meredith reminded with the stoic facade she had mastered over the years. On certain days she could almost convince herself that the years of neglect did not bother her—days her aunt usually wasn't around.

"Appalling. The way he left you, simply appalling," Aunt Eleanor forged ahead with the mercilessness of a battering ram. "Not what the earl had in mind, I warrant. Perhaps it's best the old gent did not live to see his son abandon you."

"Well, the earl will no doubt get the heirs he always wanted." Meredith sank down on the settee, arms falling limply at her sides. "Only from the wrong son."

"You should have borne those heirs. If Edmund had been any kind of husband, you would have a dozen babes by now. Not to have even consummated—"

"Please." Meredith lifted a hand to ward off the rest of her aunt's words. Some memories were too bitter to speak aloud. The night her husband had refused to consummate their marriage and walked out on her was one such memory.

"And now we will lose Oak Run to this . . . *man*, when it has been you caring for everything." Aunt Eleanor counted off on her fingers. "You've managed the house, the servants, the tenants, the dairy, the harvesting—"

"I know, I know," Meredith broke in, hot tears stinging the backs of her eyes. "I can do without the reminder." She blinked fiercely, refusing to succumb to the tears bubbling just beneath the surface. Ever since she had learned that Nicholas Caulfield was alive and stood to inherit everything, she had clung to a glasslike facade of calm. One more stone thrown would send her fragile world crashing down.

Oak Run had become the home of her heart. She'd made it so. From refurbishing to landscaping, the Elizabethan manor house had thrived under her care. She could not lose it. Not without a fight. Besides, she had more than herself to consider. She had her aunt and father to care for. And Maree and Nels. They needed her to be strong, to look out for them, to fight for their home.

"I will not lose Oak Run," she vowed, crossing her arms to hug herself. "There has to be a way."

"Well, you best discover it soon," Aunt Eleanor grumbled, adding the burden of her fate to Meredith's shoulders without the slightest compunction—as she always had. "We do not even have the vicarage to return to."

Meredith sighed, feeling the beginnings of that headache.

Her aunt rose from the tapestry floral chaise, her slender form as elegant as a painter's brushstroke as she strolled nonchalantly to the gilded mantel. Quick as a wink, she snatched one of several crystal figurines crowding the mantel and pocketed the costly trinket.

"Aunt!" Meredith's admonishment was strangled on a laugh.

Aunt Eleanor widened her eyes in mock innocence. "We must look to ourselves now, musn't we, dearest?"

Trust her aunt to always cheer her. She had been the one, after all, to comfort Meredith when she awoke in her cold marriage bed, Edmund's cutting words ringing in her ears. At the time such crushing rejection did not seem surmountable. That an earl's son actually wanted to marry *her* seemed the makings of a dream. Deceptive logic led her to believe that Edmund wanted her, for why else would he marry the vicar's frumpy daughter?

Her mind touched upon her wedding night and shied away from the memory—a bleeding wound that could never be staunched. She was no longer a dewy-eyed eighteen. She was mature, wiser, no longer expecting a knight in shining armor to save her.

Experience had taught her the world was a hard place. Only the circumstances of men kept her living in luxury one moment and indigent the next. Never again would she rely on a man for rescue. Never again would she believe love could be so easy, or at least so easy for her. So what if her heart had turned into a hard little stone. A heart of stone could never break.

But it could feel fear.

Like the fear of finding herself at the mercy of a stranger. Her fate lay in the hands of a man who would probably cast her out without a penny. They weren't blood relations, after all. Nicholas Caulfield owed nothing to her.

If she had just herself to look after, Meredith could acquire employment as a governess or lady's companion. There were, however, others to consider.

Her father, bless him, was a growing burden, scaring the household staff with his unsuitable behavior. Yesterday he had attacked the upstairs maid while she changed the linens in his room. He ranted that she was a Spanish spy come to poison him. Her father's lifelong love of history fed his dementia. He periodically believed himself in the sixteenth century with Papist spies about bent on assassinating Queen Elizabeth. The new earl would want to rid himself of such a blight. No one wanted a half-mad old man skulking about the place. Many of the staff had quit since her father had become so unstable. Only the most stalwart remained, like Maree and Nels. Formerly members of a traveling show, they could not be considered standard household servants. They relied on her, needed her.

Despair, acrid as vinegar, rose up to choke her. If only she could have inherited. If only she could have given birth to Edmund's heir. Then all would be secure. If only . . .

Meredith stopped and gave a small shake of her head. She had always wanted a child, but never before had the lack of one carried such significance. She joined her aunt before the mantel. Propping her elbow on the gilded surface, she mused aloud. "Too bad I couldn't have given birth to that heir."

Her aunt turned and surveyed her through shrewd, narrowed eyes. Meredith's nape prickled. Removing the crystal from her pocket, Aunt Eleanor carefully set it back on the mantel, gave it a gentle pat, and asked with deceptive calm, "When was that letter dated?"

"Why?"

"Merely curious," she mused, tapping her lip. "How much time do I have to spread the joyous news that my niece is carrying the late earl's child before Nicholas Caulfield arrives?"

A long moment passed before Meredith spoke. When she did, her words were slow and pained, as though trying to make sense to a dim-witted child. "That is not possible. I have not seen Edmund in years. And the two of us never . . . grew acquainted." Her cheeks warmed at discussing such a delicate subject with her aunt. "Not as a husband and wife should."

"I am aware of that. But no one else is."

Meredith's eyes widened with understanding. "Oh, you aren't thinking . . ." Her hands flew to her now scalding cheeks, unable to speak the words aloud.

"Do you have a better idea? Some other way to keep us from living on the streets? I, for one, am not suited for poverty."

"Well. No. But certainly there *is* another way. We don't even know the new earl. Perhaps he is—"

"Kind? Generous?" Her aunt snorted in a surprisingly unladylike manner. "I think not. He is kin to Edmund. I vow he's as evil as his brother."

"Perhaps he would let us stay on at the dower house." Even as she said the words, they rang hollow in her ears. Not for an instant did she expect such charity from Edmund's brother when Edmund himself did not possess a charitable bone in his body. Blood is blood, after all.

"More likely he is a heartless, greedy wretch who intends to throw all of us out on our ears," Aunt Eleanor countered, her purple turbaned head bobbing up and down. "You can live with this lie, Meredith. It is a good lie if it serves to protect us."

A good lie. An invisible band wrapped around her chest and squeezed, making it difficult to breathe. "Let us assume the new earl is horrible, and let us assume I go along with your scheme." Meredith gave a single, obliging dip of her head, deciding to humor her aunt for a moment. "What happens when he discovers I am only *pretending* to be with child? He'll have me tossed into the gaol."

"How could he find out? Will he examine you himself?"

Meredith curled her hands into fists at her sides to stop from shaking some sense into her aunt. "Would you please listen to yourself? Even limited in experience as I am, I can only surmise there comes a point when a woman increasing must deliver a baby. What then?"

Aunt Eleanor sat down and plucked her discarded needlework from the chaise, shrugging lightly. "We will find a baby."

"Find a baby?" she echoed, watching, stupefied, as her aunt worked needle and thread. Feeling dazed, she shook her head and queried in clipped tones, "Where? At market?"

"I am confident Nels and Maree could help. They are quite resourceful. Of course, we will have to take them into our confidence, but they are trustworthy." Her keen eyes studied Meredith intently. "The number of orphans in this country is shocking. Orphanages are no better than asylums. To think we could save one poor baby from such a fate. Why, we would be providing a Christian service."

It was Meredith's turn to snort. "I'm sure the Almighty will place stars by our names in His book for this deed."

Aunt Eleanor's needle paused. She angled her head thoughtfully. "A boy is the only solution. Then he could inherit. A girl would just put us right back where we are now." The needle and thread resumed its speed.

Meredith could not dispute that logic, even as mercenary as it sounded. Feeling her resolve slip a notch, she tried to lodge another protest. "I know nothing of babies—"

"Nonsense. You'll have the knack. You've always wanted to be a mother. Here's your chance." Aunt Eleanor shuddered as if the prospect of motherhood revolted her. "A good thing because you'll have to do all the work. Children are messy creatures, especially boys. You will have to see to the child's rearing."

The prospect of raising a child did not fill Meredith with dread. On the contrary. Her heart warmed at the thought. The prospect of defrauding an earl, however, tied her stomach in knots. Yet what choice did she have? It was either this or live out her days in genteel poverty, suffering the increasing demands of her flighty aunt and ailing father.

Meredith closed her eyes against the tiny hammers beating against her temples from inside her head. Suddenly she felt very small, powerless, as though a powerful current swept her along. Opening her eyes, she asked, "What if I am caught? Defrauding an earl must carry grave penalties."

"Nonsense," Aunt Eleanor said solemnly, a fierce light entering her eyes. "Who would dare question you? The plan is foolproof, Meredith."

Then, as if the matter were settled, Aunt Eleanor rose and strolled to the desk. "We need to pen a missive to that Grimley fellow. With any luck, he will arrive before Nicholas Caulfield so you don't have to confront the dreadful man alone. Just imagine how upset he will be when he learns he is not the next Earl of Brookshire." The glow in Aunt Eleanor's eyes revealed a decided lack of worry. "I hope he's not predisposed to violence."

A tremor skated along Meredith's spine. Considering upon whom his wrath would focus, so did she.

Aunt Eleanor brandished a sheet of parchment and flattened it on the desktop. Quill pen in one hand, she crooked an impervious finger at Meredith. "Come, dearest. You are the far better correspondent. You shall have to compose this."

Meredith rose and moved to the desk. For a long breathless moment she gazed at the blank sheet, allowing her aunt's plan to root and settle in her mind. A plan borne of desperation, a plan to forever link her to the Brookshire estates and money, to lifelong security. She closed her eyes in one long fortifying blink. Almost anything was worth such a guarantee.

Gathering her courage, she wrapped shaking fingers around the quill and, with a deep breath, began to write. A small spark of hope flared to life deep in her soul as the tip of the pen scratched parchment. *Lifelong security.*

Chapter 2

Nick was not a pimp.

No more than he was a man interested in engaging the services of a whore.

"I'm afraid you've been misinformed. I don't conduct business in this manner." His gaze raked the beautiful young woman in front of him dispassionately. "Nor do I substitute payment of debts for a quick tup."

Old Lord Basslye's new bride flinched, and Nick felt an annoying stab of pity. Basslye, a gamester with a vicious temper who lost a fortune every night at Nick's tables, had *lowered* himself to wed the chit—the daughter of a rich merchant who cared not that he married off his child to a degenerate, only that said degenerate came with an old, renowned title. Every bit of her generous dowry had been applied to Basslye's debts. Still, it wasn't enough. Apparently Basslye thought his wife's *charms* could make up the difference.

She wasn't a whore. That much was clear. The stark misery in her face proclaimed her humiliation. His acceptance would offer her a reprieve— at least until her husband sunk them back into debt. Then Basslye would force her to offer her body yet again in exchange for his debts. Who knew whom the lender might be the next time?

Yet the thought of using her repulsed him. The fear in her too large eyes reminded him of another woman brought low by the very man who was supposed to love and protect her. He couldn't be a party to it. Couldn't be his father. Over the years, he had done some terrible things—thieving, stealing, and, when called for, killing. But even he had his limits.

"Sorry, love. I may be a bastard, but I'm not interested. Leave the way you came." He waved his hand to the door of his room. "Be careful you're not seen. And tell your husband if he sends you here again, he'll face my pistol."

Her eyes grew even wider. Rushing forward, she fell to her knees and grabbed his hand in both of her cold ones. "Please! He'll only beat me if I tell him you refused." Her head dipped in shame, a cascade of flaxen hair obscuring her fresh young face. "He'll only send me to others until I've earned enough. He said a lot of men would pay good coin for me."

Nick felt something dark and dangerous coil in his gut and was certain that if Lord Basslye were in front of him he would gladly strangle the son of a bitch with his bare hands. He still might do just that.

She lifted her face, shiny with tears, and clutched his hand tighter, her nails digging into the back of his hand. "I would rather it be you. You're handsome. And there is kindness in your eyes . . . even though you try to hide it."

A sudden knock at the door saved him from refusing her again.

"Who is it?"

"It's me . . . Mac. There's a gent here to see you."

"Tell him to come back later."

"Don't think he'll go away."

Nick sighed and pulled his hand free. "Go home. Tell your husband the debt is cleared."

Her mouth fell open. "But—"

He sliced a hand through the air, silencing her. "It's done. Be gone when I return." He hurried out of the room before she drowned him with gratitude.

"Damn," he muttered under his breath as he made his way to his office and wrenched the door open, the hinges squeaking in protest. He couldn't afford to be soft. He had not gotten this far in life by being tenderhearted.

For the moment, he ignored the room's other

occupants, making his way to the liquor cabinet, feeling the need for a little numbing. It had been a long time since he thought about his mother, but that sad little pigeon in the other room had conjured her ghost. Settling himself into the chair behind his desk, he turned his attention to his uninvited guest. Mac Swell relaxed in a chair beside the stranger, not bothering to ask if he could remain. Equal partners in several gaming hells and betting shops throughout London, they had no secrets.

Wasting no time, Nick asked, "Who are you?"

"Grimley, sir. Albert Grimley of Snide and Grimley."

Nick frowned. "What does a solicitor want with me?"

Grimley fidgeted in the seat. "Why nothing, my lord. I am here to—"

"What did you say?" Nick broke in, a coldness gripping his heart, squeezing like an icy fist.

Grimley blinked and appeared a little frightened. "I—I want nothing."

Nick leaned menacingly over the desk.

"Not that," Mac explained with infinite patience. "Did you just call him *my lord*?"

Grimley flushed red and rubbed his forehead ruefully. "Ah, so I did. Not the best way to break the news I suppose."

"What news?" Nick persisted.

"Mrs. Grimley claims I have a habit of running away at the mouth a bit."

"What news?" Nick thundered.

Grimley's Adam's apple bobbed above his cravat. "Your half brother has passed away. You, sir, are the new Earl of Brookshire."

Mac whistled between his teeth.

Nick closed his eyes in one long blink, but it did no good. Opening his eyes, the solicitor still sat across from him, delivering the most shocking, distasteful news. It must be a nightmare. He pinched his leg beneath the desk. Hard. It did no good. This was one dream from which he was not waking.

Recovering his voice, he said, "Give it to someone else."

Grimley frowned and looked to Mac as though seeking confirmation to Nick's incredible command. No sane man would turn down an earldom.

Mac shrugged, holding both hands up in a gesture of helplessness even as his smiling eyes indicated his enjoyment of their little drama. "You heard him. Can't you give it to someone else? I wouldn't mind being an earl."

The solicitor sniffed disdainfully before turning back to address Nick, evidently not appreciating Mac's sense of humor. He cleared his throat. "I'm afraid it is not that simple, my lord—"

"Oh, but it is," Nick cut in, his voice sharp as a whip. "And don't call me that."

Albert Grimley struggled to swallow past his bobbing Adam's apple, and Nick felt a brief stab of sympathy for the solicitor. This meeting was likely not unfolding the way he had imagined. No doubt most men would have hugged the bearer of such news. But he was not most men. He preferred his life the way it was, with his roots in the aristocracy completely erased. That his father had been an earl made little difference in the world he chose to inhabit. It was a fact Nick preferred to forget.

"How did you find me?" He squeezed the bridge of his nose.

"It was our obligation to locate the closest living male relation to the late earl."

"You shouldn't have troubled yourself. Mark me off and move down your list."

"The line ends after you, my lord. Your half brother left no heirs."

"Then as you said, the line ends," Nick replied blandly.

"I cannot do that—"

He knotted his fist on top of the desk until the knuckles went white. "I'll sign whatever I have to. I don't want it. Any of it. Not the property. Not the money. And especially not the title."

"It's not that simple," Grimley reiterated with a sigh, his eyes glancing uneasily at Nick's large fist. "You own property, whether you wish it or not. You may either sell it or give it away, but that will require some paperwork, not to mention the necessity of a buyer in the matter of selling. The matter of your title is another issue. You will have to go before the courts to officially renounce your title and Oak Run since the family seat lies adherent with the title."

Nick threw his hands up in the air. "I don't want it. A refusal should suffice."

Grimley folded his hands in his lap and pursed his lips in disapproval. Clearly, Nick did not meet his expectations. Well, he could care less. The solicitor had pushed his way into his life uninvited, and he didn't owe him anything.

Grimley bent to pick up his leather satchel from the floor. "I daresay you've suffered a shock. I will leave you now to process this news. You will surely come to your senses in the morning."

"I don't think so," Nick bit out, his jaw aching from clenching his teeth.

Grimley settled his somber, brown beaver hat on his head. "Just so. I'll be in contact. Much depends upon you. Aside from the property, you bear responsibility for countless lives."

At his lifted eyebrow, Grimley explained. "Tenants, servants. And of course there are Lady Brookshire and her relations. They still reside at Oak Run."

"Lady Brookshire?"

"Your brother's widow," Grimley replied as if he should have known.

Had the man not yet figured out that he did not keep abreast of family matters? That Grimley in fact addressed the blackest sheep ever expelled from a family bosom?

"I'll show myself out. Good day to you, gentlemen."

Mac called out to the solicitor's retreating back, "Have a drink on your way out. Just tell Fred at the bar it's on the house."

Grimley's back stiffened before exiting, indicating the unlikelihood of him accepting that offer.

"Starchy fellow," Mac muttered.

Nick replied with an indifferent shrug, willing his jaw to unclench.

Mac kicked his feet up on the desk and wasted no time getting to the point. "Nicholas Caulfield, the Earl of Brookshire. Nice ring to it, eh? You inheriting it all—that's a good comeuppance for the old earl. Fancy that! I've partnered up with a nob. Wait till everyone hears. Suppose this means you'll be changing your ways? No more hanging about here. Can't be seen with riffraff like me."

Leaning back in his leather chair, Nick laced his hands over his flat stomach and frowned. "I'm the same man. I don't intend to change. Besides, I need to be here to keep an eye on business." He raised a dark brow sardonically. "You don't expect me to leave it all to your care, do you? Who would do the books? You can't add two and two. We'd be back on the streets in a month's time."

Mac tossed a hand over his heart in mock pain. "You wound me, boy. Didn't I find *you* in the streets and get you your start?"

Nick raised his snifter of brandy to his partner in salute. "I'll give you that, but I was the talent, remember? You couldn't draw a winning hand to save your life." He grinned. "Still can't."

"I haven't lost it," Mac defended, tapping his temple. "I just took enough blunt off young Lord Derring to buy that racer I've had my eye on."

Nick rolled his eyes. "Lord Derring. That pasty-faced nob does not qualify as talent. He's so in debt I could take the clothes off his back any day I choose."

Mac's eyes widened. "I had no idea he was that far gone. Why've you let him carry on, then? This is a business, Nick, not a charity."

"I don't want the reputation that will go along with devastating a duke and his family. Bad business, that. Never fear, I shall collect the young lord's debt in due time."

Mac gave a little shake of his head. "Should have known there was a business angle to it. There ain't a charitable bone in your body."

"Quite so," Nick agreed, neglecting to mention his *transaction* with old Basslye's bride just moments ago. Mac didn't need to know everything.

They sank into silence. He knew Mac was giving him time to think, to mull things over in his mind until he was ready to discuss the subject hanging so heavily in the air. It didn't take long.

"How can I be a part of that world again?" Nick spread his hands out wide in front of him. "One day I'm riding a pony between my Latin and fencing lessons and the next I'm . . ." He let his words hang in the air for a long moment as the past reared its ugly head. The old, sour taste he so loathed filled his mouth and throat. He wanted nothing from the man that had destroyed his mother or from the world that had turned a blind eye.

He took a long swig of brandy, thinking he

might have to get foxed. Voices, laughter, and the faint whirring sound of a roulette wheel floated from below. Nick knew he should make an appearance. Bess was acting hostess tonight and would pout if he didn't come down, but he wasn't in the mood to socialize. The dark shadows of his past had been roused, spoiling his humor. "I don't intend to claim the inheritance."

Mac nodded his head slowly, rolling his heels on Nick's desk. "You could do that," he allowed.

He knew there was more coming, and knew Mac well enough to know that he wasn't going to like what he heard.

"But there's power in the aristocracy, and that license we've been trying to get to open the gaming hell across the river will be ours in a blink if it's an earl asking."

Just discussing the inheritance roused a whole host of uncomfortable memories. He could not imagine actually stepping in his father's shoes, no matter what it brought him.

"Everything I've done, everything I've accomplished, has been with my own sweat and blood." He tapped the desk.

"Aye, and taking the inheritance won't change that."

"I don't want a thing from my father."

Mac scratched his head. "Isn't it technically your brother that's dead? Thought your old man's been dead for some time?"

He laughed humorlessly. "Please, don't let me relate to you the kind of brother I had. He was little better than my father." Nick stood and looked out the window at the city skyline. The lights of London flickered and blinked in the inky night. "I don't want a thing from either of them."

"I understand you got your demons, but this seems the best revenge to my way of thinking. I doubt there's another earl that pinched a pocket or heard his own belly rumble in hunger before. You grew up in Whitechapel, for God's sake. You could get in among the peerage and make some change. By God, you'll have a seat in the House of Lords."

Nick smiled indulgently. "I'm no reformer."

"Well, you could be if you chose. Hell, or don't." Mac, only two years his senior, seemed far older as he threw his hands up in the air and said, "Thumb your nose at them and take Bess to all their fine balls."

"Now that's a thought." His smile deepened at the thought of the buxom woman with her painted face, loud gowns, and brassy red hair rubbing elbows with the peerage.

"Besides, what about the tenants and people you're now responsible for? To my way of thinking, you can't simply turn your back on them."

Smile gone, Nick sighed and looked over his shoulder at Mac. "And my half brother's widow."

Mac's brows rose. "What will you do with her?"

"I suppose I'll have to set her up somewhere in grand style and cater to her for the rest of my life." He ran both hands through his hair, rumpling the locks in aggravation. "Guess I better pack."

Mac grinned, sitting forward in his chair. "Want some company?"

"I need to do this alone." He had no idea what to expect upon returning to the home of his birth, but he knew he needed to confront the demons of his past by himself.

Mac nodded in understanding, but the disappointment was clear in his face.

Rising to his feet, Nick downed the remainder of his brandy before excusing himself, glad for the solitude awaiting him. As close as they were, even Mac could not understand how the prospect of returning home rattled him.

The instant Nick entered his room, he knew he was not alone, which was too bad because he wasn't fit company. There was a slight movement on the bed. Lady Basslye's naked figure took shape as she rose to her knees. An uncertain, hopeful smile flitted about her lips. He leaned against the door and observed her lazily, his mood dangerous.

"You're still here," he said flatly.

She nodded, flaxen hair dancing against her generous breasts.

"You should have left."

"I know you cleared the debt . . . but I wanted to stay. For once I want to choose who shares my bed." Her eyes darkened as she eyed the long line of his body.

Nick pushed off the door and crossed the room, his strides long and fierce. He buried his fingers into her soft shoulders and pulled her close, kissing her savagely, releasing all the anger and frustration brewing inside him, forgetting his determination to leave her untouched.

Perhaps he was that big of a bastard after all.

He stripped his clothes and lowered both their bodies to the bed, his movements mechanical, his touch perfunctory. It was only a temporary escape. A distraction from the emptiness, from the perpetual night that lived inside him.

As she rubbed her body against his, he felt only a flicker of interest flare to life. It was impossible to feel anything when one was but a hollow shell. A living, breathing man should *feel*. Only it had been years since he had felt anything at all.

Chapter 3

"What else does a woman do when she is increasing?"

Meredith stood with hands on her hips, surveying the room that had been the Brookshire nursery for generations. She had seen her fair share of births in the managing of Oak Run, but it had not taken long to recognize she knew little about preparing for a baby's arrival.

"You are asking me? Dearest, I am quite ignorant when it comes to babies." Aunt Eleanor looked about the nursery with something akin to unease, running a finger along the edge of the crib as if it were an unpredictable animal that might bite at any moment. "Blessedly so," she added with a shiver, removing her finger from the crib.

"You practically raised me," Meredith pointed out as she sniffed the stale air and moved to open the windows wider.

"But you were such a precocious child—so well-behaved. Your father did not tolerate bad behavior. I felt like I was dealing with a peer and not a child."

Meredith grimaced at the accuracy of her aunt's assessment. She had not known a carefree, fun-filled childhood. The stern visage of her father had squashed any such gaiety. She had been an adult all her life. A solemn, proper adult. Perhaps it was best her father was unaware of the world around him. It saved her from enduring his censure for the perjury she was committing.

Shaking aside the disturbing thought, she stepped back from the window. "You will grow accustomed to a child about the place."

"Yes," Aunt Eleanor nodded in agreement. "Especially as this baby will be our salvation. Since we are going through such trouble, perhaps you should acquire two babies. One could act as a backup in case something happens to the original?" She took in Meredith's considering look and hastened to say, "Please, I only jest."

"The idea does have merit, Aunt. I shall think on it." She turned so her aunt could not see her twitching lips as she fought back a smile.

"No need for twins. One baby shall suit our purposes," Aunt Eleanor sniffed, exiting the nursery.

Meredith frowned at her aunt's departing words. They sounded so mercenary. Although reluctant at first, she had warmed to the notion of having a child. She had every intention of loving this baby—of lavishing on him all the love and attention she herself had never received. With that in mind, she examined the room critically.

Aired out, drapes drawn, it was quite cheery. She had paid it little heed over the years—for the obvious reasons—but now she felt a small pang of regret at the sight of the newly polished crib. Her babes should have occupied its confines by now. Most women of five and twenty had a string of babes for which to account. Bending, she picked up a small wooden horse sitting on a miniature child's table. One of the ears was nicked from age. Her fingers curled tightly around its sleigh bottom.

In that moment, she admitted that the need for security was not her only consideration. She desired a child, and that very desire largely motivated her agreement to her aunt's scheme. The realization frightened her. It meant her motives were not totally altruistic.

Digging deep to recover some of her earlier determination, she muttered, "The deed's done. No going back now." With a firm nod, she set the little horse back on the table and gave it a gentle push, smiling wistfully as it rolled to and fro.

"I say, this room looks inviting," someone said behind her.

Meredith quickly straightened, her cheeks flaming as she turned to see Mr. Grimley framed in the doorway. She made a quick mental note to cease thinking aloud. The habit could become dangerous now that she possessed secrets.

The Brookshire family solicitor had arrived yesterday, and Meredith felt great relief that he would be the one to inform Nicholas Caulfield of his changed fortune instead of her.

"I thought it best to ready things." She gestured to the room with a sweep of her hand.

"Yes, my Mary nested before the arrival of every one of our children. They call it maternal instinct." Mr. Grimley leaned back on his heels and rocked his paunchy frame with a knowing air.

"Really," Meredith murmured for lack of anything better to say.

"I cannot tell you how pleased the old earl would have been to see this nursery occupied again. It was his greatest wish."

She suffered a twinge of guilt. Brookshires were probably rolling over in their graves at the prospect of her passing off an orphaned waif as the next earl. She reminded herself that Edmund had every chance to exercise his rights as a husband. Instead, he chose not to. She had to do this. And not just for her. Others depended upon her.

"I say, I almost forgot why I came up here." The solicitor chuckled, shaking his head. "Your brother-in-law just arrived. The butler showed him to the drawing room, and I volunteered to fetch you."

Her heart skipped a beat. So soon? Now the farce would truly begin.

"Now, my lady, do not fret so." Mr. Grimley took her arm and led her from the nursery. "He is an amiable sort, if perhaps a little . . . fierce."

Looking sharply at the solicitor, she swallowed past her suddenly dry throat as they descended the stairs. Fierce? Vikings were fierce. Pirates were fierce. What did he mean?

"I am sure your news may serve as a surprise, but he will take it like a gentleman. I know it is hard to believe, but he was not eager to accept the title. I would not be surprised if he viewed this as deliverance of sorts."

Grimley was correct. She did find that hard to believe. Why would Nicholas Caulfield not want the property, wealth, and prestige that went with becoming the Earl of Brookshire?

Aunt Eleanor was already in the drawing room serving tea on Meredith's favorite Wedgwood. Nervous, Meredith delayed looking at the man in question, allowing Grimley to seat her on the settee beside her aunt. She took an inordinate amount of time arranging her skirts before lifting her gaze, then exhaled a great lungful of air.

The man standing across from her, towering like an oak over the unmistakably feminine furnishings, could not be Edmund's brother. This swarthy man with dark hair and matching eyes was no pasty-faced Englishman. His tanned skin stretched over high cheekbones and a square jaw, reminiscent of the Spanish pirate in that gothic novel she had secretly read and reread as a girl.

He bowed as Grimley made the introductions.

"Lady Brookshire," he murmured, his voice a gravelly rumble that did strange things to her already churning stomach.

His finely tailored jacket stretched tight across broad shoulders. She was acutely conscious of his maleness, of his attractiveness, and—as Grimley's introduction penetrated—of her own mounting horror. *This dazzling display of manhood was Nicholas Caulfield?* Her nostrils flared, catching the faint scent of clean woods and saddle leather as he took her fingers in greeting. She stared at the dark hair of his bent head and wondered if it felt as silky as it looked. He gave her a cursory glance before releasing her hand and submitting to Grimley's inane conversation.

She choked back her dismay and stared, mentally listing all the reasons why this man could not be Nicholas Caulfield. For one, his eyes were not the Brookshire blue. Edmund's small, vapid blue eyes were nowhere in evidence. How had this man sprung from the Brookshire family tree? Nicholas Caulfield's eyes gleamed dark mahogany. He was, she realized in shock, the most delicious man she'd ever clapped eyes upon. A hot flush warmed her cheeks. Mortification filled her at the vulgarity of her thoughts.

Collect yourself, she silently commanded, trying to pay attention to the conversation at hand. His attention trained on Grimley, he was thankfully unaware of her intense regard.

Aunt Eleanor, however, was wholly aware of her ill-mannered gawking and raised a brow in silent inquiry. Sternly, Meredith forced herself to focus on Grimley's words.

"You came directly from London, Lord Brookshire?" Grimley inquired. "Hope the wet roads did not spoil your trip."

Stifling her flinch at Grimley's application of the Brookshire title, she calmed herself with the reminder that it was only temporary.

"Not at all. I traveled by horseback and made good time."

"Really? Such a distance, my lord?" Grimley's eyes widened, impressed. "You must be quite the horseman."

"I prefer to ride over taking conveyances." Nicholas Caulfield's eyes settled on her, giving her more than a preliminary glance this time as he assessed her from head to toe. Something hard and relentless glittered in his eyes, convincing her she had been right to agree to her aunt's scheme. He looked ruthless, the type to kick all of them out on their ears.

The barest of smiles graced his lips. It was a practiced smile, the type bestowed on countless women. A small secretive smile to let her know he knew his effect on her as an attractive male. *Arrogant man.* To disguise her discomfiture, she lifted her chin and refocused her attention on the boring solicitor.

"I must confess that I did not expect to see you here, Grimley," Caulfield said mildly, shifting his gaze from her. "I thought we had concluded our business for the present time."

Aunt Eleanor and Meredith exchanged uneasy glances. The moment had come. Their lie would now be revealed to the one it most affected. Anxiety knotted her stomach. Mr. Grimley glanced her way as if trying to gauge how to break the news.

"Yes. Well. I received a most interesting post from Lady Brookshire. Good news, actually." Grimley's voice faded, as though he doubted his own words.

Caulfield narrowed his eyes speculatively on her, obviously expecting her to elaborate.

"I—" Meredith's voice came out a croak. Swallowing, she tried again, forcing herself to speak firmly and in no mincing terms. "I have recently learned that I am with child, Mr. Caulfield." Heat flooded her face. Never, in all her days, had she imagined herself speaking of such a delicate matter to a veritable stranger.

His dark eyes didn't so much as blink. The only disruption to his cold reserve was a slight ticking in his jaw, and what that signified she could only guess. Those deep brown eyes probed her until the silence grew strained. She wanted to look away, afraid he would decipher the truth in her face, but his penetrating gaze held her hostage. Why did he not speak?

Meredith wrenched her eyes away from his and shifted restlessly on the settee. Hopefully, he would credit her discomfort to the fact that such delicate subjects were not typically for discussion among strangers. Even estranged relatives.

Finally, he spoke. And with such calm that he

truly appeared unbothered by his change in fortune. "Grimley, I expect you're here to explain where this places us? Obviously, the prospect of a child changes everything."

"Quite an unprecedented situation we have here. I must say my colleagues and I found it most intriguing." Grimley chuckled at the *situation*. She wanted to strike the fool. Caulfield certainly found such a *situation* lacking amusement.

"After consulting with others, the situation stands with Nicholas Caulfield as the present Earl of Brookshire, with all rights to the estate, monies, and titles thereof. . . ."

Stiffening in reproach and shock, Meredith crossed her arms. Surely this was a mistake. Grimley had led her to believe Caulfield would not stand to inherit . . . so what rubbish was this? Had Caulfield's presence intimidated the solicitor?

Caulfield had not missed her altered stance and had the audacity to wink at her. Her mouth thinned at the impertinence.

Grimley continued, "In the event Lady Brookshire delivers a son, the title will revert to the child, held in trust by Lady Brookshire until he reaches his majority. If the child is female, there have been no provisions made, just as there was no jointure provided for you, my lady." Grimley cleared his throat, obviously ill at ease with the topic of her potential destitution. "A terrible oversight of the late earl, but the law must be followed accordingly."

Blast the law. She gave a slight nod and smiled

tightly, wishing she could tell Mr. Grimley exactly what she thought about British law.

"If the baby is female, I will provide for both the child and Lady Brookshire," Caulfield intoned.

Meredith gaped in disbelief.

Aunt Eleanor's eyes, equally shocked, met hers over the tea service.

Could they have been wrong about him? He would assume responsibility? As simple as that? She took another look at his hard features. Impossible. More than likely he wished to appear magnanimous in front of Grimley and did not mean a word he uttered. Even if he did, how long would his generosity extend? A year? Ten years? What would become of her if something befell him and he died? Once again she would be left scrabbling for her livelihood.

"Splendid! I was hoping you would make such a gesture, my lord." Grimley beamed. Leaning forward, he grasped both his knees. "These matters are not always dealt with so amicably. It truly speaks to the manners and breeding of the aristocracy."

"Don't rush to include me in the ranks of the aristocracy," Caulfied said dryly.

Feeling slightly sick at the possibility of defrauding a truly honorable gentleman, Meredith pressed a hand over her queasy belly. She wanted to hate him, needed him to be a greedy, villainous man, undeserving of the inheritance. *For the sake of her conscience, he had to be.*

"I have dependents, you should know. My aunt and my ailing father," she blurted out, then held her breath, waiting to see a flicker of doubt cross his face, waiting to hear him recant or simply refuse to extend his support to her relations.

Unfortunately, he did not sprout the horns and forked tail she desired. At least not yet. Instead, he replied with total equanimity, "That should not be a problem."

Meredith scowled. He and Edmund shared the same blood. The wretch in him would surface yet. "And there are certain members of the household staff—certain, um, colorful individuals—you may not wish to keep on. I feel responsible for them as well." Lifting her chin, she figured that statement would certainly rattle him.

"The rather imposing butler, I presume?"

"Yes, Nels's scar does tend to make some visitors squeamish," she allowed.

"An interesting choice for a butler, I should think."

"I feel he has just the right air of self-importance for the position."

He raised an eyebrow at her description of the former pugilist. "Yes, no unwanted guests would scurry past him."

"Indeed," she primly responded.

"Should I decide to dismiss any of the staff, they may have the option of continuing on in your household, provided they do work, of course. I will not support the indolent. And I would not have them take advantage of your generosity."

Her fists curled at her sides. As if she needed him telling her how to run a household. She had managed without a man these last years.

"Be assured, I am an excellent judge of character." *Except for Edmund,* a small voice in her head reminded. But that was long ago, when she had been a naïve girl. Dreams of love no longer clogged her vision.

"Then all is settled?" Grimley asked. "For now at least?"

How she wished she could warn Caulfield not to get too comfortable with his temporary power over her. Yet she couldn't very well inform him that she was guaranteed to deliver a son. Instead, she said, "You are too generous, my lord. Might I inquire of your plans for the interim?"

"I should like to stay here a fortnight—speak with the steward and see that the estate runs smoothly while in my possession, however short-lived that may be. You should not worry over its management in your delicate condition."

Grimley bobbed his head in agreement. "Splendid, every gentleman should take his responsibilities so gravely."

It took all her will not to pound both men over the head. Delicate condition, hah! What did men think was so delicate about childbirth? More than likely Caulfield wanted her out of the way so he could manage her life and her household to his heart's content. He was probably one of those men who had to control everything within his sphere. The gall. To think he needed to oversee matters for her when she had managed the estate for years without any man directing her.

Forcing a smile, she said, "As you wish. But I think you'll find things well in hand. I've managed Oak Run in my husband's frequent absences."

"But not too frequent?" He inclined his dark head toward her middle.

Her cheeks burned. Heavens. Was he suspicious or simply bold with his words? Either way, she quickly defended—perhaps too quickly, "I last saw my husband in Bath. My aunt and I stayed a fortnight there shortly before he . . . expired." She had worked over the details. It seemed wise, especially considering that she had not seen Edmund in three years, when he last brought a hunting party to Oak Run. Fortunately, she and her aunt had been in Bath at that time to corroborate the story. It was highly unlikely that anyone could contradict that Edmund had visited her at least once while she was there. "Edmund did not care for the country. He left the management of Oak Run to me."

"Oak Run does not have a steward, my lord," Aunt Eleanor chimed, blinking owlishly over the rim of her teacup. "My niece handles all estate matters, and quite ably. Edmund had every confidence in her," she fibbed, making it appear that Meredith and Edmund enjoyed an agreeable relationship.

"Yes," Meredith added. "I would not want to prevail upon your time. You undoubtedly wish to return to London."

"Just the same, I should like to stay for a while."

Stung by his rebuff, she tried for a demure air. "Of course, I did not wish to imply you were not welcome to do so. This is your home too." She rose to her feet. "Would you like to see your room and settle in before dinner?"

Before he could respond, the drawing room door burst open and her father strode into the room. They all froze in a surprised tableau. With his white hair wild about his head, her father looked fresh out of the asylum. The blood pounded in her temples and she braced herself, instantly recognizing he was having one of his bad days.

His flashing eyes settled on Caulfield with deadly intent. For a man of seventy years who had spent almost every one of them behind a pulpit, he was amazingly spry. Before anyone could react, he launched himself against Caulfield's chest. Meredith heard a faint popping and hoped it was her father's creaking joints and not Caulfield's ribs.

"Swine," he cried, grabbing Caulfield by the cravat. "Papist swine!"

Then pandemonium broke out.

Chapter 4

⸻∽◗◖∾⸻

Aunt Eleanor screamed. Someone turned over the tea service. China shattered on the carpet and Meredith gave the broken pieces a brief, mournful cringe. Grimley hollered for help. Servants poured into the drawing room like a small invading army, adding to the chaos by pure presence if not volume. And throughout it all Caulfield remained calm, an amazing feat considering her father strangled him with his cravat.

"Please, don't hurt him!" Meredith beseeched above the din.

"He's got a bad back!" Aunt Eleanor screeched, her hands fluttering helplessly in the air. "Watch his back!"

"He's trying to bloody choke me." Caulfield shot her a look of pure incredulity as he worked to carefully disengage himself from her father. It all happened in the span of a few moments, but time seemed to stretch endlessly before her father was restrained. Nels held her father tightly, yet gently, in his great bear of a frame.

"Daughter, do not be beguiled by that one!" Her father wagged a gnarly, arthritic finger at Caulfield as Nels escorted him from the drawing room. "He's a Papist, I tell you! They're all about the place. He'll kill the Queen." The rest of her father's deprecations faded as he was led upstairs.

"My sincerest apologies. My father is not himself these days." Meredith was helpless to suppress her embarrassment, which only angered her. Her father had once been a great man—pious, quick-witted, admired by many. True, he had been stern and not the most affectionate of fathers, but he was the only one she would ever have, and his condition was no fault of his.

"No need to apologize, my lady," Caulfield said as he straightened his cravat, his lips twisting with a wry smile. "I don't expect your father really meant to kill me."

"Oh, my lord," Aunt Eleanor gushed, clapping her hands. "You are all that is kind and good. Not everyone possesses such patience and understanding." She nudged Meredith sharply. "Is he not kind, Meredith?"

"Yes, most kind," Meredith echoed, shocked by her aunt's sudden change of sentiment. Only hours ago she was cursing Caulfield as the lowest sort of scoundrel.

"I say, my lady, I am concerned. I had not realized your father had succumbed to such a low state." The solicitor's appalled tones rang out in the drawing room. "I am most grievously concerned for your ladies' safety. And you must think to your child now. Having one given to violence under your very roof is an unnecessary risk. Perhaps you should consider an asylum—"

Anger spiked through Meredith at the suggestion. "Have you any idea the deplorable conditions of asylums? It is worse than Newgate prison, I am told. Besides, my father is not a threat. Age and disease have made a victim of him. God willing, should such a fate befall you, I hope your relations are compassionate enough not to lock you away."

Caulfield's eyes raked her with something akin to approval. Grimley opened his mouth, no doubt to put forth further unwanted opinions, but Caulfield smoothly intervened, his voice matter-of-fact as he said, "This is a family matter, Grimley. Trust that I'll see to the safety of those under my protection."

Seemingly mollified, the solicitor nodded and made no further comment. Meredith bristled indignantly at such high-handedness, even if it did appease Grimley and put an end to his badgering. When exactly had she become subject to Nicholas Caulfield? Especially when her sole goal had been independence?

A flicker of apprehension coursed through

her . . . and something else, something she could not put her finger on. It had been years since she relied on anyone. Not since she was a little girl and her father had been hearty and whole. Nicholas Caulfield's words echoed in her mind. *Under my protection.* What would it feel like for a man to protect her, look out for her, claim her as his own—

Meredith veered sharply from such unsettling thoughts. Dangerous thoughts. She'd had thoughts like those before. When she married Edmund. And what a colossal mistake that had been. No, better she maintain control of her own life than be cast to the whim of another Brookshire. Glancing at a maid cleaning the broken china, she asked with forced lightness, "Shall I send for more tea?"

He couldn't sleep. Not in this house. Funny that he had not considered what it would feel like to be back here again. He had not anticipated the resurgence of memories—memories that still occupied the nether regions of his mind. Apparently, the past wasn't dead. Not as he'd told himself all these years.

He paced his room still dressed, tempted to march downstairs, saddle his horse, and depart from this place. Nick sighed and rubbed his forehead tiredly. That would be too easy . . . and too cowardly. He had to see this through. If luck was on his side, Lady Brookshire would deliver a healthy son and he could return to his own life.

On the surface, the house appeared unchanged.

But there were small changes. Subtle differences. It seemed cleaner, the air fresher, and the rooms brimmed with light. He suspected these were Lady Brookshire's efforts. No doubt such an ice princess would demand order and cleanliness. Not like his mother, who had been content to while away her time in leisurely pursuits and neglect the running of the household.

As a boy, he had enjoyed his life here, not suspecting that it could be snatched away. His memories were fond . . . until that long ago day. Another lifetime. Another boy. That pampered child had died a thousand deaths since he last stood in this house. His father had been a distant figure, but in no way had he viewed him as an enemy. Yet what else would one call a man who tossed away both wife and child? Nick did not know if his mother had been the adulterer his father accused. He would never know that particular truth. More than likely his father had grown tired of his foreign wife, embarrassed at the public life she had led as an opera singer, and wanted to break all ties once his desire for her had been slaked. His father was a gentleman, rich and titled. A divorce would hardly ruin him. But his mother? A female? A common performer? Not only was she incapable of showing her face in Society, but she had been unable to make her living on the stage as before. No, only one profession had been left to her.

Nick left his room and walked slowly down the dimly lit corridor, the muffled fall of his feet on the carpet merging with the whispers of yesterday. He stopped before the nursery. The door stood ajar. The darkened room suddenly became alive with the past. He could still hear his nurse, Connie, pleading with his father, begging him to keep Nick. He could see his father's face so clearly, could feel that wintry blue gaze looking right through him as he pronounced those fateful words. *He goes too.*

Edmund had been there, leaning nonchalantly on the doorjamb, unaffected, indifferent to the impending exile of his stepmother and half brother.

Stepping back from the threshold of his old nursery, Nick detached himself from the memories, hating to consider what others might surface during his stay.

"My lord?" a voice queried softly, conveniently shattering his troubling reveries.

Nick turned to face Lady Brookshire, prim in a heavy cotton robe that doubtlessly hid an equally prim nightgown. Hugging a book to her chest like a makeshift shield, she bore no resemblance to the pale-faced, black-clad widow from earlier. Gone was the severity of hairstyle and dress. A long plait of auburn hair hung loosely over her shoulder. She looked young, like a virgin schoolgirl, yet he knew her to be a widow, past the first blush of youth.

"Are you lost?" Her wide, intelligent brow furrowed in concern.

Lost? No, unfortunately he knew exactly where he stood. Nodding toward the room, he stepped away from the door. "My old nursery."

"Oh," she replied, her expression uncertain. She ceased hugging the book so tightly and lowered it in her hands.

"I had a nurse. Connie. Does she by chance still work here?"

"I have never heard of her. Perhaps you could ask in the village. She may still be in the area."

"Perhaps," he replied, shaking off his strange mood. "I suppose it's time the room sees some use again."

She gave a slight nod, looking distinctly uncomfortable. "Your father would be pleased. He did not live very long after I came here, but he desperately wished to have this nursery full of children again."

How ironic that his father had craved a nursery full of children when he banished his own son from its confines. "Yes, a shame he did not live to see this," Nick said dryly. "I am certain his view does not extend this far from hell."

He waited for her shock, her denunciation, perhaps even a fainting spell—the hallmark of all women of breeding, especially from such a starchy little package like herself.

Instead, she angled her head and studied him curiously. "I take it you and your father parted on bad terms?"

Nick eyed her closely. She blinked back at him, eyes wide and guileless. She posed the question sincerely, without the faintest amount of censure in her voice.

"No gossip has reached your ears?" Nick lifted

a brow. "How surprising. I thought you would surely be apprised of all the sordid details. Edmund never spoke of me, then?"

Her gaze dropped and she plucked at the spine of her book, making him feel as though he'd asked a tactless question.

"No, he never mentioned you."

Was she so grieved by her loss that the mention of Edmund gave her such discomfort? Had she loved him that much? A sour taste filled his mouth. He looked her over again. The flyaway tendrils of hair haloing her face made her look young, fresh. Undeniably pretty. His blood stirred with both desire and envy. What had Edmund done to deserve her devotion? The brother he remembered hardly seemed the type to evoke loyalty.

"Yes, well, I don't suppose I mattered overmuch to him. But you've heard nothing of me from others?"

"No, and I certainly made my inquiries, my lord." She lifted her eyes, as if daring him to disapprove. "I learned that your mother was a performer of some kind before she married your father—that she took you and left years ago."

Nick smiled at her intrepid mien, so at odds with the solemn little girl she appeared in her prim robe. "There's a little more to it than that. The truth is my father cast both of us aside. Divorce. That ugly little word that is only whispered about in drawing rooms. I was eight years old, but he divorced himself from me just as much as from my mother." Bitterness washed over him, belying the calm tone of his voice.

Her eyes narrowed thoughtfully and she pursed her lips, evidently considering his words. The lighted sconces on the wall lent shadows that obscured the exact emotion of her eyes, but he sensed her reproach—or perhaps expected it.

"I suppose you're wondering what we did to deserve it?"

"Not at all. I don't think a father is ever justified in banishing his own child. It is reprehensible."

"Is it only reprehensible to banish one's child? What of wives?" Nick challenged.

At this, she stammered, "I—I cannot presume to know the circumstances—"

"Very politic of you. However, I wonder if you would say the same thing had my mother not been an opera singer. Tell me, do you really think that my mother was on equal footing with my father? Did he not possess the wealth and status? Does the law not grant a man more rights than a woman? Are you not right now beholden to me just as you were to Edmund?"

Her body noticeably stiffened, and he knew he had made his point. A point she clearly did not like but nonetheless recognized.

"What's wrong? Do you find it difficult to hear the truth, my lady?"

"I don't like it," she admitted. "I don't like to think of myself as subject to anyone."

"Your circumstances are not so different from my mother's. You've both been left with nothing." Nick shrugged and injected a measure of calm he didn't feel. "He accused my mother of infidelity. If the allegation was true, perhaps she deserved the miserable end she suffered."

"But what of you?" she asked. "You could not have done anything to deserve such treatment. You were a helpless child. It must have been frightening to lose everything safe and familiar. I can understand that." Her last words were uttered with such feeling, as if she truly knew how it felt to lose one's sense of security. Perhaps she experienced a bit of that right now, with her future still so much unsettled. That her future rested on the outcome of her child's gender was indeed a vagary of fate. A vicar's daughter would more than likely subscribe it to God's will, he thought wryly. Not him. If God existed, He had abandoned him long ago. Whether she gave birth to a boy or girl, it was just a roll of the die.

"I survived."

"Your father lost too, even if he did not realize it. He died a lonely man. I'm sure he regretted—"

"No," Nick interrupted harshly, slicing a hand through the air. "That bastard doesn't deserve your pity, and you'll rouse none from me. If you must pity, pity my mother who had to whore herself just to put food in our mouths and died coughing her guts up in a rat-infested hellhole."

Her face blanched. Now he had shocked her. And it felt good. Rage—that old familiar friend that got him through the hardest of times—resurfaced. It felt gratifying to lash out at someone. Everyone else he could blame was dead. She was the closest substitute. The chit had married Edmund, after all, sharing her bed and life with the very brother who had stood silent as he was banished. Edmund had been fifteen, old enough to possess a voice, to have at least spoken out on their behalf. The woman before him had married that gutless man, even mourned him. He would feel no softness for her. No matter how sweetly she listened as he bared his soul.

She dropped her gaze to the carpet, reminding him of a mouse trying to go unseen in the face of its predator. "My apologies. I spoke unthinkingly."

"Now you know."

"I'm sorry for all you suffered. I only wish others had known, so they could have helped you."

Nick felt a flash of irritation. Did she honestly think no one knew? Just because no one had stepped forward to tell her his family's sordid history did not mean no one knew.

"People knew, don't doubt it. If the same thing were to happen today, Good Society would not deign to lift a finger."

"I think you will find a good many people in Attingham that would not stand idle for such an injustice today."

Her total naiveté maddened him. "If your child is female and I decided to cast you to the wolves, the good Christians of Attingham would look the other way, of that you may be certain."

She shook her head slowly, murmuring in a voice that lacked conviction, "No."

He studied her closely, hypnotized by the way

the candlelight brought out the red highlights in her auburn hair. "What an innocent you are. I can say with absolute faith that my former neighbors did not grow a conscience in the last twenty years. But have no fear, I'll keep my word. You'll not have to test the extent of their charity."

"I can only say that the good Christians I sit beside in church—"

His scornful laugh cut short her stalwart defense.

"What is so amusing, my lord?" Disapproval rang high in her voice.

Nick sobered and answered mildly, "I'm not much for church or God." God had been his mother's crutch. Not his.

Her sharp intake of breath indicated he had either offended or surprised her. That stubborn little chin of hers went up, and he knew she was not going to let his declaration slide past unrefuted. "I don't believe that."

"What exactly don't you believe?"

"That you are faithless. I don't believe it."

He could tell her any number of stories to prove just how blackhearted he was. He could regale her with how he grew into a predator on the streets of London: stealing, assaulting, and even killing a man at the tender age of thirteen when the man insisted on becoming his *special* friend. How scandalized would she be to learn that he had broken into the mansions of Mayfair's most eminent? Perhaps then she would believe him.

"You don't believe it because you don't wish to.

It's more comfortable for you to believe that everyone is like you." He waved his hand at her. "That I am like you."

"But you must believe in God." The quaver of hesitation in her voice made him smile. She feared for his soul. Charming. She probably feared he was going to be swallowed in flames right in front of her.

Nick answered with a vague, "I believe God exists." For her sake, because she was so obviously perturbed, he would leave it at that and refrain from telling her of the years he had prayed for his mother's precious God to intervene as he endured the beatings and deprivations of the streets. The boy that had whispered desperate prayers over his mother's corpse was dead.

"But you reject Him," she finished for him.

Nick clenched his jaw, her judgment angering him. Or was it disappointment he heard in her voice? Either way, it bothered him more than it should. He didn't need her good opinion. In fact, he would much rather have her disgust. It would keep things in perspective.

"How did Edmund ever end up with such a sweet innocent like you?" he mocked, stepping closer to brush her cheek with the back of his hand. "Shocking that such a prim little thing let him into your life, much less your bed."

Gasping, she tried to step back, but his hand slid behind her neck, holding her fast. The nape of her neck felt soft as silk. He inhaled the scent of her. Mint and honey. Delicious. Her eyes dilated and her lips parted as she gazed up at him. A primal growl welled up in him and he inched closer, his eyes fixed on her lush mouth. Then the thought came, unbidden, unwanted. *This woman could have been his. She could be his now.* Nick stepped back, dropping his hands to his sides. Had he sunk so low he craved the woman carrying his brother's child? Could he be that perverse?

Her trembling voice rolled through him like warm brandy. "This has been a trying day. Especially for you. I'm sure old ghosts abound tonight. We best retire."

"I remember little of my life here. It was long ago," he lied, rubbing the back of his neck as if he could rid the silken feel of her from his hand.

"The downstairs library boasts a large selection. Sometimes I read when my mind is overwhelmed." She waved her book in a nervous little circle, watching him warily.

"A worthy suggestion. Tell me, what overwhelms you?" He reached for the book, unable to stop himself from stroking the soft inside of her wrist. As if burned, she quickly released the book. Reading the title, he asked, "You think *Gulliver's Travels* will provide distraction from your worries?"

"I'm not worried, my lord." Her voice lifted a notch as she worked to rub his touch from her skin.

"You're a poor liar, my lady."

Her eyes widened into luminous pools of green. "Of course I'm not."

He chuckled. "Indeed?"

Shaking her head, she quickly corrected, "Not a liar, I mean—poor or otherwise."

"It's not a crime to confess that my arrival has discomfited you."

"Your arrival has not discomfited me. Why should it?" she asked, fidgeting and looking nervous again.

Nick observed her curiously. Most women would have been glad to have a man step in and take charge. Not this one. From the moment he arrived, it was evident she wanted him gone. He handed the book back.

She gave a single curt nod. "Good night, my lord."

"Good night." He watched as she turned and walked down the corridor, scowling when he caught himself appreciating the natural sway of her hips. He remained where he was until she entered her room. The door closed behind her with a soft click.

Strange woman. Not the prig he initially thought. No woman could be too priggish with hair that inspired fantasies and a mouth that begged to be kissed. He stared at Lady Brookshire's door for several moments, convinced of one thing. There was more to her than she would have him see.

Chapter 5

Meredith needed to escape. Two days of staying tucked away while Nicholas Caulfield surveyed her domain proved difficult to abide. She saw him at evening meals where he exhibited a polite reserve, never again revealing so much of himself as he had that night outside the nursery, never again being so bold as to touch her—for which she felt a small pang of relief and regret. She extended only the required hospitality and was neither warm nor effusive. It would only encourage him to remain, and the last thing she wanted was him underfoot, continually measuring Oak Run and herself for worth.

After glimpsing the wounded soul within him,

she felt a curious urge to help him find the peace so obviously eluding him. A dangerous inclination. She could not bear to harbor a soft spot for the man she was cheating out of his birthright.

Outside, the lawn glimmered a verdant green from yesterday's rain. Sunshine sparkled on the morning air. Meredith decided she had hidden indoors long enough. Sending word ahead for her mount to be readied, she quickly donned a riding habit of fawn-colored velvet. She supposed the color was not entirely appropriate for mourning, but as she did not own a black riding habit, it would simply have to do. Eyeing herself critically in a cheval mirror, she smoothed a hand over her torso and hips, wincing at the evidence of too many honeyed scones. Well, a woman with child—even in the early stage—might be a little thick about the middle. She and her aunt would soon have to come up with a way to fashion a bulging tummy for her. Maree would prove helpful in that endeavor.

Her mare, a spirited creature name Petunia, was saddled and waiting for her when she emerged outside. Petunia appeared to have missed her exercise as much as Meredith. Soon they were streaking across the countryside. She gave the mare her lead, delighting at the wind on her face as they raced over hills. After a while she reined Petunia toward the Finney farm, a large tract of land on Oak Run's southern border. With a dozen children, the couple had no trouble managing so large a farm. Sally Finney was expecting yet another child and had recently taken to bed, no longer able to move about with ease. Meredith guessed the woman would not be averse to a little company.

The Finneys' yard was oddly empty when she rode up. Dismounting, she tethered her mare to a post in front of the cottage's well-tended garden. At the sound of a distant cry, she looked in the direction of the fields, where Tom Finney and his children hailed her.

Meredith's heart skipped a beat when she saw another in their midst. *What was he doing here?*

The Finney children surrounded Nicholas Caulfield, chattering and vying for his attention. Little Meg Finney clung to his hand, hero worship glowing bright in her eyes. Meredith felt little better than the child as she devoured the sight of him. His bare chest glistened with perspiration, and his hair gleamed blue-black in the sun.

"Good day, Lady Brookshire," Tom Finney greeted.

"Good morning, Mr. Finney. Children." She nodded before turning to greet the man to whom her every nerve was achingly sensitized. "Good morning, Mr. Caulfield." Even sweaty and dirt-spattered, he was beautiful to behold.

"Lady Brookshire," he returned, his gaze raking her wind-chapped face and wild hair, reminding her of her mussed appearance. Heat stole into her face and she fumbled for her bonnet.

"Have you come to call on Sally?" Mr. Finney asked. "She'll be pleased, sore for company as she is."

"I suspected as much." Meredith addressed the farmer and forced her gaze off Caulfield's lean, sinewy body. Tying the ribbons of her bonnet beneath her chin, she noticed that Mr. Finney's eldest daughter appeared equally captivated by Caulfield's physique.

"Right lucky that his lordship happened along. He helped me free the plow from the field. The children and I have been trying at it half the morning."

"Lucky indeed." Once again Meredith felt the stirrings of resentment. For all that she had done for her tenants, she never helped pull a plow free. And by the glow in Mr. Finney's eyes, this gesture from the new lord of the manor meant a great deal.

"Come inside. Sally will not like my keeping you from her, my lady."

Mr. Finney led her inside. Caulfield, Meredith noted, didn't follow. Undoubtedly, he had further things to do in order to undermine her—surely somewhere there was a baby to birth or a roof to thatch. The sour thought stayed with her as she settled herself in a chair and attempted to focus her attention on Sally Finney's extensive complaints.

"The swelling's got so bad I can't even walk. It weren't this bad the other times," Sally complained, submerged in the bed beneath the huge mound of her stomach, several pillows propped behind her back.

"Perhaps a pillow beneath your feet will help

eliminate the swelling," Meredith suggested, standing to arrange a pillow beneath the woman's feet.

Sally shrugged. "I'll try anything, milady."

Meredith took advantage of her standing position to search out the open window for Caulfield. "Has Maree brought you her special tea?" she asked distractedly.

"Aye, milady. She left the herbs and showed my Catie how to prepare it."

"Good. And don't hesitate to send for Maree when your time comes. She's experienced with these things."

"I've always delivered my babes fine, milady. I don't need a fuss." Sally batted a hand in the air as though she were shooing away flies.

"I insist." Meredith tore her attention from the window to level a stern stare on Sally. "You'll hear from me afterward if you do not."

Sally smiled indulgently. "Ah, milady, you need not fret over me like a mother hen. I've done this lots of times."

"Sally," she warned in mock severity, "I'll have your word."

"Aye." Sally threw her hands up in the air in good-natured defeat. "I promise, I'll send for Maree when my time comes."

Meredith visited a bit longer, making Sally a fresh pot of Maree's tea. Finally she stood to leave, promising to return in a week's time.

"Hopefully, the babe will be here by then, milady." Sally rubbed her abdomen absently. "Can't take much more."

"Then I'll visit both of you." Meredith smiled.

"With some of your cook's honeyed scones?" Sally asked hopefully, fairly smacking her lips.

Meredith smiled. It had become tradition for her to bring a basket of honeyed sconces and other small gifts to every tenant family that delivered a child. "Of course. And with your growing brood, I think I shall ask cook to prepare two baskets."

She departed, leaving a delighted Sally behind. Given the length of her visit, Meredith did not expect to find *him* outside. With his jacket slung carelessly over his shoulder, he was now decently clothed—although his appearance still fell short of proper. At least his lovely muscled torso was hidden from view. He went without a cravat, his very tanned throat a stark contrast to the white of his shirt, only half tucked into skintight riding breeches. Her mouth dried at the sight of his rakish mien. His wet hair glistened in the sunlight. The image of him washing up at the well, droplets of water clinging lovingly to every inch of his powerful flesh, teased her.

Shocked by her carnal thoughts, Meredith quickly averted her gaze, noticing that his horse stood tethered next to hers. Both beasts waited placidly as he chatted with the eldest Finney girl. Unnoticed, Meredith took in the cozy pair with mounting suspicion. A dark-haired girl far too buxom for fifteen years, Catie displayed more self-confidence than most women. Her fingers stroked Brookshire's arm as she leaned in. Brookshire's lips curved in the semblance of a smile, and

Meredith searched hard to decipher that smile. On the surface it seemed a touch indulgent, but surely corrupt intent lurked within that devastating wolf's grin. Perhaps he intended to play at the seduction of a young farm girl during his stay at Oak Run.

Meredith's lips tightened as she advanced on the pair, her riding crop twitching a furious staccato at her side. She had her hands on Petunia's reins before they even noticed her. Catie started guiltily and dropped her hand from his arm.

"I'm sure your mother could use you inside, Catie." Meredith glared over the back of her mare at the girl.

Red-faced, the girl glanced at Caulfield before addressing her. "Yes, ma'am." She executed a quick, clumsy curtsy to him. "Good day, milord."

Meredith swung herself up into the saddle, struggling for a moment until a large hand on her bottom pushed her into place unceremoniously. Stifling an indignant screech, she righted herself in the saddle and glared down at him. Her fingers clenched her riding crop, itching to bring it across his smirking face and erase the amusement from his eyes. Inhaling deeply, she reminded herself to behave properly . . . even if he did not.

"I did not ask for your assistance, my lord." She swiped furiously at the loose tendrils of hair that refused to stay confined beneath her bonnet.

"I thought I could be helpful." He shrugged, smiling.

"I don't need your kind of help." Looking down

her nose at him from atop her mare, she allowed just the right amount of ice to creep into her voice.

His eyes danced with laughter. "I could not resist." He splayed a hand over his chest. "It's my nature to help others."

Still feeling the burning imprint of his hand, Meredith looked in the direction of the cottage and caught sight of Catie peeking longingly out the window.

He followed her gaze.

Catie visibly started at finding herself the subject of their attention and stepped back from the window, disappearing from view.

"I think I am coming to understand your nature, my lord." Her voice rang with quiet condemnation as she looked away from the now empty window. He was a philanderer, out to seduce anything in skirts.

He met her eyes with a dark, brooding stare of his own. "You know me so well, then? You think I crave after little girls?"

With only the barest hesitation, she gave a quick nod of affirmation. He was a bold, sinful man— willing to ruin any poor country girl who stared moon-eyed after him. He had lived an improper life. That much he had made abundantly clear. A hard, godless existence. Whether of his making or not, it was nonetheless his life.

His voice dipped. "What is it you see when you look at me, Lady Brookshire?" The combination of his dark-eyed stare and that soft, rumbling voice sent a tremor rushing through her, heating her blood. Suddenly she was not so certain of what they discussed. *What did she see when she looked at him?* When the truth struck her, it could not have terrified her more.

She saw what she wanted and could never have.

Afraid to speak, in case the real, horrifying answer spilled forth, Meredith tugged her reins, but her mare did not move. She glanced down, seeing that he held the reins, impeding her escape.

His sudden, brief laugh rippled through the air and did strange things to her insides. "I don't think you come close to understanding my nature. The last thing a man like me desires is a little girl."

A man like him? A rake? Meredith could not hold back her caustic retort. "Indeed? It did not appear that way a moment ago." Wishing to appear unruffled, she strove for an even tone and added, "Naive young girls like Catie are easy prey for someone as worldly as yourself."

True enough. Had not Edmund swept her—a simple vicar's daughter—off her feet with embarrassing ease? And this man was far more dangerous than Edmund. The sight of him reminded her of mythical heroes rising naked from hidden lagoons, water sluicing down their hard torsos, bodies steaming in the cool air. Meredith swallowed and gave herself a mental shake as she reined in her daydreams. Good God. If he caused such a reaction in her—someone who had long ago shelved thoughts of passion—what manner of thoughts raced through Catie's mind?

"I take the welfare of my tenants to heart, my lord."

"Rest assured, my lady, Catie is safe from the likes of me. My tastes run to more mature—" His dark stare slid over her, taking in her tumbling hair. "—experienced women."

Meredith sensed he had just evaluated and placed her in the experienced and mature category. Ha! If he only knew that was but a half-truth. Surely he was accustomed to his choice of beautiful, sophisticated women in Town? Not a dull drab like her. Perhaps the thought of her carrying another man's child did not bother him, and he saw her as an easy conquest—a widow already with child and with no one to hold him accountable should he take an unseemly interest in her. Perhaps he even thought she enjoyed bed play and missed such sport since her husband's demise. Aside of the perfunctory peck on her wedding day, she had never kissed a man. Ironically, Catie probably possessed more experience than Meredith, a woman nearly twice her age.

With that humbling thought, Meredith wrenched the reins free. "But the mature, experienced woman has more sense than to dally with you."

He chuckled again, a knowing, intimate sound that sent shivers up her arms and made her neck and breasts tingle. "It's the experienced woman who usually seeks my company. They know I can provide what they want."

Scandalized by his provocative words, his

arrogance, and her own reaction, she sought an end to their conversation. "Just stay away from her, my lord."

"Call me Nick," he said unexpectedly.

"That would be improper." Nick. So raw, bold. Meredith looked him up and down. It fit him perfectly.

"And I shall call you Meredith." Most people pronounced her name harsh and clipped. Not him. The emphasis he placed on her name sounded strange, his deep voice softening the accents. It was all too alluring.

"I would rather you not."

He smiled that wolf smile, his teeth a flash of white in his tanned face. "Why is that? We are family, are we not? I am your brother of a sort."

Brother?

Meredith choked. Undeniably, her thoughts often became muddled in his presence, but one thought stood out clear and confusion free. *This man was not her brother.*

One look into his laughing eyes told Meredith he did not regard her in a sisterly fashion either, that he merely mocked her with the ridiculous suggestion.

"Good day, my lord." Meredith clung to the formality of his title, a much needed barrier. His hand on the bridle stopped her. "Release my horse," she demanded. Petunia whinnied, the bridle jingling as she jerked her head up and down, either sensing her mistress's distress or simply eager to be off.

All mockery gone, he asked, "I had not given it a thought until just now . . . is it wise to ride in your condition?"

She stared at him blankly, having no idea to what he referred. Then it dawned. Her fingers drifted to her abdomen, recalling the alleged life there, a life she had completely forgotten about because it did not exist. "The exercise is good for me."

He frowned. "Do not most ladies in your condition abstain from riding?"

Naturally, he was correct. Most women did not ride during their confinement. It galled her to have overlooked such a consideration before she left this morning. "Honestly, it had not occurred to me that riding was inadvisable."

His gaze narrowed. "Perhaps you need to adjust your reasoning. You no longer have only yourself to consider."

Must his high-handedness extend to her person as well as Oak Run? She could not abide his interference. He did not control her.

"Do not scold me like a child. I am quite accustomed to caring for myself . . . and others. I have been doing that exact thing for years."

"Then why did your judgment lapse today?" he countered, one black brow rising superciliously.

"Oh!" She fisted her reins in sheer frustration. "Please be so good as to mind your own affairs."

"I thought we had established that for the time being you and your child are my concern." He released the bridle and crossed his arms over his broad chest.

"Don't trouble yourself. I can look after myself."

"As long as you look after yourself *properly*, you'll hear nothing from me, Meredith."

Arrogant man! His deliberate use of her name chafed her already frayed nerves. Meredith gave no thought to how reckless she appeared as she spun her horse about and tore out of the Finney yard. Digging her heels into Petunia's flanks, she surrendered to the moment, hoping she sent dirt and earth kicking up into Nicholas Caulfield's handsome face.

Her satisfaction was short-lived. Galloping away, her head cleared enough for her to realize how foolish she must appear. If she wanted him gone long before the supposed delivery of her son, she would have to rein in her defiant streak. How was he to be fully confident in her ability to care for herself and Oak Run if she behaved so recklessly? And one thing was for certain. The man could not be at Oak Run when she "gave birth." Matters were already complicated enough without him underfoot then.

"Blast it," Meredith muttered, slowing her horse to a trot. She had to avoid acting rashly in his presence. When forced into his company, she would be modest, demure, the perfect model of gentility—boring. He would leave for no other reason than to escape the absolute tedium of her company.

* * *

The woman fascinated him.

She was not quite the frigid piece of lace he had first determined. The way her eyes lingered on his naked chest testified to that. When they quarreled, sparks flew from her green eyes like a hot-blooded virago, lighting a fire in the pit of his gut that could not be quenched by any suitable means. She did not at all resemble the prim, retiring, drawing room lady he first thought her to be. Not when she looked upon him with desire. It was growing impossible to dismiss her from his mind. Especially since she hid something from him. Her nervousness around him could not totally be attributed to physical attraction.

He could not deny his annoyance as he watched her thunder away at breakneck speed, her auburn hair streaming in a wild banner behind her, the final remnants of her plait unraveling in the wind. He had half a mind to give chase and haul her bodily from that bloody horse. The woman was a menace to herself and her unborn child, regardless of how intriguing he found her. *What was she thinking riding a horse like that?* The idea of him tapping into all her fiery energy and seeing just how passionate her nature ran seized him. Scowling, Nick gathered his reins and swung himself into his saddle in one easy motion.

How had she managed all these years on her own exhibiting such poor judgment? He sighed and urged his horse into a trot. Most importantly, why did he care? Why couldn't he just walk away?

Slink back to the life he'd made? Why did he have to feel such bloody obligation to her, a sense of obligation that only increased with their growing acquaintance?

Nick tried to ignore the answer that teased at him like a pesky fly buzzing around the inside of his head. But it was no use. He wanted his brother's widow, wanted the woman carrying Edmund's baby. He gave his head a small shake. An attraction wrong on countless levels, but there it was, nonetheless.

As a man unaccustomed to self-denial, this spelled trouble. There was only one solution. He had to leave. Soon. Before he found out it was more than her auburn mane and tempting curves that attracted him.

Chapter 6

Meredith arrived to an empty dining room. Not unusual for a Sunday. Her aunt spent so much time selecting her clothes and turban for church, she often missed breakfast completely. Especially on the first Sunday of the month, when the vicar dined with them. Her aunt always wanted to look her best.

She exhaled, not realizing until that moment that she had been holding her breath in anticipation—and dread—of facing Nick.

Morning sunlight shot through the mullioned windows in bright beams, bringing the air to vibrant life with tiny motes of unknown particles. Turning, she let the warmth of the sun soak through her dress and into her back as she helped herself to eggs and kippers from the generous spread of food on the sideboard. Maree entered the room, leading her father to his chair with a firm hold on his elbow.

"Now, you sit yourself here and I'll fetch you a nice plate of eggs and—"

"Coffee, lots of cream," her father interrupted, his voice petulant as he settled in his chair.

Her father may have changed a great deal over the last years, but his preference for cream-laced coffee had not. Meredith smiled at the exchange as she succumbed to her sweet tooth and selected a plump sweet roll from the sideboard.

As Maree prepared her father's plate, Meredith set her plate aside to pour her father's coffee, making certain to include a generous amount of cream. "Here you are, Father." She set the cup in front of him, warning, "It's hot."

Ignoring her, he took a noisy sip, puckering his lips when he singed them with the scalding liquid.

"Careful," Meredith chided, rubbing her father's back.

Paying her no heed, he tackled his cup of coffee again. She sighed and exchanged knowing looks with Maree. Her father loved his coffee too much to exercise caution.

Amid this noisy slurping, Nick entered the room.

"Good morning," he greeted, his gaze skipping over her to the selection of food at the sideboard.

"Good morning," she responded, ignoring the

stab of disappointment at the brief glance he sent her way.

Her father looked up from his coffee to stare broodingly at Nick's back. Meredith's breath suspended, anxious to see if her father would behave or not. She breathed easy when he resumed eating, indifferent to their presence as he turned to gaze out the window at the sunlight glinting off the vast landscape of green lawn.

Seating herself at the twenty-foot dining table, she forced her eyes on her plate, battling the temptation to stare at the man occupying far too much of her thoughts. Peeking beneath lowered lids, she discreetly watched him move along the sideboard. Her attention lingered on the superb fit of his breeches. Mortified by the direction of her thoughts, she wrenched her eyes away, pulled apart her sticky sweet roll and stuffed a generous portion into her mouth.

Cheeks burning, she was still chewing when he took the seat directly across from her, snapping his napkin once in the air before laying it over his lap. As she reached for her cup of tea, his gaze caught her. He watched her intently as he bit into a slice of jam-slathered toast. Dropping her eyes, she stared into the milky brown contents of the steaming cup she held with both hands.

"You look fetching this morning, Meredith."

Her gaze dropped to her dress. It was the finest of her mourning gowns, the one reserved for church, but still depressing. Only a few more frills and some black beads graced the modest neckline.

Nothing about the gown could be described as *fetching*. And she sincerely doubted her person lended any beauty to its moroseness.

"Your hair is lovely in that arrangement," he added.

Her hand flew to her hair self-consciously. She usually wore it in a softer fashion for church, taking the time and effort to arrange it into one of her less severely knotted buns. The effort had not been taken on account of him.

Then, horrified that he might draw that very conclusion, she blurted, "Thank you. I always wear it so for church."

He gave a small nod and returned to his breakfast, digging in with gusto. Clearly, he was a man who enjoyed his food. Meredith liked to cook and believed herself to be a fair hand in the kitchen. True, not many ladies could attest to such knowledge—nor would they want to. But she had not been a countess all her life. Before Oak Run her family had only two servants, and when Cook needed a hand in the kitchen, the task fell to Meredith. She watched as he bit into a sweet roll. He closed his eyes with a look of deep appreciation, and she wondered what he would think if he knew she had helped prepare them.

After several moments of awkward silence, she thought to announce, "We depart for the village church at nine, my lord."

Nick blinked once before replying. "That is very well, my lady, but do not mistake that I shall be accompanying you."

Meredith felt the heat rise in her face and suppressed the urge to snap back that she had not presumed to think he would. But that would be a lie. Of course she had thought he would accompany them to church. It was what respectable Society did on Sundays.

Instead, she merely said, "Your arrival will be known to all of Attingham by now. Your presence will be expected. There will be . . . talk if you are not there."

Setting his utensils on his plate with a soft clink, he leaned back in his chair and gave her a long, measuring look. It took every ounce of will not to squirm beneath his heavy regard.

"As you come to know me, you will find that I rarely do what is expected, nor do I live my life for the satisfaction of others."

She scarcely registered the clench of her fingers around her knife and fork—only heard her biting retort. "How very convenient to live life with no concern save for yourself." The instant the words left her mouth, she wondered what it was about the man that had her blurting the first thing to pop into her head. That had her *reacting* rather than pausing to think.

With narrowed eyes, he replied, "Phrase it however you like. I simply do not subscribe to the hypocrisy of sitting in a church surrounded by an overprivileged Society that sings alleluias on Sunday and practices hedonism the rest of the week."

"I have never heard such sacrilegious drivel in all my life!"

He lifted an eyebrow and asked blandly, "Indeed? Country living has left you quite sheltered, then."

She scowled, not appreciating his insinuation that she was *limited* in some way. "I don't dispute a great many churchgoers fail to practice what is preached on Sundays. They are only human, after all. However, the majority does aspire to live rightly, including members of the very *overprivileged Society* you yourself are part of."

"That is where you are wrong. I may have been born to this world, but I don't belong to it. My father saw to that." The sudden angle of his head and angry glint of his eyes should have warned her to let it go, to accept that he was a man outside her realm of knowledge and she had no business tangling words with him. Besides, she was doing a poor job of behaving demurely and modestly, as she had only recently avowed.

Even bearing this in mind, Meredith heard herself saying, "But you are here, acting very much the part of lord of the manor to my eyes."

"Temporarily, I assure you. Even if you should deliver a daughter, I shall find a way out of my obligation to Oak Run, the title . . . and you."

She experienced a contrary twinge of hurt at that last bit. Which was absolutely absurd. She did not want to be bound to him any more than he to her. He returned his attention to his food, and Meredith breathed a bit easier, released from his intense scrutiny.

"I will be free again," he muttered so softly she

barely made out his words. They sunk into her head gradually, like a pebble sinking through water and settling at last into a riverbed.

Slumping back in her chair, her eyes narrowed with sudden insight, as if seeing him for the first time. *He really wanted no part of Oak Run.* His apparent indifference to the news that she carried Edmund's child was because he was in fact . . . indifferent. He did not long to take up the title. For him, it was a yoke about his neck—the shackles and dictates of Society. He lived by no code other than his own. His rules were none but his own. Respectability, responsibility, Oak Run, the earldom . . . he viewed it all as a prison sentence.

Armed with this knowledge, she idly wondered if he would even care about her deception. Perhaps he would help her carry it out. No, an unlikely possibility and not worth the risk. Still, she felt better knowing she was giving him what he wanted. A way out. Rising to her feet, Meredith dropped her napkin on her plate.

He lifted an eyebrow. "It's not yet nine. Are you off already to join the pillars of Society?" He snorted faintly. "Don't be fooled by them, Meredith. None possess the charity in their heart that you hold in your little finger."

Convinced she misunderstood his words, that he did not mean to compliment her, she gave him a puzzled look. He did not know her well enough to make such a judgment, and he would hardly think her charitable if he knew the fraud she perpetrated against him.

As if to erase his backhanded compliment and remind her of his innate shamelessness, he added, "Was my half brother such a saint too? Did he attend church with you?"

Meredith suffered the laughter in his eyes and immediately recognized that he knew Edmund. Probably better than she ever did. Which was not saying much. Edmund's tailor probably knew him better than she had. The only thing Meredith knew about her late husband was that he had wanted nothing to do with her. Had found her so distasteful that he could not bear consummating their marriage.

Despite her desire to remove the smirk from his face, she could not refute his mocking question. She shot another glance at her father, unsure whether to leave him alone with Nick. Her father, however, appeared blessedly oblivious to their conversation. A good thing. He would have been appalled to know he sat beside a pagan.

Meredith moved from the table in a dignified swish of skirts. "Excuse me, my lord. I don't want to be late for the service." In the threshold, she paused to add, "The vicar dines with us tonight. Perhaps you can engage him in a discussion on the lack of charity among his parishioners." With the barest smile tugging her lips, she exited.

Nick stared broodingly at the door where Meredith disappeared, feeling like an utter ass for needling her. It never seemed to fail. Minutes into a conversation, and she provoked him. He stabbed at a bit of egg, cursing under his breath. It had been a long time since he found himself in the company of a genuine lady. Perhaps he could blame his breach on not recalling how to behave.

But it was more than that. He found it diverting to bait her. So diverting that the room felt empty without her animated presence. It was as if all life and energy had been sucked out with her departure. The sudden, loud slurping of Meredith's father drew his attention, reminding him that he wasn't alone. Nick shook his head, a wry smile twisting his lips at the prolonged noise. The old man set his cup on its saucer with an unsteady hand and resumed his absent stare out the window.

The full loss of Meredith's company settled like a heavy weight on Nick's chest. For the first time in years, he yearned for the company of someone else. Strange that it happened to be Edmund's widow. A woman he should dislike on principle alone.

Chapter 7

"I don't know why you are so upset, dearest," Aunt Eleanor pouted.

Meredith sighed and tried to explain her disappointment once again. "I simply wish you would have consulted me before inviting half the neighborhood to dinner."

"You exaggerate. Mr. Browne, Sir Hiram, and the Stubblefields hardly constitute half the neighborhood."

"Felicia Stubblefield is the biggest gossip around. Inviting her is inviting the entire neighborhood. And you know Sir Hiram makes my skin crawl."

"What else was I to do? They know the new

earl is here, and the vicar was already coming to dine. I couldn't very well exclude them, not when Felicia angled for an invitation."

Meredith took hold of her aunt's elbow, stalling her outside the drawing room where their guests waited. "Did it occur to you that perhaps Lord Brookshire does not want the neighborhood raining down upon his head? *That I do not?* Especially as his presence here is only temporary." She hissed this last bit.

Aunt Eleanor's hand flew to her mouth. "Oh, dear," she whispered woefully, and turned to stare at the drawing room door as if a snake lurked within instead of the guests she had invited. "I had not considered that."

How their circumstances could ever be far from her aunt's mind when it consumed hers at nearly every moment was unfathomable to Meredith. Her deception marred the horizon like a perpetual cloud, at times worrying her so much that she hesitated to go about her day, afraid that someone might run up to her at any moment pointing and shouting, "Liar, liar!"

"I realize that, Aunt." Meredith gave her aunt's shoulder a comforting pat, helpless against the long-ingrained need to console her. "Don't fret. We shall manage."

Drawing a deep breath, she strove for an air of optimism. Some good might come of her aunt's poor judgment. An evening with local gentry might be just the thing to chase Nick back to London.

Pasting a smile on her face, Meredith entered the drawing room, black skirts swirling around her ankles. The three gentlemen rose to their feet and bowed. Baron Stubblefield's daughter, achingly pretty in pink muslin, lounged on the chaise like an empress. She gave Meredith a brittle smile that failed to reach her eyes. Only nineteen, Miss Felicia Stubblefield reigned as the diamond of Attingham. Even so, Meredith found it hard to like the girl whose cold blue stare always slithered over her with such disdain. Struggling against feelings of inadequacy, Meredith raised her chin and complimented Mr. Browne on his morning's sermon.

Felicia glanced to the door. Her tapping foot clearly indicated her impatience. Meredith could guess the cause of it, and her suspicions were confirmed when Felicia finally broke down and asked, "Is Lord Brookshire not joining us? Miss Eleanor said he would dine with us this evening."

Meredith did not miss the way the girl glared accusingly at her aunt. "Lord Brookshire is a man full grown and not accountable to anyone but himself."

"Have no fear, Miss Felicia, no man would miss out on such lovely dinner companions," Sir Hiram inserted, the elegant sweep of his hand indicating all three ladies present.

"Quite right, Rawlins," Baron Stubblefield chortled, patting the considerable bulge of his belly to add, "And Lady Brookshire's cook is the finest in these parts. No gentleman would miss an invitation to dine at Oak Run."

They all laughed. Except Mr. Browne, who took a small sip of tea through pinched, disapproving lips. The vicar's sermon had been longer than usual and given to more ceremony today. Meredith suspected he had taken great pains, expecting Lord Brookshire to be in attendance. The vicar's immediate questioning of her following the service on the issue of Lord Brookshire's whereabouts only confirmed her suspicion.

They visited for another half hour before Nels announced dinner. Meredith and her aunt exchanged uneasy glances as their small party filed into the dining room. It appeared Lord Brookshire would not join them. Meredith's hands fisted at her sides and she felt an embarrassed flush creep up her face.

The head of the table stood conspicuously vacant. The empty seat seemed to glare at all of them, reminding everyone of the slight implied by his absence. Doing her best to ignore the empty seat, Meredith steered conversation away from the mention of Lord Brookshire. Even so, Mr. Browne and Felicia's eyes constantly drifted to the unused place setting, then back to her, clearly holding her responsible for the empty chair.

Then, before the first course was served, he arrived. "Forgive me," he offered with a casual smile. "I lost track of the hour."

Meredith felt the tension inside her snap. "Perhaps you need a timepiece, my lord?"

Her aunt gaped from across the table, letting Meredith know, in case she had any doubts, that she had been unpardonably rude. Nick, however, appeared unruffled as he seated himself at the head of the table. His eyes danced with amusement, but he only responded with a light shrug.

Aunt Eleanor quickly performed the introductions. In record time Felicia engaged Nick in conversation to the exclusion of everyone else. Meredith leaned as far to her left as she dared without falling out of her chair, trying to catch their words, finally giving up when she realized Sir Hiram was repeating himself due to her inattention.

"Might I inquire as to your future plans, my lady, now that Lord Brookshire has taken control of Oak Run?"

Meredith fidgeted, twisting her linen napkin in her lap. The news of her approaching motherhood had not yet spread, and she dreaded the revelation, fearing the reaction from those who knew of her estranged marriage. Gossip was inescapable.

Sir Hiram especially knew her relationship with Edmund had been less than devoted. Edmund's abandonment had paved the way for his amorous attentions these many years. A widower of middle years, he lacked the sophistication to be called a rake. Left alone to raise a set of troublesome twins that had successfully terrorized every resident of Attingham at one time or another, Meredith believed his attentions were motivated solely by his desperation for companionship.

Especially as no female was inclined to take on his two terrors in a more permanent arrangement. The fact that Meredith never showed the slightest interest had not swayed the man. A neglected wife such as she appeared the natural companion for dalliance.

Sir Hiram's eyes gleamed hopefully, as if he believed his chances improved now that she was widowed. Still awaiting her answer, he touched her hand where it rested on her knee beneath the table. She jumped at the touch, sending her knees—his hand included—crashing against the table and jarring both their place settings.

Hiram winced and pulled his hand free, clutching the injured appendage to his chest. Nick looked on, his eyes hard with interest . . . and something else.

"Yes, where will you go now?" Felicia tore her attention from Nick long enough to pick up Sir Hiram's line of questioning. As if the prospect of Meredith leaving were of no account at all, she continued chewing, her cheeks stuffed fat with food. A quick glance around the table revealed that everyone waited for her response. Evidently, no one expected her to stay on.

"Lady Meredith is not going anywhere."

All heads swiveled in Nick's direction. He stabbed a small roasted potato with his fork. At that moment, he appeared indifferent to their stares, simply a man enjoying his food. He took a swig of wine before adding, "Lady Meredith will remain here of course. This is her home."

"And live with you?" Felicia exclaimed, her golden ringlets swinging as she looked back and forth between Nick and Meredith. For the first time, something besides disdain frosted the girl's eyes. Jealousy shined in the china blue depths. "That is highly improper, my lord."

"Is it?" Nick asked in a tone indicating his lack of interest in what was proper.

Meredith wanted to laugh at Felicia's reddening face. If the girl's outrage weren't at the cost of her own reputation, she would have been overjoyed.

Mr. Browne's unsolicited opinion rang out in strident tones. "It cannot be appropriate for two unattached persons to live together out of wedlock—"

"With her aunt to act as chaperone?" Nick shook his head in dissent. "I hardly think we are stretching the bounds of propriety." His eyes drilled into the gentlemen present. "I dare anyone to sully Lady Meredith's good name by implying differently."

Mr. Browne sniffed at the indiscreet warning, but wisely chose not to offer further opinion.

"Besides," Nick added in seeming afterthought, "Lady Meredith is increasing with my brother's child—a better safeguard to her virtue I could not fathom."

Meredith pressed her eyes shut against the immediate commotion that erupted around the table. Opening her eyes, she met Nick's curious gaze and read the question there. *You haven't told them?*

In a voice that sounded small and weak even to

her own ears, Meredith tried to explain. "I did not know the best time to announce the news . . . what with Edmund's recent passing there never seemed—"

Felicia had no trouble getting to the point. The young woman's voice rose over her father and Mr. Browne's well wishes. "Well, are you the earl or not?"

Nick leaned back in his chair, appearing to enjoy himself as everyone watched him with bated breath, anticipation writ on their faces. "That depends."

"Depends?" Felicia snapped, clearly anxious to know if he was a prize worth winning. "On what?"

"On the sex of the child."

All eyes swung back to Meredith, drilling into her with unnerving intensity—as if they could strip away her clothes to seek the answer buried within.

At her side, Sir Hiram's voice dropped to a frantic whisper. "Lady Meredith, how can this be?"

Indignation welled up inside her. Who was he to ask such a question of her? She desired nothing more than to relieve Sir Hiram of his propriety air. Instead, she swallowed back the stinging set down she wished to vent. "I do not understand your meaning, Sir Hiram."

As Sir Hiram struggled for words, Nick voiced his own question. "Yes, what do you mean, Rawlins?"

Apparently realizing how close he was to insulting his host and hostess, Sir Hiram abandoned his line of questioning and lifted his glass in a toast. "Felicitations and many blessings on the safe delivery of your child."

Meredith nodded in polite acknowledgment and smiled weakly as the others joined Sir Hiram in raising their glasses.

She watched Nick drink deeply, his dark eyes trained on her over the rim. She gave him a small, grudging nod of gratitude for smoothing things over. Perhaps she even owed her aunt gratitude. By tomorrow all of Attingham would know she was with child. The matter of breaking the news would be out of the way. Even if no one believed it.

Meredith could not say what exactly woke her. She lay still in bed for a few moments and waited, listening to the silence. Then she heard it.

Voices. Floating from the first floor. They rumbled in the air like a distant drone of bees. The hour had to be very late. The night sky was pitch-black out her balcony window and the air almost unnaturally still. Grabbing her night rail, she pulled it over her cotton gown and hurried to investigate. She stopped at the top of the stairs, eyeing the scene below.

Young Ben Finney stood on the threshold, his hands waving wildly with his excited speech. Nels stood there as well, nodding as he listened to the boy.

"Nels?" Meredith called from the top of the stairs,

clutching her night rail to her throat. "Is anything amiss?"

"Mrs. Finney's time has begun. The lad here is to fetch Maree."

"Give me a moment. I shall accompany her."

Meredith hurried back to her room and made short work of dressing, changing into one of her old, brown wool dresses. She didn't bother with arranging her hair, simply allowed it to remain in its loosely bound plait. Perhaps she would have taken more care had she known she would face Nick in the foyer.

"My lord? What are you doing here?" she asked as she descended the stairs, coming to a halt before him.

"I heard voices." His dark eyes examined her, roving over her plain clothing and untidy hair.

He appeared to have dressed in haste as well. His white lawn shirt flapped open to the middle of his chest and was tucked untidily into dark breeches. The tan of his skin presented a dark contrast to the stark white of his shirt, and Meredith experienced a strange tightening in her breasts the longer she looked at him.

"I am sorry you were disturbed. Mrs. Finney's baby has chosen the middle of the night to greet the world," Meredith explained.

Just then Maree ambled toward them, lugging a heavy basket. Nels rushed to help her. "I've got everything except the stove. Oh, did we wake everyone?"

"I will accompany you, Maree," Meredith volunteered. Maree gave a grunt of acceptance, accustomed to Meredith's presence at the birthing of tenants' children.

Nick followed them outside and took her arm to assist her into the Finney wagon. Their eyes locked as she settled on the hard seat. She felt certain his thoughts were on the last time he had *assisted* her. Warmth flooded her face at the memory of those strong hands on her derriere. She felt the heat of those black eyes boring into her back as they rode away in the wagon, but she dared not look back.

"That one appears to do a good deal of looking at you," Maree murmured.

Meredith cut a sharp glance to the boy at her side. Thankfully, Ben appeared too lost in his worries to pay attention to their conversation. She replied in hushed tones, "I don't know what you mean."

Maree's keen eyes and worldly aura reminded Meredith that this woman had done her fair share of living outside of Attingham. "He's not your average man. I never seen no gentleman like him in all my days. Don't travel with a valet. Brought just one bag with him . . . and no coach, just a horse." Maree made a clucking sound and shook her head in wonder. "Sure he has manners enough to be Quality, but take one look in his eyes and you can see it."

"See what?"

"You ever look an ol' beat-up dog in the eyes?

He's got that same look. Like deep down he's dead inside. Like there ain't nothing in the world that can reach him. Not even you."

Meredith frowned. Nick possessed a wounded spirit, with that she would agree. With his past, how could he come away unscathed? But she refused to think him dead inside. That would mean he was lost, and for some reason she would not allow herself to believe that of him. No soul was ever completely lost. Besides, his eyes burned with life. Especially when they looked at her.

"He's not dead inside," she said a touch defensively. "He fairly hums with vitality."

Maree squinted at Meredith's face, as if trying to distinguish her features in the shadows. "Oh, Lord." She laughed. "He's already got to you."

Meredith opened her mouth to deny the outrageous words, but Maree did not give her a chance to speak.

"One look at him should have warned me you'd fall for him. Be careful, Meredith. You can't afford to fall in love with him. Not this one." She patted Meredith's belly in reminder, her thick brows dipping meaningfully. "You've made other plans. Keep that in mind and steer clear of him." Her voice lowered to a hushed whisper. "He won't be the gentleman if he finds out. Men don't like being fooled, and something tells me this one would be more than you could handle."

Meredith bit her lip in concern, considering Nick's reaction should he uncover her deception.

He might not want the inheritance, but he would not thank her for being deceived. Maree was correct on that score.

The wagon hit a rut that jarred her from her troubling reflections. Her fingers dug into the rough wood bench beneath her for support.

"Easy, boy," Maree huffed, clutching the basket to her ample bosom as the mules took a turn in the winding road that nearly lifted the wheels of the wagon. "We'll be no good to your ma if you over-turn this box and break our necks."

Both Meredith and Maree breathed a sigh of relief when they reached the Finney farm without mishap. Tom Finney waited in the yard with his sons. He rushed to help the two women down.

"So glad you came. It's taking so long. It didn't take Sally this long with the others . . . well, maybe just the first one, but that's the way they say, with the first one," he rattled as he followed them to the cottage door.

It appeared all of the Finney males would have followed them into the cottage if Maree had not blocked their way. "We'll have enough bodies in here with all the girls. The rest of you wait out-side."

A putrid smell assailed Meredith upon enter-ing the cottage. Sally Finney's low moans rent the air. Three young girls peered wide-eyed from the loft above. Meredith could see the fright in their little faces as the eldest girls, Catie and Hannah, tended their mother.

Maree wasted no time and set to work examining Sally. "Have you started any pushing yet, love?" she asked from between the woman's trembling thighs.

Sally shook her head jerkily on the pillow, sweaty strands of coppery hair clinging to her cheeks.

"I'd say it's about time then," Maree declared.

"Thank God," Sally sighed.

"Can you hold your legs up or do you need help?" Maree asked, taking a bowl of water from Catie.

"I can do it—" Sally began, trying the pull her shaking legs back, but gave up, letting them collapse heavily on the mattress. Meredith grasped one knee to help her. Catie took the other.

Sally smiled weakly at Meredith. "This is the last one, I tell you. I'm not going through this again."

"You said that last time, Ma," Catie teased, patting her mother's knee.

"Aye, well I mean it. From now on your father can sleep in the barn."

They all laughed, the levity welcomed.

"God has a way of making you forget the pain. Then you're left with a beautiful babe who soon grows and leaves you pining for another." Maree grinned from between Sally's sweat-slick legs. "Right, love?" she asked in soothing tones.

Sally gave a wobbly smile. "Aye."

"Fine, whenever you feel it building up on you, push," Maree instructed.

Sally pushed, her face purpling from the strain.

Tiny wheezes of breath escaped noisily through her gritted teeth. Before long Sally's groans grew into agonized screams. Over the din, Meredith heard a toddler weeping in the loft.

"Hannah," Meredith commanded. "Take the little ones outside. They don't need to be here."

Hannah obeyed, fetching them from the loft and ushering them out while their mother labored.

At last a mewling, slippery life arrived. Maree held it upside down, slapping its bottom and eliciting a furious howling. Sally fell back on her pillow, a contented smile on her face. "What is it?"

"A girl," Maree beamed.

"Go get the family, Hannah." Sally weakly waved her daughter to the door. "Tell them to come greet their little sister."

Maree rubbed the baby vigorously with a blanket before handing her to Sally.

"She's beautiful," Sally pronounced, watching her new daughter latch onto her finger.

"You do make pretty babes, Sally," Maree agreed.

The entire Finney clan filed into the room, laughing and exclaiming over the infant. Sally relinquished the baby to her proud father. It was a happy time for a happy family, and Meredith felt a little lonely and apart from the scene. She took solace in the knowledge that she would soon have a child of her own, a baby to hug close. Even if she would not give birth herself, she would forever have a child to love. Someone who would not reject the offering of her heart.

As Maree tended to Sally, Meredith watched Tom Finney kiss his wife. Holding his daughter in one arm, he placed his other hand on Sally's sweat-beaded brow in what could only be described as a possessive, devoted gesture. Looking on, she felt like an intruder, acutely reminded of her aloneness in the world. For a brief second she wondered how different her life would have been if Edmund had been a real husband, if he had not turned from her on their wedding night.

Meredith moved to stand by the door, unnoticeable and out of the way, but near enough should Maree need her. A chill draft fluttered the hairs along her nape and she rubbed her arms for warmth. Through the happy clamor, an all too familiar voice spoke near her ear. "It's quite a celebration."

She looked over her shoulder at Nick standing in the threshold, before turning back to observe the Finneys. "What did you expect? They're a happy family."

"Well, I have no experience with that."

Meredith gave him a long, considering look. "No," she murmured. "I suppose not." After a pause she asked, "What are you doing here?"

"I told Nels I would drive the carriage over to collect the two of you."

"You should not have troubled yourself, my lord." She latched onto his title like old, familiar armor. "One of the Finney boys could have returned us. You should not lose sleep on our account."

He shrugged. "I sleep little as it is."

She hugged herself tighter, clinging to any conversation that kept her from lonely thoughts, and at the same time wanting to destroy the kinship she suddenly felt with him—another soul who knew what it felt like to be alone. "Is that so? Have you no need for sleep like the rest of us?"

With his arms crossed, his eyes glittered like hard chips of coal. "I didn't say I need less, only that I sleep little. For some, sleep does not come easily."

"My lady," Maree called, waving Meredith over to the bed and saving her from responding to Nick's enigmatic words.

Approaching, she looked to the bottom half of the bed as Maree indicated. The sight horrified her. The foot of the bed was drenched in blood. Too much blood for any human to lose and still sustain life.

Chapter 8

Meredith and Maree stood solemnly at the foot of the bed, unnoticed by the others. Even Sally, growing paler every moment, only focused on her family's joy as they exclaimed over their newest member.

"Get them out," Maree whispered.

Nodding, Meredith struggled past the tears clogging her throat and adopted a cheerful tone. "That's it. Enough excitement. Leave Baby with Father. Out while your mother gets cleaned up." Meredith waved the children out the door. Nick's eyes met hers knowingly before exiting the cottage.

Meredith shut the door, then turned back to Maree. "What do you need me to do?"

Maree flipped the covers back and examined Sally. "She's bleeding out. If it doesn't stop we'll lose her. Something must have torn inside when the babe was born."

Sally, now aware of the danger, quietly said, "Let me hold my daughter."

Meredith fetched the baby from Tom Finney's arms and placed the bundle in Sally's arms. Tom looked beseechingly to Maree and Meredith, but their helpless expressions said it all.

He shook his head violently. "No!" he shouted at Maree as she applied pressure between Sally's legs. "Do something!"

"I'm doing all I can."

Shock, disbelief, anger. Meredith read the emotions flickering across Tom Finney's face, felt them in her own heart. As Sally cooed to her baby the last lullaby she would ever sing, he placed a hand over her brow. His features screwed tight with pain and shudders racked him. "Don't go, Sally. Don't leave me."

As the lifeblood drained from her, her head lolled on the pillow, her eyes growing glassy, dead. Her bloodless lips worked silently in one last attempt at speech. No sound ever came. Seconds passed before Maree removed the babe from Sally's still arms and handed her to the sobbing father.

Then, very deliberately, Maree set about cleaning Sally one final time. Meredith helped, knowing she felt no grief like that of Tom Finney, and needed to offer whatever assistance she could.

They removed the blood-soaked bedding, maneuvering the dead woman's body while they fitted the new linens. At last Maree nodded. "We're done."

Meredith braced herself and stepped outside. Maree followed close behind. Tom Finney's sobs had no doubt carried to the yard.

"Children," Meredith softly announced to the waiting young ones, "your father needs you now."

Catie raced inside. The others hung back, their fear a palpable, living thing on the air. The girl's agonized scream shattered the night. The other children stood paralyzed, clinging to one another, eyes wide and haunted. Maree pulled little Bess and Hegar into her comforting bosom.

Suddenly, Meredith couldn't breathe. Grief clogged the air like smoke, suffocating her. Stumbling, she rushed from the yard, heading for the fields, instinctively searching out space, ready to embrace the solitude she had earlier resented. Once alone, she took in huge gulping breaths and attempted to erect a wall against the ugliness behind her.

She had learned death's lessons early. When her mother died, her father forbade grief. According to him, grief was the devil's instrument. Only nonbelievers wallowed in grief. One should rejoice when another joined the Lord. It was that simple. No tears had been spent the morning Meredith awoke to discover her mother gone. For a time, she had missed her, but by the time she was old enough to understand her true loss, the opportunity for tears had passed.

Tonight had revealed that death was not simple, nor a quiet departure to go unremarked upon. It was messy, ugly, and heartbreaking. Not everyone could accept death with her father's stoicism. Meredith dreaded returning to the raw pain waiting for her at the Finney farm.

"Meredith?" Nick's voice sounded behind her, its gravelly rumble sliding over her like velvet, comforting in its familiarity, in its nearness. She forgot that she did not want him at Oak Run, that she resented his presence, his interfering ways. All that mattered was that he was there.

She spun around, her eyes seeking his shape through the gloom. He moved toward her, his feet crunching over dry leaves. She covered the distance, flinging her arms tightly around his waist and pressing her cheek against his hard chest, seeking solace in another human being. There was the barest stiffening before he relaxed beneath her cheek and wrapped his arms around her, returning the embrace.

He placed a large hand on the back of her head. "It's all right."

Meredith clung to him, inhaling the clean scent of him as he murmured soft unintelligible words of comfort. "I don't want to go back there. It's selfish to say, but I can't bear it."

Reluctantly, she pulled back and stepped out of the circle of his arms. Wiping furiously at her tears, she muttered, "You must believe me weak and selfish to carry on so when it's the Finney family who suffers. I did not carry on like this when I lost my own mother."

"Then perhaps that is why you grieve now," he suggested.

She pictured his chiseled features in her mind as she addressed his shadow. "She just bled to death right there on that bed. There was so much blood. It happened so fast. To be alive one second . . ."

"Death rarely makes sense." His hands were firm as they grasped her arms, their warmth seeping through her cloak to her flesh. "I know it's unfair, but at least there was a life given in return tonight. Few deaths can claim to bring such good."

Meredith considered his words before nodding in agreement. "Yes, of course. It should be looked at just that way. We could have lost both of them." A shaky smile twitched her lips. "You see to the heart of things."

"I suspect something else bothers you. Another reason why you were so affected by tonight's happenings."

"What?" Meredith hedged, having an idea of what he intended to say, and not wishing to hear it.

"Could you not be afraid for yourself when your own time comes?"

Meredith stared up at him dumbly, once again disturbed that he could be capable of such consideration—especially for her, the very wretch deceiving him. But then he did not know that she was such a wretch. She released a shuddering sigh, a headache starting to form at her temples.

"I don't think—" She halted and shook her head, pressing her fingertips against her temples. "I am not afraid for myself. The women in my family have always held up well in child labor."

She freed herself from his grasp and began walking back to the farm, her steps quick and clumsy as she made her way in the dark—almost as if she could flee from her lies.

He fell into step alongside her, taking her elbow to guide her along. "It's only natural to have such fears, and tonight probably did not afford you much confidence."

"Of course," Meredith replied, awash with guilt. She preferred him difficult and domineering. He was easier to dislike that way. Not like this. Not kind and caring.

"Which is why you may wish to consider relocating to London for the remainder of your confinement. The finest physicians are to be had in Town. It would be a wise recourse, just to be safe. There are physicians specialized in the delivery of children. I could investigate and obtain the services of London's best."

Meredith's guilt grew, making her nervous. The man wanted to acquire a physician for her? She could just imagine the fellow's face when she delivered a one-pound pillow. Why would Nick want to put himself to such pains for her? They hardly knew one another. She glanced suspiciously at the man beside her. Perhaps he was not so kind after all and really suspected the truth . . . that she was not with child. Or even worse. Perhaps he was more nefarious than she imagined and wanted to arrange for a physician that would do harm to her or the baby, ensuring that he gained his inheritance. Had he fooled her just as she fooled him? She felt sick at her wild assumptions.

"When my time arrives, I would prefer the comforts of home."

"Meredith." He halted their progress and forced her around to face him. "I realize it's only my suggestion. I will not force you on the matter, but you should consider what is for the best and not simply what is comfortable." The concern softening his voice vanquished her earlier suspicions and even made her a bit ashamed. There was nothing but genuine kindness to his suggestion. Kindness she did not deserve and had attempted to deny by turning him into something ugly and villainous.

"I appreciate your concern." She could still hear the resistance in her voice, although she tried to mask it, feeling that a show of acquiescence would be best.

He sighed. "You are a stubborn woman. I'll leave off for now, but I'll not give up. Remember that I witnessed tonight's tragedy as well. It leaves me worried for you."

Worried for her. How long had it been since someone worried over her? Had anyone ever really worried over her? Meredith hugged herself as they resumed walking, vowing that his concern did not endear him to her in the least.

Why had she listened to her aunt? This lying business could get very complicated. Now she was even lying to herself.

Nick had to go. His kindness from the night before had been unexpected and unsettling. His interfering ways, his audacity, even his mockery, she could bear. But kindness was the final straw. If he stayed even one more day and bestowed so much as a single thoughtful word on her, she would break down and confess all. Yet she knew he would not leave until he deemed it time. Meredith shook her head and confronted the depressing truth that his leaving or staying was out of her hands. She could have pounded her head against the wall in frustration.

Instead, she sought solace outdoors, hoping the air would clear her head and she could arrive at some strategy to encourage his departure.

The millpond beckoned like an old friend, ready to soothe taut nerves. The water was too cold this time of year, but Meredith could not resist removing her boots, stripping off her stockings, and dunking her feet below the surface. The mill stood abandoned at the end of the pond. Even with its clapboards rotting and fallen to disrepair, it was a picturesque reminder of the past. She had not seen to its repair mostly because its charm rested in its neglected air. Giant oaks and weeping willows shaded the pond as though they wished to hide the lovely little sanctuary from the world.

Gritting her teeth against the frigid water, she gathered her skirts at her knees and sloshed the water into froth with her legs. Moss tickled the balls of her feet like a silky sponge. Freeing her hair from its topknot, she leaned back and flattened her palms on the moist earth behind her. Staring up at the branches swaying overhead, she relaxed, enjoying the solitude. She loved this place. She felt like a wood sprite ruling over her own private, enchanted world. Nothing could trouble her here.

"I see you found one of my old haunts."

Meredith jerked at the intruding voice and turned to look over her shoulder at the one who dared to invade her personal refuge. Nick loosely tethered his horse to a bush. With a few long-legged strides, he stood even with her along the bank.

"How is it you have become my shadow?" she grumbled.

"Purely by chance." He grinned.

Meredith snorted in disbelief.

"Perhaps there are forces at work," he suggested, a glint of mischief in his dark eyes.

She observed him skeptically, a crick forming in her neck. His long lashes dipped, casting crescent-shaped shadows on his cheeks as his eyes inspected her exposed limbs. Meredith pulled her legs from the water and covered them with her dress. The fabric clung wetly to her flesh, but she felt better at the shield it offered from his roving gaze.

The memory of her body pressed against his popped unbidden into her mind. Had she really been so bold as to embrace him? Heat suffused her face. She locked her arms around her bent knees and gazed out at the water's rippling surface, trying to ignore his presence. An impossible task. Her peaceful solitude was ruined. She felt his presence right down to the burn of his gaze on her body.

Unable to ignore him, she asked, "I take it you have been here before?" She tried to hide the resentment from her voice. For years she had thought of this place as hers.

"As a boy, yes. Many times." His gravelly voice rolled over her. Awareness spiked through her at the warm sound.

She risked another glance at his profile as he surveyed the pond.

"I pretended this pond was a moat and I had to swim it to storm that castle." He nodded his head to the dilapidated mill.

"And rescue the fair maiden within?" Meredith guessed, sure she had not been the only child with foolish romantic dreams.

"Of course there was a maiden . . . sometimes two." He grinned again and her heart tripped. "Strange how much smaller it seems." His smile slipped. "As a boy I thought this pond the ocean. Now it's clearly a pond. And a small one at that."

Meredith bristled at the veiled attack on her

beloved sanctuary. "Everything looks bigger through the eyes of a child."

Pushing to her feet, she wobbled for balance on the uneven ground. His hand darted beneath her cloak and grabbed her arm to steady her. Her skin tingled where he touched her, but she didn't pull away, couldn't if she wanted to. She could only gaze up at him, hostage to his dark, fathomless stare.

His eyes skimmed the length of her, resting on the naked, muddied toes peeking from beneath her hem. Her toes dug into the soft earth, burrowing for cover. She tossed a heavy flank of hair over her shoulder and tried to appear the dignified countess—unbound hair, muddy toes and all. His eyes followed the movement, surveying the rioting mass.

"How did you meet Edmund?" he demanded abruptly, a strange light glittering in his eyes. She wet her lips nervously, and his eyes darkened to black as they followed the movement of her tongue.

"In the village. My father was the vicar, remember?"

Tension lines bracketed his mouth as he demanded, "Was it a love match?"

"I am carrying his child, am I not?" The defiance in her voice rang out.

His fingers flexed on her arms, the pressure increasing as he drew her nearer. "What has that to do with whether you loved him?"

Meredith stared up at him, confused. "Why should it matter to you?"

The muscles along his jaw knotted. "Answer me. Did you love him?"

His piercing gaze demanded an answer. One she was unprepared to give. Yet in no way could she admit the truth. That she had been *infatuated* with Edmund, that she had *wanted* to love him . . . until her wedding night and the death of her romantic dreams.

"You are prying, my lord."

Suddenly he smiled. "You didn't love him."

Meredith flinched. "I did not say that."

His hands gentled on her arms, his thumbs rotating in small, seductive circles. His face inched closer, his warm breath a puff of air against her lips as he murmured, "You didn't have to."

One of his hands slid the length of her arm, his touch feather-soft. He grasped her wrist and brought her hand to his chest, splaying her palm directly over his heart. "What of desire? Did you desire my brother? Did you look at him the way you look at me?"

Meredith gasped. Convinced she could feel the strong beat of his heart beneath her hand, she whispered, "You mustn't speak such things."

"Why?" He angled his head, dark eyes studying her intently as he placed his other hand at her waist, his touch burning through her dress, branding her. "It's true. I see the way you look at me. I imagine it's the same way I look at you."

She shook her head fiercely and tried to tug her hand free.

Nick pressed her hand deeper against his chest. "Meredith—"

"No," she hissed, refusing to let him weave sweet words of seduction around her. "You'll not get your revenge on Edmund by seducing me."

His expression turned rigid before her eyes. He released her as if stung and stepped back. In a cold, flat voice he replied, "You are ever astute, my lady. That is exactly what I was about."

With an uncertain nod, Meredith hobbled off barefoot, stopping a good distance away to bend and slip on her stockings and boots. She watched the unyielding set of his back from beneath her lashes, wondering if perhaps she had been unfair. Perhaps he in fact desired her. *When her own husband could not stand the sight of her*? She shook her head. With one final look at his stubborn stance, she turned away.

Chapter 9

"I depart in the morning."

Meredith stared into the murky depths of her soup bowl, fearful of lifting her gaze and revealing how much his words affected her. She should feel only relief, not this deep ache beneath her breastbone.

Aunt Eleanor's voice carried from across the table. "We shall miss you. I confess I have grown accustomed to your company."

"Unfortunately, I have business that needs my attention in London." Although he answered her aunt, his eyes drifted her way, dark and unreadable beneath his dark brows. "Lady Meredith has everything well in hand here."

"You reside permanently in London, my lord?" Aunt Eleanor asked, dipping her spoon into her bowl of soup.

"Yes, business keeps me in Town most of the year."

Then why had he stayed here so long, upsetting the course of her life?

"What exactly is your business?" Meredith asked between sips, savoring the rich broth.

Aunt Eleanor's frown told Meredith she did not approve of her line of questioning. For some silly reason polite Society deemed it lowly for anyone to work for a living. Meredith supposed the proper thing would have been to ignore Nick's mention of an occupation, but she found nothing disreputable about earning an honest living, and was curious what kind of business would occupy a man like him.

Those brilliantly dark eyes of his settled on her in amusement. "I operate gaming establishments."

Aunt Eleanor fidgeted across the table. Her father had never approved of gambling, although it was a commonly accepted pursuit for gentlemen. Aunt Eleanor shared his opinion that a hint of sin lurked in the indulgent pastime, but Meredith noted that did not prevent her aunt from occasionally partaking in a friendly game of whist.

"Indeed?" Of course she had never been to any gaming establishments on her infrequent visits to Town. Ladies rarely endeavored beyond a drawing room game of whist.

"I spend most of my time at the Lucky Lady, my largest gaming operation."

Meredith's spoon clattered in her bowl. He owned the Lucky Lady? She and her aunt shared looks of incredulity. Even a provincial like her had heard of the Lucky Lady. Only gentlemen of the highest means patronized that establishment. It was purported to specialize in high stakes gaming only.

His inheritance could not amount to much when compared to the wealth he already possessed. She had assumed he possessed adequate means but not any true wealth. By his own confession, Nick and his mother endured poverty. How had he risen to such prosperity? She studied him with new respect. Not because of his wealth, but because of the obstacles he had overcome in reaching it.

Meredith suddenly felt buoyed. There was no need to feel guilt over cheating the man from an inheritance he did not need.

"You must be quite skilled at the cards, my lord," Aunt Eleanor commented.

"I'm a fair hand."

"Meredith is quite good herself. She beats all the neighbors. You two should play whist after dinner."

Meredith glared at her aunt. "I'm sure Lord Brookshire does not play cards with amateurs. There would not be much fun in it for him, I fear."

"I beg to differ," Nick objected. "I'm sure cards after dinner would be vastly entertaining."

Meredith eyed him closely but could read no

mockery in his expression. She shrugged. "If you wish." Perhaps it would be diverting. Her aunt refused to play with her anymore since she always won. Some competition would be nice.

After dinner, her aunt settled down with her needlework as Meredith removed the cards from a small lacquered box and set them on the center of a small marble-topped table.

The fire crackled in the hearth and its flames cast fascinating shadows across the clean-cut lines of Nick's face as he seated himself across from her.

"You deal," Meredith directed.

He waved an elegant hand at the cards. "I defer to you. It is your home."

Meredith's nails dug into the tender flesh of her palms at the unwelcome reminder. He was no mere guest. No matter how loath she was to admit it, he was lord and master at least for several more months.

Setting her chin at a stubborn angle, she pushed the cards toward him. She preferred no pretense. For the time being, she lived as a guest in her own home, a leech surviving off the whims of his will. For him to pretend ignorance of that fact only offended her intelligence.

"You deal, my lord." She pasted a smile on her face. Let him enjoy the upper hand while he had it.

There were gentlewomen who frequented Nick's establishments—widows and ladies with husbands less than rigid in overseeing their wives' habits. Independent women of good family and fortune. Yet even these women seemed somehow soft and weak compared to the one sitting across from him. He could never picture them tending to the tenants of their country manors with the same zeal and dedication. Never could he see them assist in the messy delivery of a tenant's baby, then suffer right alongside the family in the loss of the mother. Interestingly enough, he thought Meredith more aristocratic than those other ladies because of her unorthodox behavior. Not despite it.

How the vain brother of his childhood memories ended up with a wife of her mettle mystified him. He supposed marriage to an earl's son was a fabulous match for a vicar's daughter. Perhaps his brother had possessed the foresight to see that Meredith would make an excellent countess. Over the past week, he had learned that she was an outstanding landlord. Oak Run truly required nothing from him while in her care. The tenants praised her. The household staff respected her. She even saw to the crops. Her establishment of a school for the tenants' children to attend when they were not needed at harvest spoke to the level of concern she held for the inhabitants of Oak Run.

He studied her closely, eyeing the hair neatly coiled atop her head. The firelight brightened her hair to a burnished brown, contrasting sharply with her pale skin. Bess could never duplicate such color from one of her jars of dye. The thought of her smooth, water-speckled legs had tormented him all day. He especially wondered how they would feel sliding around his hips. Too bad his brother got to her first. Nick had dropped his guard yesterday, allowed her to see his desire for her. Such a breach would not happen again. This was one woman he could never have.

He shuffled the cards with ease. They flew through the air like so many moths. A soft gasp escaped her, her lips parting in awe over his expertise. He chuckled, strangely pleased to have impressed her. She possessed a pleasant mouth. Wide, lush, and inviting. Frowning at his thoughts, he reminded himself that she was carrying another man's child. Edmund's child. That alone should cool his ardor and put her in the untouchable category right above nuns.

He dealt and studied his hand before returning his attention to her. She was an easy read—biting her lip when she disliked her hand. Grinning when she did.

He beat her the first game and quickly discovered that Lady Brookshire was a poor loser.

"How delightful!" her aunt crowed, looking up from her needlework. "No one has beaten Meredith before."

Nick's lips quirked in amusement as a becoming flush stole over Meredith's cheeks. It appeared the noble lady suffered from excess pride.

Her aunt stood and rested her needlework on the settee. "As pleasant as the evening has been, I'm wearied. I believe I shall retire." She looked to her niece expectantly.

Meredith's eyes locked with his, glittering with determination. Fine eyes too. A lovely green, dark like a shady glen. The desire to best him sparkled in their depths. Lovely hair, shapely legs, and fine eyes would carry a woman far, he decided. Not to mention such kissable lips.

"Another game, my lord?" Challenge rang in her voice.

"How can I refuse?"

Her aunt yawned behind her hand. "Then I am off to bed. I suppose the night is for the young."

If Meredith felt uncomfortable at being left alone with him, she did not show it. She focused on her cards, silent and engrossed. Plenty of time for him to consider her. The rusty tones of her hair, the way she worked her mouth in concentration. It all attracted his notice. Again he recalled her pretty legs, the delicate arch of her foot. Triumphant laughter broke his musings. She displayed her winning hand with a flourish.

He frowned, then spoke evenly, deliberately, knowing intuitively what words would irritate her most. "I guess we're tied then."

Her eyes flared brightly, emeralds caught in sunlight. "One more game," she countered.

This time Nick wasn't taking any chances. He did something he hadn't done in years. He slipped a card up the inside of his sleeve. Yet when he won, she appeared so deflated, like a child with a broken toy. He could not resist showing her the card. It was only a game after all. The one thing he had learned from a lifetime of playing the game was that one should never take it seriously. Apparently she did not see the humor. Lurching from her chair, her green eyes darkened with fury.

"You sir, are no gentleman!"

A smile played about his lips. She hovered above him, glowering like an avenging angel. Her breasts rose and fell with the intake of each breath, filling the modest neckline of her black dress to capacity. He tossed the cards back and forth between his hands and tipped back in his chair, admiring the view. "True. I was not raised one."

She blinked at this reply, but her anger ran unabated. "Is this how you earn your living? If I were to walk into one of your establishments should I expect to be cheated?"

His smile deepened. "I expect not. I reserve that for drawing room diversions such as this."

"Perhaps you find it of no import to trick a woman. If I were a man, I doubt you would have dared."

He stood. Even with the table between them he towered over her. He let his gaze crawl over her with deliberate slowness. "If you were a man, I would not have lost the second game to begin with."

"Indeed," she scoffed. "Why is that?"

Nick circled the table, closing in on her. "Because I would not have been distracted. Because I would have watched the cards and not you."

Her eyes widened and she looked around her, taking in the empty room. Biting her lip, she shuffled backward, fleeing his predatory advance.

He suddenly saw himself taking that lip between his own teeth and licking the bruised flesh. "Nothing to say, Meredith? You never seem at a loss for words."

Her back collided with the wall, rattling several framed paintings. He placed his hands on the wall on either side of her head, trapping her, caging her in.

"H-How do I distract you?"

Nick had anticipated the question. He knew women well enough to understand they had to know the meaning and reason behind everything. His meaning would be clear to a man. He wanted her. In his arms. In his bed.

Her eyes dropped to his mouth. Something hot erupted low in his gut. No stranger to desire, Nick recognized it when it thrummed to life in his blood. Never before had he withheld himself from any woman he desired, not when the opportunity presented itself. He had made his success by grabbing opportunities when they arose, and she was an opportunity even he could not deny. So for a brief moment he allowed himself to forget her identity and that she carried Edmund's child.

Removing one hand from the wall, he caressed her face, letting her creamy cheek fill his palm. He dug his fingers into the silky hair behind her ear and tilted her head back.

His thumb brushed her mouth, tracing its shape,

memorizing its smooth texture. Her lids drifted shut. He brought his mouth closer, only his thumb barring her lips from his. She parted her lips and he tasted the honey sweetness of her breath. He watched, transfixed, as the pink tip of her tongue darted out to lick the rough pad of his thumb.

His manhood hardened instantly, craving more, craving all. He sank his hips against her soft curves, pressing her into the wall, grinding himself against her welcoming heat. Her eyes fluttered open, heavy-lidded with desire.

Then, as her gleaming eyes watched him, she took his thumb into her mouth. White-hot desire spiked through him as she sucked. Gentle at first, then harder. *Good God, her hot tongue laved his thumb like a piece of sugar candy.*

A groan of pure hunger tore from his throat, and he caught himself from offering his mouth in place of his thumb. Startled by the force of his arousal, he pushed himself away. Apparently he wasn't quite the opportunist he thought.

She looked up at him, eyes dazed and filled with longing, breasts heaving with rapid breaths. He staggered back, aching from lack of fulfillment, yet mortified at the mounting desire between them.

"My apologies." He looked away and ran his hand through his hair, disgusted that he would act in a carnal fashion toward Edmund's widow. "It won't happen again."

He swung about and left the room, forcing

himself not to look back. His hands clenched open and shut at his sides, empty appendages that ached for the feel of her. *God, how he wanted her.* Hell. In truth, he could not remember wanting another woman more. Tomorrow would not be soon enough to leave this place and whatever Lady Meredith stirred within him.

He took the steps two at a time, wondering how he would have behaved if she had not been Edmund's wife, if she wasn't carrying his brother's child.

Nick gave a harsh, derisive laugh. What was to wonder? He would have stripped her naked and satisfied both of them right there against the drawing room wall.

A gloomy dawn lit the sky when Meredith heard the jingle of a halter followed by a horse's whinny. Sleep eluded her. Images of Nick skittered through her mind like flashes of lightning in a dark night. Shame that she had allowed him to touch her, that she had been so bold as to take his thumb in her mouth—and regret that he had not done more—battled in her head.

She had lied to herself all these years, actually believing she was above such a base emotion as lust. If he had not stopped, she would surely have allowed him further liberties.

Meredith swung her legs off the bed and dropped to the floor. Her bare feet padded silently across the carpet. She pushed the damask drapes back and wiped the fogged windowpane, her fingers squeaking against the cold glass as she viewed the emerging day. Nick descended the stone steps to where his horse was held in wait by a sleepy-eyed groom. There was an anxious energy to his movements as he launched his tall frame into the saddle and took the reins.

At the last moment—as if he felt her stare—he raised his head. Their eyes met. In the muted light of dawn she could read nothing in his gaze. Did he feel even a fraction of the turmoil that surged through her? Giving her a brief nod, he spun his horse about and galloped down the drive.

She pressed her fingers against her mouth, unable to stifle her strangled sob. For days she had prayed for him to leave. She watched until he was out of sight before releasing the drapes. They fluttered back, a whisper on the air.

In the back of her mind a desperate voice asserted itself, making itself known. *Don't go.*

Chapter 10

Meredith packed the earth tightly around newly planted foxglove, pausing to wipe a hand across her brow. Leaning back on her heels, she squinted up at the sun. The day was unusually warm, and the extra padding across her midsection that Maree had fashioned added to her warmth. The padding—packed tight with horse's hair—attached to her corset and lent her the appearance of a woman not too far along in her pregnancy, but a woman definitely bearing the signs of pregnancy no less. At first she had wrinkled her nose at using horse's hair in the padding. But then Maree explained horse's hair was used to stuff furniture cushions and would make the padding firmer should someone be so bold as to touch her belly.

"My lady?" Nels called, coming down the garden's pebbled path. Meredith shaded her eyes with a hand to look up.

"Good morning, Nels. What do you think?" She waved a hand to indicate the tall stalks of lavender foxglove.

He nodded, sparing only a quick, distracted glance at the flowers. "Lovely, my lady. Donald just informed me there's a gent here."

Her heart raced and her mind immediately leapt to the image of a certain darkly handsome gentleman.

"Donald saw the fop scuttling about the place, almost as if he were up to no good. He has not approached the house or made his presence properly known."

Disappointment stabbed her. It couldn't be Nick. Frowning, she slapped her hands together, shaking loose the dirt from her gardening gloves. "How curious. Where is the gentleman, then?"

"Donald last saw him heading toward the family cemetery."

She rose to her feet and pulled off her gloves. "I shall find out who he is forthwith."

"I'll accompany you, my lady—"

"That is not necessary, Nels." Meredith gave his arm a pat, hoping to relieve his worry.

Nels crossed beefy arms over his muscular

chest, bringing to mind a very devoted bulldog. Meredith's lips twitched. "Oh, very well, Nels. Just try not to frighten the man."

They exited through the garden's rear gate, which led to the back lawn. From there the lawn began to slope gently upward. They made their way up the hill to the small fenced-off cemetery that was the resting place for generations of Brookshires. Edmund's grave, freshly mounded over with rich, dark soil only beginning to seed with grass, was easy to locate. It was there she found him.

A quick inspection revealed that he was not from these parts. His attire consisted of a dove gray jacket, silver brocade waistcoat, and black trousers. No gentlemen in these parts dressed so extravagantly, not even when attending an assembly. She blinked at the bright violet of his impeccably arranged cravat, certain she had never seen such a splendid color.

"Good day, sir. Might I help you?" Meredith asked in pleasant tones, mindful of Nels hovering next to her like a titan.

He looked up from Edmund's grave, his blue eyes moist. "Pardon my trespass, I simply wished to pay my respects to the late Lord Brookshire. We were quite good friends." He doffed his head. "Adam Tremble at your service, ma'am."

"Forgive me, Mr. Tremble, but I do not recall meeting you at the funeral. How is it you were acquainted with my husband?"

"You are Edmund's wife?"

She nodded as Tremble's gaze swept over her, stopping to rest on her swelling belly. His eyes flew back to her face with sudden intensity. "You are *increasing* with Edmund's child?"

Taken aback by his impertinence, she did not immediately react. But Nels did. Stepping forth, he grabbed the gentleman by his bright cravat and gave him a shake hearty enough to rattle his teeth out. "You'll watch your tongue, young fop, if you want to keep your pretty face, eh?"

Adam Tremble sputtered, clawing at Nels's fist.

She placed a hand on Nels's shoulder. "Nels, release him. I'm sure he meant no offense."

He dropped Tremble, who quickly attempted to set his cravat to rights. He glared at Meredith and Nels belligerently, the brightness of his face competing with that of his cravat.

"Few people are aware of my condition, Mr. Tremble. Even I did not know at the time of Edmund's funeral that I carried his child. Understandably, the news may come as some surprise to you," she allowed, hiding her anxiety behind a gracious smile.

Surely this man did not know Edmund well enough to know the exact nature of their marriage—or rather the nonexistent nature. That would hardly be the thing two gentlemen would discuss, would it? And even if he did suspect, he could not disprove her. She was his legal wife. It would take more than one man's suspicions.

"I am sure you are overjoyed, my lady." The words were said kindly, but his eyes glittered with an unidentifiable emotion. "You must be greatly consoled." His voice was scathing, heavy with implication, and Meredith knew that he did not believe her. Lifting her chin, she met his stare, daring him to openly contradict her. Despite her shaking hands, she knew he could prove nothing.

"Yes, it is some comfort," she agreed, smoothing a hand over her belly.

Tremble pursed his lips and sent another long look at Edmund's grave. Meredith felt convinced he relayed a message to the deceased Edmund. When he looked back up, his eyes shone with purpose. He fingered the mussed folds of his cravat. "You need not invite me in. I must get back to Town. Until next time, my lady." He bowed stiffly.

Replying with equal hauteur, she said, "I doubt we will meet again, Mr. Tremble. I rarely see my way to London."

"Oh, I am certain our paths will cross again." A smile played about his lips as he strolled past, giving Nels a wide berth.

Meredith and Nels stood there for some time watching Adam Tremble leisurely stroll down the hill.

Nels finally spoke. "He knows."

She understood Nels's meaning perfectly. She crossed her arms and shivered a little in the warm afternoon. She looked up at Nels's heavily lined face, then back at the retreating figure of Adam Tremble. "What can he do?"

"I can see that he loses his way and never gets back to Town."

Meredith swung her gaze to the grim set of Nels's craggy face and knew he did not jest. She sighed. Her moral fiber might have taken a considerable nosedive of late, but she was not so far lost she would conspire in another's demise.

She squeezed one of his beefy paws. "That's not necessary. He's of no account. We won't give him another thought."

Although she uttered the words convincingly enough, they were more to reassure Nels and dissuade him from harming Tremble. Because she was in fact destined to worry over Mr. Adam Tremble for many days to come.

Ensconced in a heavily padded and richly upholstered armchair, Nick wondered when he had exactly grown weary of evenings like this. The thick fog of smoke, the crush of people, the din of voices, the whir of roulette wheels, the shouts of jubilation—all served to irritate him. That he grew richer every night the Lucky Lady filled to capacity, nobs tossing their money down a bottomless hole that led directly to his pockets, didn't mean a hell of a lot anymore.

He craved . . . something else. The reminder of Oak Run, of air redolent with woods and earth, of land ripe with the seeds of honest labor—of *her*—lurked in his thoughts.

"Derring is up to his old tricks," Mac murmured, waving his cheroot in the direction of the duke who sat playing cards with several others. Nick watched the nobleman run an aggravated hand through his hair, sending the locks into wild disarray.

"Appears he's losing again," Nick observed dryly.

"Ah, hell. Look what's crawled out of the gutter." Mac grimaced and nodded toward the tall, gaunt man winding his way through tables, a curvaceous blonde on his arm. No doubt a hired companion. Pock scars horribly disfigured Skelly Fairbanks's face, yet as proprietor of several brothels throughout London, he possessed enough blunt to afford pretty companions. For some reason, Skelly viewed Nick as a business rival. Although not proud of his past, Nick would never place himself in the same league as the Skelly Fairbankses of the world.

"Come to check out how the other half lives?" Mac asked as the pimp stopped in front of their table.

Skelly's lips stretched into a semblance of a smile, revealing brown, rotted teeth. "It's smart business to know your competition." His eyes settled on Nick. "Never could figure out how you attract all the swells to your place, Caulfield."

"Easy." Nick fingered the rim of his glass. "I run a superior operation. You run a low-grade whorehouse."

"Full of yourself, aren't you?" Skelly's lips twisted into a nasty sneer. "I'd take care, even the mighty fall."

Cocking his head, Nick returned the man's fulminating stare. "Is that a threat, Skelly? Come, don't be vague. If you wish, we can take care of our mutual dislike for one another at dawn. With pistols. Or do you prefer swords?" He knew a duel was too honorable a method for Skelly to settle his differences. He was the type of man who jumped his enemy in a darkened alley, where a knife could find its home in his enemy's back.

"Always with your airs, thinking you be a fine gent." Skelly waved long, bony fingers at Nick in contempt. "Just cause you cater to the swells don't mean you're one of them. At the end of the day you're just like me, a thief and a swindler brought up from the streets."

"Actually," Mac proclaimed with undisguised relish, "he is a gent. And a titled one."

Skelly's laugh died a quick death as he took in the seriousness of Mac's expression. "What do you mean?"

Mac's hand swept the air in front of Nick with a flourish. "You're looking at a bloody earl. The Earl of Brookshire."

Nick scowled, wishing Mac would stop his blathering. He was not keen on the idea of anyone, much less degenerates like Fairbanks, knowing his personal business. Growing up in Whitechapel, Nick had his enemies—and the less informed they were, the better.

"You're an earl?" Skelly's eyes bugged from his gaunt cheeks like overripe berries. "But you grew up on the streets."

Nick shrugged. "My father didn't raise me."

"All those airs weren't a put on. He's the genuine article," Mac guffawed.

"Bloody nob," Skelly sneered, the hate in his eyes glittering like polished marble. "Shoulda figured you was one of them." He gestured roughly to the crowded tables around them.

"You've seen enough. Why don't you take yourself off now?" Although worded as a question, the steel in Nick's eyes left no doubt that it was a command.

With one last sneer, Skelly turned and headed for the door.

Bess approached with a bottle in her hand. "Have a care with that one. He's got a mean temper. Heard he works his girls over real good, even killed one of them when he learned she was holding out."

"He'll never challenge me to my face."

"His type never does," Mac agreed. "He'll bully a woman but never stand up to a man."

"That's what worries me. Insult him and he'll get to you in some way." Bess sat on the arm of Nick's chair, trailing her fingers through his hair as she poured more brandy into his snifter. He pulled away from the unwanted intimacy and glanced at her in annoyance. Her painted lips drooped in a pout. Standing, she flounced away, an exaggerated sway to her hips that at one time would have won his appreciation.

Mac chuckled. "You two have a lovers' spat?"

"We aren't lovers."

"That so?" Mac rubbed his chin dubiously.

"Not anymore," Nick explained. "Bess grew too cloying. Acted as though she had a monopoly on me. No woman owns me."

Mac stared at Bess, who peeked over her shoulder to make sure Nick watched her provocative method of departure.

"My guess is she thinks there's a chance of changing your mind," Mac suggested.

"We were never exclusive. She'll get over it."

Mac studied Nick with a bemused look on his face. "When did all this occur? Sometime after you returned from Oak Run?"

Nick sliced Mac with a sharp glance. "What does that have to do with anything? We had simply run our course. Bess and I had a good time while it lasted."

"Well," Mac mocked, "if Bess knew the reason for your disinterest was another woman, she might relinquish her claim—"

"There is no other woman," Nick interrupted, mouth grim. "Why must there be another woman for a man's interest to dwindle?"

"Hmmm," Mac mused, his eyes dancing with mischief. "You said very little on the subject of your brother's widow. Leads me to wonder. Was she a fetching piece of baggage?" Mac held up a hand. "I'm picturing a delicate, fair-haired angel clad in mourning black."

Nick snorted. "That's not Meredith."

"Meredith, is it? Enlighten me. What's *Meredith* like?"

"She's a brunette. Well, in a way. Her hair is

reddish brown, especially in sunlight—" Nick clamped his mouth shut at Mac's knowing look.

"You seem to have made a study of her hair."

"She's nothing to me," he asserted, perhaps too forcefully. "She carries another man's child. I feel a responsibility toward her, that is all. She is a gentlewoman, the prim, proper churchgoing type. The kind who needs a man to take care of her." He nearly choked on that colossal lie. He had never met a woman who needed or desired a man's help less.

"If you've a yen for her, take her." Mac shrugged. "Her child needs a father. Perhaps it's time you settled down, became respectable."

"What in the hell are you talking about?"

"You're not getting any younger, Nick. Perhaps it's time you take a wife."

Nick leaned forward in his chair and looked around him as if searching for someone. Appearing not to find whomever he searched for, he swung back to Mac and pointed at him. "Have you seen Mac? Because I bloody hell don't know the man sitting across from me." Nick ceased pointing and slammed his hand down on the table between them, heedless of the stares sent their way. "I don't see you with a wife and gaggle of kids."

Mac's eyes widened with dismay. "Me? No woman would marry the likes of me. Some men can't be civilized."

"Oh, and I can?"

Mac's expression grew serious. "Aye. You're the type."

"Nick, love," Bess interrupted. Given the conversation, Nick was grateful. "This fella wants a word with you."

Nick eyed the gentleman behind her and blinked. The scarlet red cravat at the fellow's throat was blinding. Nick waved his hand to a vacant chair. "What can I do for you, sir?"

The man glanced pointedly at Mac as he eased himself into the chair. "I prefer that we speak alone, Lord Brookshire."

He arched an eyebrow. "Anything can be said in front of Mr. Swell, we are business partners."

Waving a lace handkerchief beneath his nose as though the smoky room offended, the gentleman warned, "This is a personal matter, not business."

"Since you're a stranger, I doubt what you have to say is too personal."

The stranger's eyes alighted in challenge. "Oh? Have you no personal involvement with a Lady Meredith?"

The hair at his nape began to prickle. Voice hard, he demanded, "Who are you?"

"My name is Adam Tremble. I was a close friend to your brother."

"Half brother." Nick felt compelled to point out the distinction.

"Yes, I know." Tremble fluttered a hand as if that were of no consequence. "I recently met Lady Brookshire."

"You and her husband were close, but you never met her before?" Mac asked skeptically.

"Of course not," the man replied haughtily.

"Edmund had nothing to do with her. He hadn't seen her in years, which is why I'm here." Tremble's eyes fixed steadily on Nick. "The brat she's carrying is not Edmund's."

Nick clenched his snifter tightly and narrowed his eyes on Tremble. "You better be certain about what you're saying. Perhaps Edmund visited her without your knowledge. You could not know the man's every move. I don't care how good a friend you were."

"I am certain. I tell you, she's trying to pawn some other man's bastard off as Edmund's. I knew Edmund well enough to know that he only married her to satisfy his father. The old man pressured Edmund to wed, threatening to disinherit him if did not. Edmund did not so much as consummate the marriage."

"Now I know you're lying," Mac snorted. "What kind of man wouldn't take an available and ready chit to bed?"

Tremble sniffed in disdain, his fine-boned features strained as if he smelled something foul in the air. "Edmund, for one. And I, for another."

Nick studied Adam Tremble across the table. He took a long sip of brandy, trying to suppress the rolling emotions in his gut, murmuring, "How long were you and Edmund *friends*?"

"For ten years, but we were *special* friends for eight."

"Gor!" Mac sputtered, lurching up from his armchair, at last coming to the conclusion Nick had already reached. "You mean you and he—" Mac looked at Nick for confirmation. "Your brother was a . . . a . . ."

"Apparently that is what Mr. Tremble is trying to tell us, if we are so inclined to believe him," Nick said drolly.

"Why would I lie? I have nothing to gain." Tremble pulled his handkerchief away from his nose to give Nick the full benefit of his glare.

"You are certain Lady Brookshire and Edmund never actually consummated their marriage?" Nick pressed.

"How much more clear must I be?" Tremble gesticulated wildly, handkerchief flying. "Shall I shout from the rafters that I was Edmund's lover? That he had no desire to be with a woman? That he had never been with a woman?"

"Perhaps he wanted a taste of something different," Mac offered helpfully.

"I think not. Edmund taking a woman to bed would be as intolerable to him as you taking a man to bed, I suspect." Tremble smiled archly at Mac's grimace. "Besides, he did not describe his wife in flattering terms. Said she was quite the frump. Red hair. Freckles. Nose in a book. If Edmund wanted to experiment with a woman, it would not have been her. I do hope you stop her from this . . . this fraud. She could be trying to pass off some miscreant's brat as Edmund's. It would simply mortify me for our friends to think that Edmund had been unfaithful to me and fathered a child with his wife." Tremble's expression grew pained and he shuddered as if a snake slithered across the toe of his boot.

"Aye, how unnatural," Mac muttered, rolling his eyes heavenward. "His own wife."

Nick stared at Adam Tremble, but saw only one thing—a pair of large, guileless green eyes. "This is my concern now. I appreciate you coming forth with your information, but I'll handle it from here."

Tremble stood. "Just be sure she gets what's coming to her."

Nick smiled thinly, thinking of all the lies she had woven around him. He quickly recounted the times he had expressed concern for her and the baby. Now he knew it hadn't been his imagination. She had been hiding something. Every second they had been together she must have been laughing over what a fool he was. He had even gone so far as to contact the Royal College of Surgeons upon his return to London to acquire the names of a few specialists. "I assure you, she shall get what she justly deserves."

As soon as Tremble left, Nick rose to his feet.

Mac set his drink down with a thud. "Where you off to?"

"Oak Run, of course. I'm quite eager to have an audience with Lady Brookshire." Nick stalked from the table, seeing little beyond the red haze of rage clouding his vision.

Mac followed, muttering, "God help her."

Chapter 11

Nick gave the brass lion head knocker two solid raps and waited, tension thrumming through his veins. Several moments passed before Nels opened the front door, nearly filling the threshold to capacity. He eyed Nick and Mac in guarded silence.

"Nels," Nick finally greeted, inclining his head.

"Lord Brookshire, we were not expecting you." Nels's words were polite enough, but his craggy features did not crack a smile.

"I was not aware I need warn of my arrival in my own home. Is Lady Brookshire in?"

"She's in the salon with her aunt." Nels hovered in the doorway like a giant sentinel, barrel chest puffed out. He did not in any way appear ready to move.

"Might we see her?" The edge to his voice made it clear he would gain entrance one way or another.

"Wait here. I'll announce you."

Nick glanced at Mac, who raised his brows over such a coarse, seemingly out of place butler. Stepping over the threshold, Nick shut the door behind them with a firm click and fell in step behind the butler. He wanted to see Meredith's face the precise moment she learned of his presence.

Nels looked over his shoulder and hesitated, indecision flickering in his eyes when he realized they had ignored his command. Clearly, he debated whether to protest. Nick almost wished he would. In his present mood, a good brawl would relieve some tension. With a final glance at Nick, Nels sighed and led the rest of the way to the salon, knocking once on the door before pushing it open.

"My lady, Lord Brookshire is here," Nels announced, before bowing out of the room. The soft click of the door resounded in the still air.

Meredith looked up from the book in her hands, the color draining from her face as their gazes clashed. Careful to suppress the fury he had nursed since Adam Tremble's informative visit, Nick pasted a cool smile on his face. A shrewd gambler never tipped off his hand.

Her book slipped from her fingers and slid down her skirts to the floor with a swish. He stepped forward and picked it up. His eyes sought and found the swell of her abdomen beneath her dress. Fury spiraled inside him. From all appearances, she looked to be increasing with child. And that could be the case, he warned himself. She could be carrying a child. If that were so, he would have the man's name and gladly kill him.

But the gambler in him was willing to bet she wasn't pregnant. That was why he had brought Mac along. To help flush out the truth. Despite the conclusion jumped to by Adam Tremble, he knew in his gut that she had never known a man, not intimately at any rate. The signs had been there. He could recognize that now, even if he hadn't been able to admit it before. She might possess a treacherous, black heart, but her modest manner— her nervousness around him—declared her a virgin.

"Good afternoon, ladies." Bowing, Nick extended the book to her, noticing that her fingers shook as she accepted it.

"Lord Brookshire," Miss Eleanor greeted, "how splendid to see you again. I see you have brought a friend with you."

"Mackenzie Swell, ma'am." Mac clicked his heels together smartly and bowed to both ladies in an exaggerated manner.

Despite the dark emotions rolling through him, Nick felt tempted to laugh.

"Won't you gentlemen have a seat?" Miss Eleanor graciously indicated two high-backed chairs opposite them.

Sitting and running his hand over his slicked back hair, Mac said, "It is not often that I am included in such lovely company, madam. This is a rare pleasure."

Nick, now seated in the other chair, frowned at his friend, hoping to convey that he should tone down the drama. "Swell here is a member of the Royal College of Surgeons," he inserted.

"Oh my, how impressive," Miss Eleanor murmured.

Nick did not fail to miss the uneasy look she darted to her silent niece. Meredith's hands worried the book she clutched, blinking wide eyes on Mac.

"How are you feeling, Lady Brookshire?" Nick inquired.

Her eyes jerked back to him. "Fine. Well. Very well." Her voice wobbled, lacking conviction. As if on cue, Mac propped his little black bag on his lap. Meredith's gaze flew to the bag like a moth to flame. If possible, her eyes grew wider.

"Happy to hear," Nick murmured, fighting the urge to grab her by the shoulders and shake her until the truth tumbled out. Unsure how to proceed, he asked, "And the Finney family? How are they?"

She tore her gaze from Mac—or rather, his imposing bag—and looked at Nick with a good deal of suspicion. "Doing as well as expected. It shall take time, but they are coping. I doubt they will ever fully recover."

"One never does," he agreed, holding her gaze.

The sight of those brilliant green eyes—so deceptively innocent—fueled his anger. "Such a tragedy. I'm haunted by that night, and I cannot tell you how it has worried me over you." He pressed a hand to his heart in mock concern.

"Me?" Her hand fluttered to her throat and her blinking worsened, as if she were trying to rid some particle from her eyes.

"Yes," he answered, never removing his probing stare from her. "The dangers of childbirth should not be taken lightly."

"Indeed," Miss Eleanor agreed, then clamped her lips together at the fulminating stare her niece cast her way.

Meredith swung her gaze back to him. "Fret not on my account, my lord. I hope you did not come all this way to express your concern for my health. I could have written a letter to assure you of my fitness." Although she softened her setdown with a smile, it was clear she did not want his interference. He had known as much from the start. Only now he knew why.

Nick fixed a courteous smile to his face. "I realized the only thing that would set my mind to rest was to do the very thing I offered."

With growing satisfaction, he watched her eyes drift again to Mac. Her dread crackled in the air, a perceptible, tangible thing Nick could reach out and touch. Clearly, she understood his meaning and what this visit signified.

Exhilaration and triumph raced through him. He had caught her in her own game, snared her in her own web of lies. Deceitful chit. Did she really think she could carry off such a scheme?

"Wh-What do you mean?" she stammered, suddenly examining her nails.

He grinned, enjoying her discomfiture. "I have acquired the service of a physician for you." He gestured to Mac. "He has agreed to examine you."

"What?" Her voice rose several octaves. She ceased studying her nails and gripped the arms of her chair.

Nick blinked in seeming innocence. "Swell here will make certain that you and the baby are faring—"

"That is not necessary."

"You have seen a physician, then?"

She hesitated, and he could see the wheels turning in that devious brain of hers.

"No," she said slowly, "but Maree is quite skilled in these matters. Her care is more than sufficient."

"Yes, Maree is very knowledgeable." Miss Eleanor finally recovered from the shock of his announcement to second.

"I would feel much better if you let the good doctor see you. He comes highly qualified." Nick's eyes narrowed, and he added a hint more forcefully, "I know that your foremost concern is for your child. That's the case with all *good mothers*. You would not want to dismiss the opportunity of having one of Britain's finest surgeons under your nose."

Silence hung thick in the air as their eyes clashed in an unspoken battle of wills. Was she ready to admit her deceit and be done with it? He had effectively backed her into a corner. How could she possibly continue to refuse his offer and not appear insensible in her stubbornness? One thing was for certain: he wasn't going anywhere. If she did not confess, he would stay until he had the truth.

"Have no fear, my lady." Mac patted his black bag, and her eyes widened in dismay. "I've a gentle hand." Then Mac had the audacity to wink.

Meredith gasped. Miss Eleanor made a small choking sound and reached out to grasp Meredith's hand for support, her head lolling against the back of her chair as if her neck could no longer support the weight of her considerable turban.

Nick didn't know whether to laugh or strangle Mac. Did his friend think he was coaxing a tavern wench into bed with him?

Extricating her hand from her aunt's, Meredith surged to her feet and pointed a shaking finger at Mac. "I am not letting this stranger lay one finger on me." She swung her finger next at Nick. "And you, sir, have overstepped yourself. To have the gall to show up here with a physician to examine me. It is as though you question whether I am—" Her voice died abruptly, the only evidence of her inflammatory words the sudden dip of her gaze. A charged silence fell over the room.

Nick rose to his feet and took the two steps that separated them. Ducking his head so he could meet her gaze, he finished for her, "As if I question whether you're pregnant?"

Her chest lifted on a hitched breath. "That is absurd."

Nick spoke slowly, succinctly. "No, I don't think it is. I think it's the bloody truth."

Shock crossed her features, followed by a look of desperation. He could hear the wheels in her head screech to a halt and shift gears, searching for a way out of the hole she had dug.

Nick pressed further. "The truth. I want it now."

She opened her mouth several times, but no words spilled forth.

He shot a glance at the room's other two occupants. "Out. Both of you," he barked.

Mac jumped to his feet, ready to comply.

Miss Eleanor wrung her hands uncertainly, not moving from her seat. "Meredith?" she asked in a shaky voice.

Nick jerked his head at Meredith's aunt. "Mac, would you escort Miss Eleanor from the room?"

"I don't think a private audience is in order, my lord." Meredith's voice wobbled pitiably on the crackling air. "I am offended by your accusations and request you leave at once." She raised her chin a notch and somehow accomplished the appearance of looking down her nose at him. Nick had to hand it to her. She had backbone. Most would have thrown their cards in by now.

Mac took Miss Eleanor by the elbow and helped her to her feet. The woman looked on the verge of tears, and grabbed Nick's arm as she was led past. "Please, my lord. You don't understand. Meredith is a good girl. She was just frightened you would throw all of us out."

"Aunt Eleanor," Meredith snapped, losing her haughtiness in the face of her aunt's heedless plea.

Miss Eleanor shut her mouth with an audible snap. She looked between a fierce Meredith and a smug, satisfied Nick. The dear, stupid woman had as good as confessed on behalf of her niece. Nick couldn't help himself. He threw back his head and let loose a laugh.

It took a second for Miss Eleanor to realize she had given up her niece by way of her loose tongue. Her face blanched and she erupted into noisy tears, striking Mac on the chin with the top of her turban as she collapsed into his arms. Mac looked uncomfortable at this new development. Calming a sobbing lady was something with which he had little experience.

"Oh! I've ruined it all!" Miss Eleanor twisted Mac's coat in her white-knuckled hands. Mac led her out, awkwardly patting her shoulder.

The door clicked shut behind them and they were alone at last. Nick ceased to laugh. Meredith's bottom lip jutted defiantly, reminding him of a thwarted child. He was hard pressed to remember she was a woman full grown. Stepping back, he let his eyes skim the black sack she wore. The generous outline of her breasts, although put to extreme disadvantage in her hideous dress, was in clear evidence. It sufficed as a reminder. She was all woman. And as dangerous and deceitful as they came.

"What do you have to say for yourself?"

"About what exactly," she hedged, eyes flitting nervously past him, clearly searching for an escape route.

His annoyance grew . . . along with his disappointment. This was not the scene he had played out in his mind. In his mind she was weeping at this point, begging for his forgiveness, his mercy. It was over. She was caught. Could she not at least try for an air of contrition?

"Oh, I don't know. About your lying," he growled.

"There was nothing personal to it. You must understand that," she explained with a coolness that further fanned his temper. She slid several steps back and lowered herself onto the edge of a chair.

He moved forward, gripped her by the arms and lifted her up. "Did you enjoy making a fool of me?"

Her eyes widened and she shook her head vigorously in denial. "It was never like that—"

"No?" he ground out. "You didn't get a thrill in sending me packing knowing that this place rightly belongs to me?"

The ice princess evaporated. "Oak Run is not *rightly* yours! A circumstance of birth does not make it yours! You've not given it a passing thought these many years," she dared to contradict, eyes sparking like flaming tinder.

He gave her a small shake, ignoring the wild pulsing of his blood in response to her flashing eyes. "And how is Oak Run any more yours than mine? Don't I deserve something from the man who fathered me? Thus far, he has contributed very little to my life."

"That may be," she allowed, "but before I came here this place was just wood and stone. I made it a home. I made it prosper."

He shook his head at her logic. "Tell me one thing. Are you pregnant?"

She jerked in his hands as if struck. "No, of course not. How—"

"You've proven yourself nothing but a liar," he broke in, forcing a careless shrug. "How am I to know you do not carry another man's child?"

"Unhand me!" With renewed vigor she tried to wrench her arms free. Nick felt certain that if he had not been holding her, she would have slapped him. After all her revealed sins, he marveled that she should be offended by such a reasonable question.

"Then there isn't another man?" he asked, strangely relieved.

At this, she ceased struggling. The pins had fallen loose from her hair, framing her face in a fetching tumble of waves. "No. There was never a man." Her words were soft, almost sad. Her eyes looked haunted in her pale face, the light spattering of freckles on her nose especially prominent.

There was never a man. He studied her, denying the primitive surge within him to be that man, the first one to introduce her to passion, to feel her untried body arch beneath his. He released her and stepped back, clasping his hands behind him. Safer than touching her.

Clearing his throat, he asked, curiosity demanding to know, "How did you intend to pull off this deception? I applaud you for your shrewdness. No doubt you intended to have a son. However did you plan to acquire one?"

"Must we do this?" she whispered, her hand fluttering to her forehead as if she were suddenly suffering a headache.

"Yes, I want to hear all of it."

Those lovely eyes of hers searched his face before answering. "There are plenty of orphans in need of homes."

"Ah." He rocked back on his heels.

"I know it seems horrible, but if you could just try to look at it from my perspective."

"*Seems* horrible? That you would go to such lengths for money? Or was it the title that you could not part with?"

"It wasn't the money." Her nostrils flared and she beat a fist into her palm. "And I don't care about the title. My family—"

"Spare me your pretty excuses," he cut in.

She flinched. "You'll not hear me out, then?"

He stared down at her for a long moment. She made a tempting picture with her flushed cheeks and bright, tear-filled eyes. A part of him still wanted to believe her good and innocent. He straightened his shoulders. "No." He dared not. She'd weave a spell around him if he let her.

He recalled that last night at Oak Run, when he had almost kissed her. The only thing to stop him had been his belief that she carried Edmund's child. The thought of following in Edmund's wake had repelled him. But now that he knew the truth, that the marriage was unconsummated, little had changed. She was still off limits. Now more than ever. Attractive or not, even he would not risk touching such a viper.

His eyes drifted down. Curiosity prompted him to reach out and touch her swelling stomach. The padding felt firm and surprisingly real. She cried out, slapping his hand. "Don't touch me."

Perhaps it was her tone. Or her defiant attitude. But he deliberately ignored her. He had a right to investigate the means she took to deceive him.

Meredith, however, did not hold the same opinion.

It was as if a dam broke. She attacked him, his hands no longer her primary target. Her fists rained down on him as great sobs tore from her throat. He suspected more than his bold touch galvanized her. It was her loss, her failure . . . her elaborate scheme blowing up in her face.

Grim satisfaction filled him to witness the last of her composure crumble. Evidence that she was not the fine, dignified lady. She did not differ from the many women he had encountered throughout his life, all looking out for themselves and turning vicious when thwarted. No wonder Edmund had married her. They had been well suited—Edmund's sexual preferences withstanding. Both were self-serving.

He hauled her against him to stop her from swinging another fist at his face. She tossed her head to glare at him through the tangled mess of her hair.

"Let me go," she sobbed, green eyes wet and furious. The dangerous toes of her slippers lashed out and kicked him. One kick was particularly effective, grazing his shin.

Hissing in pain, he squeezed tighter and lifted her off the carpet. Tossing her down on the sofa, he straddled her and trapped her arms to her sides with his knees.

Leaning back, he wagged a finger at her. "Listen, you she-devil, you're lucky I don't call the authorities on you."

She lifted her head off the sofa and bellowed into his face. "Do it! I expect no less from you."

"Oh, I'm the villain, am I?" He crossed his arms over his chest. "Shall I recount your sins? I think they outweigh mine."

"You can't even try to put yourself in my place, to see why I did it, to try and understand. You're cut from the same cloth as your brother—selfish to the core."

He felt her accusation as keenly as a knife to the chest. The separate life he led away from his family certainly guaranteed that he bore no resemblance to either his father or brother. Didn't it?

Leaning his face close to hers, he whispered, "Rest assured I am nothing like my brother. I would have no problem consummating *my* marriage. More specifically, I would have no problem bedding you."

If possible, her eyes grew even bigger, green saucers in her pale face. She went as still as a stone beneath him. "How do you know Edmund never consummated our marriage?"

He ignored the question, instead ran a finger along her jaw and down the column of her throat. Her breathing hitched. He stopped his finger at the throbbing pulse on the side of her neck. "It's an easy enough matter to verify. Perhaps that's what you need, hmm? A man in your bed to rob you of your rebelliousness? You could use a little taming."

Wordlessly, she shook her head from side to side, rendered speechless for a change.

"No?" he queried softly, letting his fingers continue their path down her throat. "You've never wondered these many years?" His fingers stopped at the deep well between her breasts, as far as her neckline would allow him. "Never wanted to know a man?" She made a choking sound and her breasts lifted higher, straining the seams of her bodice. "Never wanted to take a man deep in your body?" His hand came over her breast. Her nipple rose up through the fabric of her gown. He grazed his palm back and forth across the hard little peak, increasing pressure as he did so.

"No," she gasped even as her body arched beneath him, betraying her.

His hand froze and he studied her passion-heavy gaze. *God, he wanted her.* Wanted to bury himself inside her again and again until he had his fill and no longer wanted her.

"Still a liar, I see," he said hoarsely as he removed himself from her. His hands shook as he straightened his rumpled jacket. His erection strained painfully at the front of his trousers. She did that to him. The little witch.

She lay there immobile, staring up at the ceiling like a piece of marble. "How did you know?" Her lips barely moved.

He knew instantly what she meant. "Adam Tremble. He was quite helpful in illuminating what kind of marriage you and Edmund shared."

She closed her eyes where she lay, and Nick could almost see the waves of humiliation wash over her. Why should she feel shame? It was through no fault of hers that Edmund had preferred men. Of this, at least, she shouldered no blame.

"Whether my marriage was consummated is none of Adam Tremble's business. Or yours."

He stood quiet for a moment, undeniably disturbed at the pain he heard in her voice, and why it should be there. Had she loved Edmund so much she could not bear his lack of ardor for her? Inexplicable anger lanced through him. Why would she have wasted her affections on someone who could never return her love?

"The subject of your marriage is of no real interest to me, only insofar as it establishes you are a liar set out to defraud me."

She swung her legs to the floor and sat up. When she looked at him, the heat in her eyes was gone, weary acceptance in its place. "Do you intend to go public?"

His anger eased, deflated by the submission in her voice. "I have no wish to see you in prison. Word will be spread that you suffered a miscarriage."

She bowed her head and gave a single nod.

"I want you packed and gone by the end of the week. You will leave voluntarily, quietly, no fuss."

She nodded again.

"I claim no responsibility for you. You may take your relatives and whatever staff with you. I will grant you a small settlement that should keep you fed, clothed, and sheltered. If you manage your finances, you should be able to live a comfortable, modest existence." Nick paused for breath, adding, "Given the circumstances, I think I am being more than generous. It is more than my father ever gave my mother or me."

She continued to nod, a ceaseless bobbing of her head, unable or unwilling to offer up a response. Strangely, that only annoyed him. Where had her fire gone?

"If you run out of funds, don't come to me. Understood?" He grasped her chin with hard fingers and forced her to look at him. "Say you understand," he demanded, ignoring the softness of her skin, as tender as any newborn's beneath his fingers. "I'll have your word that you will disappear from my life completely."

"You have my word." He watched her swallow. Her eyes deepened to a dark green, the color of a shaded forest glen. "I will be only too happy never to see you again."

Satisfied, he spun on his heels, stopping at the door to look back at her for one interminable moment. She met his stare head on, fisting the fabric of her gown.

"You made a fool of me," he admitted, hating even that small admission. She had elicited his concern and compassion, emotions he could never remember feeling toward another woman. Emotions too damnably close to those he felt for no single soul save his mother.

He tore his eyes from her before he could examine that insight closer and left, letting the door bang shut after him.

Chapter 12

Eleanor crouched behind a large potted fern near the salon door, her hands clenched tightly in determination. From her location she had managed to hear most of Meredith's conversation with Lord Brookshire. It had taken a little time to get rid of the physician. She correctly surmised that his belly would be his weakness—the case with most men—and abandoned him in the kitchen with a plate of Cook's gingersnaps. She had overheard Lord Brookshire's dreadful plans for them. Sending them on their way with a mere pittance was not to be borne.

She ducked low, crouching behind the fern when Lord Brookshire quit the salon and again, moments later, when Meredith departed. Both went in opposite directions. She upstairs. He to the library.

No doubt her niece intended to start packing. Eleanor adjusted her turban as she stepped out from behind the fern. She stared resolutely at the library doors where Lord Brookshire had closeted himself. One thing was for certain. She did not intend to spend her final years in a cottage the size of a shoe, squeezing the blood from every coin while her senile brother breathed down her neck and ranted about Papist spies. The time had come to take matters into her hands. Releasing a deep breath, she squared her shoulders. She would see about changing Lord Brookshire's mind.

Facing Napoleon's army could not have intimidated her any less than confronting Lord Brookshire. Yet his wrath seemed reserved for Meredith. He had no inkling of her own involvement, that the scheme had in fact been her idea—heavens be praised. At any rate, she suspected his anger was more wrapped up in male pride than true outrage over her niece's actions.

Eleanor paused in front of the library. The clinking of glass could be heard beyond the double doors. Lord Brookshire was no doubt availing himself of the brandy, an ostensible vice of gentlemen.

What Meredith needed was a husband, Eleanor thought, not for the first time. A man worthy of her. Perhaps then she would find the happiness eluding her. Oh, her niece *appeared* satisfied with her life, busying herself with the care of Oak Run and its inhabitants—not necessarily out of love, Eleanor suspected, but to fill the gap in her life. She knew her niece needed more. Meredith was not like her, a woman content with her spinsterhood and averse to the presence of a meddling man in her life. The girl would never admit such a thing—perhaps she was even unaware of it herself—but Eleanor knew Meredith wanted a child. Someone who would not reject her love as Edmund had, or her father, or even, to some extent—Eleanor had to admit—herself.

Eleanor had long been aware of her limitations. She sorely lacked any maternal instinct and had done a poor job filling the void left by Meredith's mother. Not only had she been a poor mother substitute, she had barely been the adult, leaning on her niece rather than lending support. When she first arrived in Attingham, Meredith had been such a solemn little girl, trained well at the knee of her father in piety and stoicism. And that unhappy little girl had grown into an unhappy woman.

Taking a fortifying breath, Eleanor vowed to help her niece. Perhaps for the first time. Meredith might not realize what she needed, but she did.

Shoving open the door, she found Lord Brookshire pouring a drink. The dark thunder of his countenance made her hands tremble. Gathering together the fleeting scraps of her courage, she cleared her throat.

He swung around with a glare, a lock of dark hair falling across his brow. "Ah, she sent reinforcements, did she?" He saluted her with his glass. "Never say defeat."

Eleanor laced her fingers together in an effort to still their shaking. "She does not know I am here, my lord."

"But you are here to plead on her behalf, yes?" He managed to point at her while holding a bottle in one hand and the snifter in the other. "Let me save you the trouble and send you on your way."

Settling herself on the sofa, she decided to omit her part in the scheme. "My niece was only trying—"

"The woman needs someone to knock sense into her head. She's lucky I have no desire to mete out the punishment she truly deserves. Time in prison would be more than appropriate for her." He downed his brandy and refilled it again, muttering under his breath, "But I would not dream of inflicting her on those poor, hapless guards."

Eleanor grimaced over his harsh denouncement. On a good day, she found Lord Brookshire intimidating, but in a foul temper, he terrified her. "I can't fault you for your anger. She does need someone to take her in hand. I'm only an old woman. What power do I have over her? As it is, my time on earth runs short. Meredith needs a husband." She hardly saw herself as nearing death's door, but hoped it might arouse Lord Brookshire's pity.

"She had a husband," he pointed out.

Dropping her hand from her chest, she said with ill-concealed disgust, "A true husband. A husband who actually resides in the same home with her would be a start."

"What man would want such a deceitful wife?" Brookshire stabbed his finger toward the ceiling, where Meredith presumably packed.

"She's not unattractive," Eleanor defended. "And quite capable of running a household. She's been left to her own devices for so many years and still managed Oak Run better than any man before her. She would be an asset for any husband."

"You have described nothing more than a good housekeeper." He waved his snifter in a small circle. "Now that I know your niece for what she is, I can understand why a husband would abandon her."

Eleanor gasped. "That is most uncharitable, my lord. Edmund never gave her a chance to be a real wife."

"Well, no," Lord Brookshire grudgingly admitted. "He wouldn't have."

She tilted her head curiously at his unexpected agreement. "You agree, then?

"I do know a little of my half brother's . . . nature."

"A proper husband and a few children should keep her in check." She nodded reflectively, as if this were a revelation for her and not a theory she had mulled over for several years. "Meredith would become his responsibility and not yours."

He considered Eleanor for a long moment. She ducked her eyes from his piercing gaze and held her breath, hoping she had achieved her point. Elated that he appeared to be listening, she decided to push further. "Once married, Meredith would no longer be your responsibility. None of us would." Her hand fluttered to her throat, indicating her person, should he have forgotten that she was part of the burden.

His snifter stopped halfway to his mouth. "Buyers keepers?" he asked dryly.

"Well, let's not be vulgar about it, my lord. My niece is not property."

"You are absolutely correct, ma'am. She is not. She is of age." He twirled his brandy in the snifter and took a swallow. "She does not have to remarry to free me of responsibility. I can simply declare myself free."

Eleanor smiled. "That's easier said than done. Society will look to you for her care and management."

"I've never cared much for what Society dictates."

Eleanor ignored her little frission of alarm. She had to make him see marriage as the best solution for everyone concerned. "Meredith was married to an earl. With a reasonable dowry, she would be quite a catch for some gentleman. It should not be a difficult matter to wed her off."

"Have you some poor fool in mind already?"

"No, but the Season starts soon. An excellent

opportunity for Meredith to make a suitable match."

He sat in silence, studying her before shifting his attention to the now empty snifter in his hand. Her knuckles whitened where they gripped the sofa arm.

"Are you suggesting your niece have a Season? Isn't she a little old for the marriage mart?"

"There are many gentlemen who prefer a mature woman over a child bride. Especially should she possess a respectable dowry. Weren't you planning to settle something on my niece?" she asked, having already overheard from his own lips that he would.

"I intended to give your niece a one-time settlement in lieu of the jointure my half brother failed to provide. I told her as much."

She leaned forward. "That could just as easily be her dowry." From the furrowing of his brows, Eleanor knew he was close to relenting.

"Just think, she would no longer bear your name, no longer share your title." She leaned back in the chair. "With your name, she would forever be linked to you, whether you like it or not. But then . . . that might be to our benefit." Eleanor sighed, tapping her lips in mock consideration, pretending to reconsider her own argument.

And that seemed to do it.

"Very well. I will make the arrangements and send word when you should set out for Town." He frowned. "I am only doing this to rid myself of your niece," he reminded crossly. "I'll not be put through all this trouble for nothing, so she better make a match—and pity the fool."

She stifled the urge to leap up and hug him. "Oh, she shall, my lord. I will do everything in my power to see that it is done. I cannot wait to tell her the news. Or should you be the one to tell her?"

"By all means, you. I have no desire to see your niece again. Correspondence should serve as adequate communication until she weds."

"But there is the matter of a sponsor. She was never officially presented. Will you handle the arrangements? I'm afraid I don't know anyone of sufficient rank capable of gaining Meredith a presentation at court, and she simply won't be accepted without—"

He waved a hand in a weary manner. "Fine, fine. I'll see to it. I'll send word once the arrangements have been made." A flicker of doubt crossed his face. "I hope this isn't more trouble than it's worth."

Beaming, she quickly assured him, "Look at the long-term gain. And it's only a brief inconvenience. Soon she will be some other gentleman's responsibility, her ties to you severed completely."

The slam of the library doors reverberated behind Meredith, making her wince—even if she was the one responsible for the racket.

"We had an understanding," she began without ceremony. "You cannot simply command me to marry. This is not the tenth century and you are not my lord and master." She pulled up short at the sight of Nick asleep on the sofa. His booted feet hung heedlessly over the sofa arm.

He opened his eyes and cringed against the morning sunlight pouring in from the windows. With a groan, he flung an arm over his eyes. "Must you scream and carry on?"

"I am not screaming," she said, lightly kicking the empty bottle of brandy on the carpet with her slipper. "You're obviously suffering from the effects of overimbibing, my lord. In your condition a whisper would sound like a scream."

"Be that as it may, my lady, *I* would appreciate it if you lowered your voice a spot." This polite request came from behind her.

She spun around to discover Dr. Swell occupying the chaise behind her and clutching his head. He still wore his garments from the day before— the worse for wear after spending a night in much the same manner as Nick. Another empty bottle littered the floor near him.

"Dr. Swell," she began with some embarrassment as the events of yesterday flooded her memory. Her hands flew to her no longer padded tummy self-consciously. "Good morning."

Had Nick explained her deception to him? If not, the good doctor would certainly make the correct deductions now. He would never believe that she had miscarried the night before and was up and about the following morning. There was only one explanation for her appearance this morning. If Nick had not told him already, the physician need only look with his own eyes to learn of her perfidy.

Despite her less than dignified entrance, the gracious hostess revived herself within Meredith. "I am sure the staff prepared a room for you. You did not have to sleep in the library."

Swell sat up, scratching his dark hair with both hands. The action sent the hair flying in every direction. He studied her through bleary eyes, working his mouth as if it were exceptionally dry. If he noticed she lacked yesterday's belly, he did not reveal it.

"Nick seemed inclined to sleep here. And it's a sad, sorry thing for a man to drink alone, so I decided to keep him company."

She masked her surprise at their familiarity. "How unpardonable of Lord Brookshire not to see to your comforts. You must be famished, Doctor. Shall I ring for a tray?"

"Er, Nick." Swell ceased his scratching, looking beyond her to Lord Brookshire. "Gonna help a chap out here?" He looked back at her with a somewhat sheepish expression.

"He's not a physician," Nick muttered with a bothered, annoyed, rather-be-asleep edge to his voice.

The blunt statement had her whirling around to glare at his prostrate form. He remained motionless, one arm flung over his face, as if he had said nothing of significance.

"What?" She spun back around to face the "alleged" physician. "Who are you, then?"

"Mac Swell. Nick's business partner." Mac shrugged uncomfortably as he darted for the door.

"Well! *Mister* Swell! You . . . you . . ." She groped for words scathing enough to hurl at his retreating, cowardly form, but he shut the door behind him before she could manage. Meredith felt tempted to give chase, but then realized the one truly deserving the full force of her wrath was still in the room.

"You're screaming again," Nick muttered.

"You're bloody right I am!" She swung back around, too furious to give thought to her rough language. Hands on hips, she unleashed the full extent of her ire. "How dare you bring that man into my home, tell me he's a physician, and attempt to have him examine me."

"It would never have gone that far. I bluffed and won."

She pounded one fist into her palm, recalling the audacity of Mac Swell's wink. "I should have known the moment he winked at me."

"Stop your caterwauling. You never knew what you were up against. I take advantage of people for a living. Now, did you have a reason for barging in here or can I go back to sleep?"

She fought past her stinging pride and exhaled deeply. There was a larger issue to address than Mac Swell not being a physician. She began calmly, praying the information her aunt had relayed to her was incorrect, a simple misunderstanding. "My aunt informs me that you have decided I must remarry."

He grunted. Not exactly the denial for which she had been hoping. She smoothed her hands over her starched paramatta skirts, struggling for patience. "Of course, this begs an audience."

Silence stretched, and she began to suspect that he had fallen back asleep.

"This was not what we had discussed."

Still no response. She inched closer, bending at the waist, trying to peer at his eyes hidden beneath his arm. He must have heard some movement, for he suddenly moved his arm, looking out at her from slit lids. Practically nose-to-nose, he asked, "You're still here?"

Her nose twitched, assailed by the stench of alcohol. Straightening, she pursed her mouth in disapproval. "You stink like a brewery." She pressed the back of her hand to her nose at the offensive smell.

Slowly, he sat up, sliding his Hessian boots to the floor with a heavy sigh. "Lady, you are one royal pain in the ass." He dropped his head into his hands, rumpled the dark, soft-looking locks and spoke without looking at her. "As to our agreement, I've changed my mind. Sending you away to cause further mischief is not nearly as satisfying as marrying you off to someone. Then you become his problem. Not mine."

Her hands clenched at her sides. "I'd rather be sent away."

"Indeed?"

The complete apathy of his tone indicated he cared little for her desires, and she wondered a bit desperately what had caused him to change his mind in the course of one night.

"I would prefer to remain unwed," she continued. "I'll as good as disappear. I give you my word on it. You need never be burdened with me again. It would be just as final as my marrying."

He lifted his head from his hands to look at her through bloodshot eyes. "Your word does not amount to much in my estimation."

She ignored the affront to her honor. It was to be expected, even deserved. Still, she had to try to persuade him.

"Surely arranging a Season is a great deal of inconvenience for you. You don't need that aggravation."

The corners of his mouth lifted in a smirk. "How kind of you to look out for my sensibilities. You are a true altruist. But to rid myself of you permanently is worth a few months of inconvenience." He once again dropped his head into his palms. "If you're going to drive some man mad, it should at least be your husband. He has the legal right to beat you."

She inhaled, groping for patience. "I realize I don't deserve your trust." Meredith swallowed past the pride sticking in her throat, moving on to say, "But I have no reason to further trouble you—"

"You never did to begin with." His voice sounded weary, contemptuous. "You are the worst kind of liar. You justify your actions. If you see a need, your arrogance precludes you from ever considering that there may be an alternative aside from your scheming and manipulations."

Heat climbed up her throat to her cheeks. Was she as selfish as all that? Had her deceit been so unforgivable? No. She refused to believe it. He simply did not understand her motives. She had been desperate and afraid and concerned for the lives of others, not just her herself.

But you did want a baby, a small voice in the back of her mind reminded. She ignored that voice to focus on her current battle for freedom. Later, she could examine whether she was as selfish as he claimed.

"And what of you? You have no qualms about sitting back, snapping your fingers and commanding me to marry. This is why I lied to begin with. I feared you would barge in here like some tyrant and start ordering my life to suit yourself with no consideration for me and those depending upon me." She stamped her foot on the carpet. "I don't want to marry. But that is of no consequence to you, is it? It's about what is easiest for you." Breathless, she waited, watching him closely, praying he would reconsider.

"You will marry." He shrugged, apparently unmoved by her outburst.

One look at his rigid expression, the inflexible set of his jaw, and she knew there would be no changing his mind.

"Take comfort," he said, the flippant quality of his voice grating her already frayed nerves. "You are only subject to my tyranny until that blessed event. So make the best of your choice. As you say, it is your life." He rose to his feet, stopping and clutching his head as though dizzy before striding from the library.

She hugged herself, terror filling her at the prospect of marrying again. Her heart couldn't take another rejection like Edmund's. Then and there she resolved to use her head and not her heart. There would be no illusions this time around and little in the way of expectations. She would pick a sensible, boring man. And her heart would be safe.

Chapter 13

A brief inconvenience. Nick sourly recalled Miss Eleanor's words as he stood in the pouring rain on the steps of the Derring's Mayfair mansion. The butler regarded him as if he were a bug to be scraped from the bottom of his shoe, not bothering to invite him inside the foyer.

"Your card, sir?" the butler intoned for the second time, his haughty accents even more disdainful than when he first asked.

"I already told you, I don't have a card—"

"Then I am sorry, sir," the butler cut in, his icy regard indicating he was anything but apologetic. "No one gains entrance without a card. And if you should acquire a card and Her Grace agrees to see you—" The butler sniffed disdainfully, the fellow's eyes raking him with great skepticism at this possibility. "Her Grace receives only on Tuesdays and Thursdays from two to four."

Nick raised his voice against the rain's increasing volume. "How about I just tell you my name, and you can pretend you're reading it off a card."

"I am sorry, sir—"

Nick's patience snapped. "What's your name?"

"My name?" The butler blinked. Had no one seeking entrance to Her Grace's lofty residence ever inquired his name before? "Finch, sir."

"Well, Finch, I'm Nick Caulfield. Remember it, because I'm the one who owns the house you're standing in and everything else Lady Derring's grandson has gambled away. Now, unless you want me for your new employer instead of Lady D, you'll grant me an audience with her ladyship, and we'll see what she can do to salvage the fine mess her grandson has made of the family's fortune . . . or should I say lack of fortune?"

Finch held silent a long moment, the steady beat of rain the only sound. Even with rain sluicing down his face and obscuring his vision, Nick suffered the butler's intent regard without blinking. At last Finch stood aside. "May I take your coat, sir?"

"Thank you." He stepped into the expansive foyer and shrugged out of his coat, wiping ineffectually at his face with his hands in an effort to dry it.

"Follow me, please."

He followed the butler to the drawing room, leaving puddles in his wake on the Italian marble floor.

"Her ladyship shall be with you momentarily." Finch closed the doors behind him with a click.

Nick strode to the fire and extended his hands to its warmth. A small noise prompted him to glance over his shoulder. The tall doors were still closed and an empty room stared back. Delicate furniture of pastel shades crowded the room, save for a single oversized chair with a fat cushion—undoubtedly reserved for guests of substantial girth. Numerous figurines stared at him in silence from various surfaces. Shrugging, he turned back to the fire.

"Who are you?" a voice asked so softly that he could have imagined it.

He whirled back around, wondering if he had in fact imagined the question when he did not immediately see anyone.

"I asked who you are." This time the whisper took on an imperious tone.

His eyes landed on a wide pair of bespectacled eyes peering over the top of the pianoforte. It was a girl, no more than sixteen and quite plain, dressed in a gown an atrocious shade of daffodil yellow. Her midnight dark hair made the bright yellow of her gown all the more blinding. The dress possessed too many flounces and ruffles for her slight frame. He suspected the flounces on the bodice were an attempt to disguise a flat chest.

"Nicholas Caulfield."

"I've never heard of you," she replied, rising until she stood behind the pianoforte and no longer crouched.

"No surprise." He lifted one shoulder in a shrug. "Why are you hiding?"

"I'm hiding from Mr. Humphrey."

"Who is Mr. Humphrey?" he inquired, his voice lowering in a whisper to match hers.

"My dance instructor, but he is simply beastly." Her hands fluttered about her in distress. "He raps my knuckles as if I were a child when I miss a step."

"How old are you?"

"Seventeen."

"A bit old to have your knuckles rapped, I should think." He folded his hands together behind his back.

"My sentiments precisely." She nodded, her spectacles slipping down the bridge of her slim nose. "But I am to have my come out this year, so my dance lessons have increased to three times a week instead of once. Not that it shall implant the amount of grace needed to satisfy my grandmother." She sighed, then eyed him speculatively. "I know all gentlemen of my grandmother's acquaintance, especially the young ones. Grandmother sees to that. You're in her drawing room, therefore I should know of you."

"I'm not the type of man she would introduce to you."

"Then you're probably the type of gentleman I want to meet."

He threw his head back and laughed. "What's your name?"

"Portia. But please be quiet." She wagged a finger over her lips a bit desperately. "I don't want them to find me."

"Forgive me." He smiled at the precocious girl.

"What business is it you have with my grandmother?"

Nosy too, he noted. "I'm afraid that is private."

She gave a world-weary sigh. "Then I'm certain it has to do with Bertram."

"Why do you say that?"

"The only thing that could be considered private is that my brother has ruined the family fortune, but then everyone knows, so that isn't really private, is it?" She cocked her head.

"You're quite the clever girl," Nick mused, nodding his head approvingly.

"Yes, my greatest flaw, or so my grandmother tells me." She suddenly smiled, revealing a pair of dimples that made her appear almost pretty. "It is also open knowledge that the family is counting on me to nab a rich husband to save us."

"Quite a burden to bear," he murmured.

"Indeed, especially since my looks are not to be counted upon, or so Grandmother tells me. And, as you said, I'm clever." Another sigh. Yet despite the sigh, he sensed she did not despair over her lack of beauty, only the disappointment it caused her grandmother.

"And what is wrong with being clever?"

"It's not a trait gentlemen care for in a wife, or so Grandmother tells me."

"Tell me something. Do most of your sentences end with 'or so Grandmother tells me'?"

The girl laughed, but quickly slapped a hand over her mouth to suppress the noise. Through parted fingers, she whispered, "Clearly you have not made my grandmother's acquaintance. You will understand once you do. Most people regard her as something of a tyrant."

"Ah, then it's no wonder you refer to her so deferentially." He nodded in sympathy.

The girl indicated her agreement with a solemn nod of her own.

"More than good looks can attract a gentleman." He felt compelled to encourage the gangly girl.

"Really good-looking people always say that," she retorted with a good deal of cheek for one of such tender years.

Before he could respond to that piquant remark, the door opened. Portia ducked back behind the pianoforte just as her grandmother grandly entered the room.

The dowager duchess did not so much as glance at him until she settled on a chaise. Then, with both hands knotted about the top of her silver-headed cane, she leveled an icy glare on him, her wide nostrils flaring. "What's this I hear? You presume to claim ownership of this house, man?"

"Point in fact, I do." He patted his waistcoat. "I

have vouchers from your grandson if you would care to see them."

At that pronouncement, the dowager lost some of her haughtiness and suddenly looked just like she was—an old woman.

"Bertram," she muttered, flexing her fingers on her cane. "He'll be the death of me."

"He is quite possibly the worse gambler I have ever encountered. Perhaps he should find another pursuit for his time. Some gentlemen like the hunt, I understand."

The lady's haughtiness returned in a flash. In ringing tones she replied, "I assure you my grandson has a new occupation and that is to wed an heiress. With his title, that should not be difficult. My granddaughter should soon make a match as well. No doubt you will charge an exorbitant interest, but we shall pay our debts to you, *Mr. Caulfield*." She muttered his name as if it dirtied her tongue. "In the meantime, I would appreciate it if you would not call upon me in my home again. You may hold those vouchers in your pocket, but I have powerful friends, and I will not stand for your bullying tactics—"

"What if I said I would be willing to waive all debts?"

She shut her mouth and squinted pale blue eyes at him. Over her shoulder, Portia popped her dark head up from behind the chaise, her spectacles askew on her surprised face. Somehow the girl had crawled from behind the pianoforte and managed to position herself behind the chaise her grandmother occupied. His mouth twitched with amusement.

"I would say such a gesture does not stem from your innate sense of generosity." Suspicion laced her voice. "What is it you want?"

"A favor."

She studied him warily. "Have out with it."

"I need you to sponsor my half brother's widow this season."

Lady Derring puffed herself out, expanding her generous bosom. "I don't sponsor just any chit. Do you know how many girls have vied for my sponsorship? Who is this woman? How shall I know she won't embarrass me in front of the *ton*?"

"She was raised a gentlewoman—"

"But she married a relation of yours?" the dowager interrupted, disdain and skepticism writ across her countenance. "She can hardly be suitable to move about in Good Society."

Clearly, the lady thought he had crawled out of some hole and could not possibly be respectable, nor could any member of his family.

"I don't see why not. My brother was an earl."

It was somewhat satisfying to deliver that bit of news and observe the dowager's small blue eyes bulge out of her fat cheeks. At least the title carried some rewards. Leaving the pretentious dowager dumbfounded gratified him.

"You're jesting. If your brother was an earl then you're—"

"Titled? Yes. I am the new earl."

He grimaced in the face of her open transformation from wary foe to agreeable hostess. In seconds he had become worthy, estimable . . . someone deserving of her company.

"Caulfield . . . Caulfield." She muttered the name to herself several times, tapping her cane on the floor as she scanned her memory. He waited.

At last he decided to help her out. "My brother was Edmund Caulfield, the Earl of Brookshire."

"Ah, yes. The recluse. He never went about Town much." Her eyes alighted with sudden recollection. "But his father created quite a scandal in his day, marrying an Italian opera singer and then divorcing her—" She ceased her prattling and inhaled sharply, her shrewd eyes suddenly bright with understanding as they absorbed his swarthy good looks.

"Now it comes together?" he asked, one corner of his mouth quirking.

"Quite so," she murmured. "Now, about this sister-in-law. Anything I should know about her should I agree to do this? And I do mean *should*."

Where to begin? By explaining that she was a lying, devious conniver who would go to any lengths to get her way? That might raise her in the dowager's estimation.

"She is quite unassuming, having lived her whole life in the country. She'll have a respectable dowry, I'll see to that. You just see that she gets a husband. I'll send her to you before the start of the Season so that you may prepare her as you see fit."

"What of her looks?"

Lovely hair and a wide, lush mouth flashed in his mind. He brushed the images aside and waved his hand dismissively. "Unremarkable."

"Another wallflower," she sighed. At that comment, Portia popped her head up and stuck her tongue out at the back of her grandmother's head. Apparently the girl was acquainted with that unflattering application.

He suppressed his laughter, not wanting to give the girl's presence away. "I trust you'll see to the arrangements. Naturally, I am not equipped to introduce a young woman to Society, which is why I require your assistance, my lady."

"If she has not been presented, that shall have to be rectified before she can make the rounds." She snorted in disapproval. "Though why the wife of an earl would not already have been presented at court is beyond my comprehension."

"As I said, she is from the country and not savvy with the fine points of Town Society." Something, he admitted, he had found to her merit.

"I suppose I will take her on, but I'll have those vouchers." She extended a bejeweled hand and wiggled her pudgy fingers.

He patted the front of his jacket. "Not until Lady Brookshire has accepted an offer of marriage."

"You surely jest." The dowager dropped her hand. "This is based on whether she actually snares a husband. I can only guide and point her in the right direction. Whether or not a suitable gentleman proposes is out of my hands."

"I want to make sure you put forth your best effort, my lady. I'd hate for you to be too focused on the marriage prospects of your own grandchildren that you neglect Lady Brookshire's matrimonial needs." He met her outraged gaze. "I don't want her to simply enjoy a Season; I want her affianced and wed by the end of it. Let her become some other poor clod's responsibility. Understood?"

"I am not a magician, but I understand your desires. Now, know mine. You are an earl." She leaned forward, her wily eyes intent. "And as such, imminently respectable. Not to mention wealthy and handsome."

He raised a dark brow in amusement. "Moments ago I couldn't even gain entrance without threatening the butler."

She fluttered a hand to silence him. "Clearly, you possess wealth through your own earnings, but with your newly acquired inheritance, I cannot fathom how deep your pocket goes. The *ton* will be standing in line to introduce its daughters to you. With your title, you will be the most sought after bachelor of the Season."

He shuddered. "Thank you, but I have no intention of attending soirees where nobles can pelt their daughters at me."

"That is where you are mistaken. If I am to do this, I will need your cooperation. Your attendance at key functions this Season is crucial."

Dread gnawed at the pit of his stomach. "Crucial?" He shook his head stubbornly. "How?" He had envisioned himself ensconced snugly before his fire while Meredith paraded through the Season under the vigilant eye of Lady Derring, comfortable with the knowledge that in due course she would land herself a vapid, watery-eyed second or third son with whom she would wed and retire to some far corner of England, never to be heard from again. He didn't need to play the nobleman and waltz with every insipid debutante to ever flutter her eyes.

"Your presence is vital to successfully marry your sister-in-law. That is what you want after all, is it not?"

"Explain why my participation is necessary," Nick insisted, needing to be convinced before he subjected himself to the torture of a London Season.

"It will visibly remind everyone that Lady Brookshire is your relation and that by marrying her they will be forming an alliance with an affluent family. You." The dowager's eyes shifted to the floor as she added slyly, "And if you were to single out my granddaughter for a dance or two, it would make her all the more intriguing to other gentlemen."

"Grandmother!" Lady Portia erupted from behind the chaise in a quivering mass of ruffles and lace.

The dowager screeched, her cane clattering to the floor as she clutched her heaving bosom. "Portia! How dare you eavesdrop—"

"How dare you bribe someone to dance with me?" she countered, flinging her slim arms wide in a flurry of yellow ruffles.

"I wouldn't precisely call it a bribe—" he interjected, enjoying himself.

"And you!" Portia dropped both hands to narrow, almost boyish hips. "Does this poor woman know what you're planning? Listening to you discuss her future so unfeelingly makes my blood run cold. *Commanding* my grandmother to see that she is wed by the end of the Season. The very idea."

His grin slipped. "It's exactly what she needs."

"I'm sure she will be grateful to be foisted on some . . . *clod*, was it?" She flung the word at him as if it soured her tongue.

"Perhaps *this* young woman simply knows her place," the dowager sharply intoned. "Perhaps *she* is grateful for those taking an interest in her life and seeing that she makes a suitable match."

His lips quirked with wry amusement. That hardly described Meredith. In fact, she would probably be a greater trial for Lady Derring than her own granddaughter. Best not mention that.

Lady Portia resembled a fish, opening and closing her mouth several times, at last recovering her voice to burst out with, "I won't dance with him." Then she darted from the room, leaving the dowager and Nick staring at one another.

"She'll come around," the dowager said with an unperturbed shrug. "But back to the point, I'll have your oath that you will be available for a requisite amount of engagements."

He could hear Mac's laughter now when he learned that Nick was going to be rubbing elbows with the peerage he had sworn to avoid. With a heavy heart, Nick nodded his acceptance. "I'll do my part. But don't expect me to attend every ball, soiree, and tea you attend."

"Of course not. That would take far too much of your time." She nodded her head in easy agreement. "I should only need you to attend perhaps two . . . three dozen affairs."

Bloody hell.

"And one more item," she called as he turned to leave. "Do try not to address your sister-in-law as Meredith in public. People shall wonder at your informality."

Chapter 14

"**A**re you certain this is the correct address?" Meredith craned her head back to take in the stone mansion looming at least five stories high.

"Yes. Lord Brookshire's letter was quite to the point, dearest. He said that after we settled in at the Brookshire townhouse, we were to call upon a Lady Derring at this address."

Meredith had taken advantage of the last few weeks to reflect and accept that she had no choice but to remarry. Despite her wishes to the contrary.

The wisest course, she decided, was to find a husband who suited her needs. Unlike before. She would make the best of her time in London by finding the *right husband*. Though deciding what constituted the *right husband* had taken a great deal of contemplation. She had lain awake many a night before arriving at several necessary requirements.

First, she need not feel love or physical attraction. Second, he must be financially secure and agreeable in assuming the burden of her relatives. And third, but not as critical as the first two conditions, he should be a gentleman disposed to country living. She would simply expire if she had to live in Town. A retiring, country gentleman, financially secure—who would not mind her few eccentric relatives and servants—satisfied Meredith's requirements perfectly. In one word: *safe*.

Accustomed to her independence, she admitted that a man she could manage would not be entirely amiss. But she could not expect too much. Not if she wanted to find a match in the span of one Season. The last time she rushed into marriage, she had paid the price. This time around she would not be so impulsive.

And there was one final thing required in a matrimonial candidate. Perhaps the most vital. He must be willing to have children. She would have to be clear upon her desire to have children. If she was going to such lengths as to remarry, then she would have the one thing she desired most out of the union.

The butler ushered them into a drawing room.

"Her ladyship will be with you shortly," he intoned as he bowed his way out of the room.

"Must be a very fine lady indeed," Aunt Eleanor murmured, her eyes taking in the room's elegant appointments. She stroked the muzzle of a large, porcelain bulldog situated near the large fireplace. "Very lifelike," she murmured, watching the statue uneasily as she backed up and seated herself on a striped chintz sofa.

Meredith lowered herself into a wingback chair and nodded. "Yes. I wonder how Lord Brookshire knows Lady Derring. They must be well acquainted for her to agree to sponsor me."

Her imaginative mind immediately leapt to all manner of conclusions and a stab of jealousy shot through her. Lady Derring was no doubt the kind of experienced, mature woman Nick preferred. No doubt a fashionable blond beauty, popular, sophisticated, and worldly.

The sound of the door opening captured her attention. A bespectacled, dark-haired girl stood in the doorway, hands on her hips in an unladylike pose.

"Are you Lady Brookshire?"

Certainly not a fashionable blond beauty, Meredith noted. Could this be Lady Derring? She hardly looked out of the schoolroom. Perhaps a relation?

"Yes."

"You are prettier than he let on."

She flushed, instantly certain who *he* was, and mortified to know that he had discussed her looks, or more specifically her lack of looks, in the company of others.

The girl walked into the room with long, assured strides. "His dislike of you must blind him."

"Lord Brookshire said he disliked my niece?" Aunt Eleanor demanded in affronted tones. "How *rude*."

"Aunt," Meredith warned.

"Well, it is," Aunt Eleanor whispered in loud tones, as if the girl in front of them could not hear her every word. "I don't care what you've done, it is unspeakably rude for him to slander you before others. I shall take this up with him upon our very next meeting."

"I don't think we will find ourselves in his company anytime soon," Meredith reminded. His aversion to the *ton* had been declared from the start. She suspected he would not take advantage of his ascent into the echelons of Society by making the rounds this Season. It was for the best. At least for her. She could not bear to see the cold contempt in his eyes at every soiree and ball she attended.

"Oh, he did not directly say he disliked Lady Brookshire, but it was easy to infer as much. I suspected there was no fondness."

"Rest assured, it is mutual," Meredith muttered, doing a poor job of feigning indifference.

"My name is Portia. And yes," she added, as if they had inquired, "my mother was an avid reader of Shakespeare. Highly unnatural and unfeminine, according to Grandmother, that a woman should be an avid reader of anything. But then she had not liked my mother very much, called her an anomaly of womanhood . . . and all because she was a scholar." Lady Portia paused for breath. "I suspect we shall grow to be quite the bosom friends since we'll be going on the auction block together, at least if Grandmother has her way. And she always does." Portia finished with a dramatic sigh.

"Grandmother?" Aunt Eleanor queried, appearing a little dizzy from the energetic girl's prattling.

"Grandmother . . . who you are here to see . . . the Dowager Duchess of Derring."

"A duchess?" Aunt Eleanor gasped before looking gleefully to Meredith. "What a coup to be presented by a duchess."

"Yes, I wonder how Lord Brookshire finagled such a feat," Meredith murmured. Apparently they could not have been paramours as she had first thought, unless Nick had a yen for grandmotherly types, and she did not think his tastes ran toward those *that* experienced and mature. So how did he manage to get a duchess to sponsor a nobody like her?

"Blackmail," Portia answered blandly, clearly reading the direction of Meredith's thoughts.

"What?" both Meredith and Aunt Eleanor enjoined, their voices a touch too loud.

Portia blinked and seemed to reconsider her choice of words. "Well, not exactly blackmail. I suppose it was more like an equitable trade."

"What kind of trade?" Meredith pressed.

"Oh, Lord Brookshire was more than fair. He offered to return my family's wealth, property . . . essentially everything my brother has gambled away in exchange for my grandmother's sponsorship of you."

"Well," Aunt Eleanor began uncertainly, "I suppose that is more than sporting of Lord Brookshire."

"It's perfectly dreadful." Meredith's eyes flared wide with outrage. "It is blackmail. He foisted me upon your poor grandmother. She has no choice but to sponsor me. How she must dread the chore."

"She's not thrilled about it, but it is really such a small task when you consider we are receiving our livelihood in return. And there is nothing *poor* about Grandmother. She is a perfect harridan. Don't pity her. The woman intends to sell me, her only granddaughter, on the auction block against my wishes. She's a slave monger!"

"What is this auction block you keep referring to?" Aunt Eleanor asked, perplexed.

"Some call it the marriage mart, but it is slavery, pure and simple." The girl settled her fists onto her narrow hips in a militant pose. "The only thing debutantes don't do is have their teeth inspected by prospective grooms."

Meredith felt her mouth curve into a smile. Possibly the first in many weeks. "Perhaps you should look at it differently," she suggested.

Portia cocked her head. "How?"

"That it is the men who are on the auction block. We do have the prerogative to say no."

Portia laughed mirthlessly. "Perhaps you do, but not I. Grandmother will be doing all the accepting and declining on my behalf. And I don't really think you have much of a prerogative when it comes right down to it either. Lord Brookshire intends for you to accept the first proposal to come along and be done with it."

"He said that?" Meredith clutched her reticule tightly, her indignation stirring.

"More or less."

"The decision will be mine," Meredith firmly insisted, her fingers digging into the soft poplin of her reticule.

"But you will choose someone?" Aunt Eleanor voiced nervously. "That was part of the agreement, dearest."

"Yes, yes. I will marry this Season. Because I must." She waved a hand in the air. "But I will go about this hunt in my own way."

Portia grinned. "Ah, I do like that. The hunt. And we are the hunters, not the hunted. Hmmm, that does change one's perspective of the situation." She tilted her head thoughtfully.

Just then Lady Derring descended upon them. "Portia, I see you have already acquainted yourself with our guests," she announced in clipped accents, her disapproval evident. Clad head to foot in black bombazine, she reminded Meredith of the angel of death. Leaning heavily on her cane, she thumped her way to stand before Meredith.

"You are Lady Brookshire?"

"Yes, Your Grace."

The dowager glanced at Aunt Eleanor beside her. "And you are?"

"This is Miss Eleanor Buchanan, my aunt," Meredith introduced.

The dowager gave a brief nod in acknowledgment at Aunt Eleanor's quickly executed curtsy before returning her attention to Meredith. "Stand up so I may have a look at what goods I am charged with dispensing this Season."

Meredith stifled an impertinent retort, not especially liking being labeled *goods*. Portia looked meaningfully at her, an I-told-you-so expression on her face. A perfect harridan indeed. Meredith rose to her feet and endured the dowager's hard-eyed scrutiny.

"The widow's weeds will have to go—"

"It has only been five months," Meredith said, bold enough to interrupt. "I should not want to raise eyebrows."

"Long enough not to stir any gossip on that account. Besides, the task here is to see you wed. No man will approach you in a frock like that." She waved her hand contemptuously at Meredith's dress.

Secretly, Meredith had always craved pretty gowns of vibrant colors, all in the height of fashion. If the dowager said that convention could be set aside, then why should she object?

"You've recently suffered a miscarriage?" the dowager inquired, interrupting her thoughts.

Heat flooded her face. She had not expected to be questioned on that point. Not so bluntly at any rate. Had Nick told the dowager? Certainly such gossip would not have reached London. She was on no one's *on dit* list.

"Yes."

"Well, you appear quite recovered. Some women languish about after such an episode. I see you have the burden of a few pounds to shed, but I'll see to that matter and instruct Cook on what manner of food to prepare for you. Never fear, you'll be back in top form soon enough."

She was torn between laughter and mortification that the dowager would credit her extra pounds to a pregnancy that had never existed and not the true source: too many honeyed scones.

"Thank you, Your Grace," she muttered.

"And the red hair has to go," the lady added, nodding grimly.

Meredith touched the hair peeking out beneath her bonnet. It was not truly red, but auburn with reddish highlights. "Go?" she asked nervously, envisioning herself bald. How could she rid herself of her hair? Surely she did not mean . . .

"Red hair denotes a foul temper and low breeding."

"Queen Elizabeth had red hair," Portia chirped, "and Boadicea and—"

"Portia, be so good as to keep quiet." The dowager sighed in vexation, not sparing a glance at her granddaughter as she continued to address Meredith in starchy tones. "Not to mention red hair is very unfashionable. It is difficult to find the right gowns to complement red hair."

"What do you suggest?" Meredith asked, trepidation lacing her voice.

"We dye it, of course."

"Dye it?" Aunt Eleanor looked as though she would faint. "Isn't that . . . *common*?"

"No more common than to possess red hair," the dowager replied with cutting ruthlessness, her expression hard and unrelenting. "If the goal is to see you wed, this is what must be done." The dowager raised her brows in challenge. "Just how serious are you about matrimony?"

Meredith had never particularly liked her hair. As a child it had in fact been been the color of carrots and the bane of her existence. She had been quite relieved when it had darkened to auburn over the years. A part of her felt uneasy over tampering with what God gave her. What if the end result was worse than what she already possessed?

Still, the dowager's question hung in the air. A test. After a moment she nodded. "Very well. I trust you have someone experienced to do it?"

"Have no fear, Henriette won't botch it. She is excellent with hair. No one will even know it is dyed."

Meredith drew a deep breath. "Fine. Anything else, Your Grace?"

After another survey, the dowager concluded, "With the right hair and wardrobe, I think you may not be as unattractive as Lord Brookshire claimed."

The words shouldn't have hurt, but they did. Hot tears smarted at the back of her eyes, and it took every ounce of willpower not to cry. She would not give the old harridan the satisfaction of making her cry on their first meeting.

"We have much to do in a short time. Next week I'm giving a dinner party, a small fete. The Season has not officially begun so the guest list is not overly large, fifty or so, but selective. There will be plenty of gentlemen for you to meet."

"She has not yet been presented," Aunt Eleanor reminded.

"That will not matter for such a small affair. She will be presented at the end of the month with Portia. You both shall reside here, I trust. That would be much more convenient."

Meredith looked desperately to her aunt. The idea of being under the dowager's roof, where she would suffer her constant attentions, filled her with no small amount of dread. At least at the Brookshire townhouse she would have privacy. "We've already settled our things at the Brookshire townhouse in Grosvenor."

"It will be easy enough to send a servant to fetch your things."

Meredith tried to lodge another protest. "But—"

"That is very considerate of you, Your Grace. Thank you," Aunt Eleanor accepted.

Meredith glared at her aunt.

Aunt Eleanor looked at her in mute apology.

"Think nothing of it. I've been charged with seeing you wed, Lady Brookshire. I shall put as much energy into sponsoring you as I shall with my own granddaughter."

"Pity you," Portia mumbled under her breath.

Meredith offered up a wobbly smile and tried to look grateful, but she was convinced that every minute of her stay would be oppressive. The dowager was clearly a managing sort. Much like herself. And she was of the firm belief that two managing types could not coexist peaceably in the same house.

Perhaps she would take the first offer that came along just to get out from beneath the dowager's roof.

Chapter 15

"When did this come?" Nick barked the question at Feebler, all the while fairly certain who sent the anonymous note.

"Late yesterday, sir." The old sailor's hands shook from age and years of too much drink. Nick had found the man starving and begging for coin in the streets. Out of pity, he had hired him. It had been simple enough to create a job that would demand very little. He used Feebler for small errands, such as sorting mail and delivering messages. Nick gazed down at the day old missive crumpled in his hands. Apparently even the prompt delivery of messages was too taxing for him.

"And why am I only now receiving it?"

"I left it here on the table for you, sir," Feebler sputtered. "It was late, and I did not wish to bother you below . . ."

Nick did not hear the rest of his words. No time to waste, he took off for the stables behind the Lucky Lady, where he quickly saddled his own horse. A short while later he rapped on Lady Derring's door. Finch opened the door, his expression as grave as ever.

"Yes, sir? What can I do for you?"

Nick wondered how the man managed to look down his nose at him when he was a full head taller. "You can stand aside and let me pass. And no, I still don't have a bloody card, but you know who I am and you *will* let me inside if you have no wish to end up tossed in the street."

Finch stepped aside and gestured to the drawing room. "The ladies are having tea, my lord. Would you care to announce yourself?"

Nick was too bent on his present course to take offense at the butler's sarcasm. He strode across the marble-floored foyer, his mind burning with the contents of that letter. The double doors stood open, and he halted in the threshold, his gaze sweeping the room's inhabitants. His gut tightened when he found no sight of Meredith among them.

Lady Derring looked up in astonishment at his unceremonious arrival. Miss Eleanor looked only relieved, further convincing him that she was the one responsible for sending him the missive. Lady

Portia set her teacup down and relaxed back on the chaise as if settling in for a good performance.

"Lord Brookshire, this is an unexpected visit." Lady Derring managed to inject just the right amount of disapproval in her voice. "A little early in the morning for a social call. We did not expect to see you until next week's dinner party. I assume you plan to attend, though you failed to reply to the invitation? Very bad form that, my lord."

"What is this rubbish about dyeing Meredith's hair?" he demanded, ignoring her question. He had received the invitation and had vacillated on whether or not to attend, despite his agreement with the dowager. Nick had a longstanding agreement with himself never to join the ranks of the pompous elite whose very code of superiority destroyed lives . . . most notably his mother's.

Lady Derring blinked and looked to each of her companions suspiciously. "How did you find—"

"That is unimportant," he snapped, cutting one hand through the air impatiently. "Is it done, then?"

"Not yet," she began, "but Henriette is working on Meredith as we speak—"

"I'll have no more of you *working* on her without my approval. From now on I want to be consulted on any decisions regarding a change to her appearance," he ordered, glaring at the dowager. "Dyeing her hair? What were you thinking, woman?"

The dowager stiffened in affront. "Have a care how you speak to me, sirrah. You charged me with getting her wed, and that red hair of hers is totally unsuitable."

"So you would dye her hair like a common doxy." Nick shook his head, unconcerned if his language offended her. "Take me to her so that I can put a stop to this madness."

"I'll show you the way," Portia piped up, a wide grin on her gamine face.

Without waiting for her reply, he followed her out of the drawing room and up the winding rosewood staircase, his feet pounding out his irritation with each step. He could feel himself scowling. What was Meredith thinking to go along with such a thing anyway? Wouldn't the daughter of a vicar be more conventional? Portia breezed into one of the upstairs bedrooms without knocking. Nick followed fast on her heels.

"Oh, excuse us, Meredith." Portia's cheery voice lacked true apology as she strode dauntlessly into the middle of the room. "I should have knocked. I did not realize you were in dishabille. I've brought Lord Brookshire with me, but then you're practically family. No harm, I'm sure."

Meredith stood atop a pile of linens, barefoot and clad only in her chemise. Her hair was wet, at least he hoped it was only wet and that was not dye soaking the long strands. Water sluiced down her neck and collarbone in fascinating rivulets. The thin cotton of her chemise clung to her body. She was shapely, curved as a woman ought to be, a fact her hideous black gowns had disguised. He admired the well-rounded cheeks of her derriere reflected in the mirror behind her and felt the blood thicken in his veins.

Portia's words penetrated his head. Family? Nick looked on Meredith with anything but brotherly love. She stood as still as a frightened doe, her mouth a small *o* as she gazed up at him.

"My lord?" She clasped her hands in front of her breasts, drawing his attention to that part of her anatomy. "What are you doing here?"

"I've come to stop you from dyeing your hair."

She touched one of the long wet strands absently. "Henriette is just preparing the mixture."

The grinning maid stirred a mixture reminiscent of something mucked out of the horses' stall every morning.

"You're not putting *that* on your hair." He nodded at the maid. "You can take that foul mixture from the room at once. We won't be needing it."

The maid did not bother even to look at Meredith for confirmation, simply obeyed. *"Oui, monsieur."* With a quick curtsy, she departed.

"What are you doing here?" Meredith's brow puckered in bewilderment. "You wish to stop me from coloring my hair?"

For the first time, he allowed himself to question why he should care whether she dyed her hair—why he had allowed himself to storm upstairs like an outraged husband. He shouldn't care if she went so far as to shave herself bald.

"If it is your wish to find a husband, I suggest

you present yourself as you are . . . not as something else." He paused. "But perhaps that is too honest an approach for you."

She sucked in her breath. Fire lit her green eyes.

Portia, whose presence he had forgotten, made a whistling noise with her teeth, her head turning back and forth between the two of them with keen interest.

He reminded himself that he had not come here to insult Meredith, only to stop her from making a horrible mistake, but now that she stood in front of him he could not refrain from antagonizing her.

"Portia." Meredith spoke evenly. "Would you leave us, please?"

"Alone?" Portia looked pointedly at Meredith's lack of attire.

"Yes," Meredith continued in that cool, even tone, her blistering stare never leaving his. "And close the door behind you, please."

Portia turned to leave, a definite pout to her lips. The soft click of the door ignited Meredith.

"How dare you come into this house, into my chamber, and order me about! How dare you insult me in front of Portia."

She was an amazing sight, trembling with rage, only a scant chemise covering her. Her wet hair hung over her shoulders, and he caught tantalizing glimpses of her breasts through the transparent fabric. Her temper must have made her forget her state of undress, a point he did not know whether to give thanks for or not.

"If you acted in a sensible manner, then I wouldn't have to rush over here in order to stop another one of your foolish schemes."

Bright color flooded her face and neck—all the way to the tops of her creamy breasts. Nick could not help wondering how far her blushing extended. Such speculation sent a bolt of desire through him. God, he wanted to strip away that flimsy chemise and find out.

"What I do in order to catch a husband is of no concern to you. I was only following the advice of the woman you appointed my sponsor." She stepped closer to jab a finger into his chest, bringing with her a familiar waft of mint and honey. "If you don't like me dyeing my hair, perhaps you should take it up with Lady Derring."

"And you can't exercise a little common sense?" He grabbed her wrist to cease the annoying, incessant jabbing of her finger. "Harlots and doxies dye their hair, and they are not the kind of women any gentleman I know would marry."

"Perhaps I have no wish to marry any gentleman with which you would acquaint yourself. I would not want to run the risk of him being anything like you."

He laughed coldly, his hand a vise around her wrist, tightening as he said, "Yes, you would not want a gentleman with a modicum of good judgment. He might be too difficult to dupe."

His hold on her wrist had her dancing on her tiptoes. "A gentleman at all would be quite a welcome change from you," she hissed.

"In our short association, I have been more the gentleman than you have been the lady."

Her free hand moved quickly, a flashing arc on the air. He had no time to stop the stinging slap she delivered to his cheek that jerked his face to the side.

Turning his head slowly, he looked down at her in wonder. Her eyes rounded and she appeared as shocked as he by her outburst of violence.

His fingers flexed at his side and he realized with horror that his hand itched to strike back. Of all his crimes, he had never committed violence against a woman. She must have read something of his need to retaliate in his eyes for she panicked and began to struggle like a wild thing in his arms, panting and wheezing in a way that made his blood grow hotter. And not with anger.

As he hauled her damp, wiggling body against him, Nick acknowledged that it was either strike her or kiss her. He much preferred kissing her. His mouth covered hers, drinking the pitiable sounds rising from deep in her throat. The instant their mouths collided, he realized he chose the greater evil. He should have struck her.

The kiss was a furious meshing of lips. Nick did not know at what moment it became a mutual exploration, but his punishing kiss altered, became a desperate fusion of lips and tongues that tasted, savored, discovered. He marveled at the hunger that filled him. And beyond that there was *feeling, emotion*—two things long dead to him. Or so he had believed.

He wanted to crawl inside her. His hands slid to her back, her waist, her buttocks. He lifted her against him, kneading the firm cheeks as he pressed her softness into him as tightly as their bodies would allow, rubbing his erection against her heat. A perfect fit. But it would never be enough. Not until he was inside her.

And that could never happen. He needed to get rid of this woman, to rid himself of these feelings and banish her from his life. Not take her to bed.

The kiss ended as abruptly as it began. He shoved her from him and stood with legs braced apart, hands clenched upon her waist as though he had to hold her there and force distance between them. Battling the frustration he felt for giving into the lust for a woman he found objectionable on countless levels, he slowly dropped his hands.

He had spent too many years vilifying his half brother to long for the bloody man's wife. It didn't matter that the marriage had not been consummated. It didn't matter if she had loved Edmund or not. *She had been his wife.*

And of course there was the not too small matter of her deception.

She stood still as marble, a perfect image of scandalized virtue, one hand pressed to her lips as if they were afire. Those big, childlike eyes. Her wide, pale face. Everything down to the smattering of freckles on her nose added to her appearance of innocence and made her deceptions all the more galling. He felt like ten kinds of fool, knowing she had played him false. And he had gone ahead and kissed her anyway. He must be losing his edge. Or his mind.

"Pardon my lack of control." He waved a hand at her person. "Perhaps you should dress."

She glanced down at herself, gasped as if just realizing her near nudity, and scurried to don a robe. She hastily belted the sash about her waist, calling attention to the lush flare of hips from a rather small waist. Nick closed his eyes as though in pain. This woman was made the way a woman ought to be. Somehow she had escaped the notice of other men, but he suspected that would not remain the case here in Town. Lady Derring would zero in on her assets, and that body would no doubt be shown to advantage. A deep ache filled his chest, almost as intense as the ache in his trousers. He wondered if he could stand to witness it.

"Are you ill?" Her hand, feather soft, touched his forearm.

He shook it off and stepped back as if her touch burned. And for all intents and purposes it did. Her touch burned a fire through his blood right to his gut.

"I wish we could erase what just happened, but since I can't we will put it behind us and pretend it never occurred."

"Oh." Unmistakable hurt flickered in the dark green of her eyes before quickly vanishing, replaced once again with her cool reserve.

"Don't mistake this for anything but lust. That's how lust works. Even people who hate each other can experience lust." He spoke harshly, deter-mined to convince himself as much as her.

"Well, that is a relief," she replied, the coolness of her gaze carrying to her voice. "I did wonder how I could return the kiss of someone I so detest. Thank you so much for the lesson. I have not had much experience in this sort of thing and would not want to come across as too callow for my fu-ture husband. To kiss someone I admire will be a delight and something to look forward to." She raised her chin a notch. "But don't forget that you were the one who instigated the kiss, not I. In the future, please keep your distance. It won't do for me to dally with the likes of you while I hunt for a proper husband."

He nodded somewhat approvingly. The kitten did have claws.

"You have my word. I won't make the same mistake twice." He turned to leave, pausing in the doorway. "I have heard the last on this hair dye-ing nonsense?"

"My hair is mine to do with as I see fit," she snapped.

He deliberately ignored her indignant words. "Just as long as you understand that you will leave it be."

"I didn't want to dye it in the first place," she snapped, an adorable vision of pique with her arms crossed over her chest, her breasts pushed enticingly forward. "But if it was my choice, you couldn't stop me." She jabbed a finger in the air.

"So long as you do as I say," he called over his

shoulder, imagining her face reddening in further aggravation. "Until you're wed, you will obey me."

He was out of the room before she had an opportunity to retort. Something crashed against the wall behind him, and he heard a muffled exclamation as he strode away, satisfied at having delivered the last word.

Chapter 16

"I look like a blueberry."

"You look lovely. The color complements your dark hair," Meredith assured Portia, who, dressed in a gown awash in ruffles and flounces every conceivable shade of blue, did look a bit like a blueberry. Lady Derring, however, insisted it created a soft, sea foam effect.

"I wish I was a widow, then Grandmother would dress me more like you." Portia eyed the clean lines of Meredith's peach gown enviously. "She has set notions of how a debutante is supposed to dress, and nothing I say can sway her." Portia twisted a handful of ruffles at her slender waist in a gesture of distaste.

"Speaking of your grandmother." Meredith inclined her head to the dowager bearing down on them with the ferocity of an invading army.

"Is there no God?" Portia sighed. "She's got Teddy with her again. I do believe she has already selected him for your future husband."

"Isn't he a bit young?" Meredith asked, taking in Lord Havernautt's soft, boyish features and eager countenance. Lady Derring, after whispering in nondiscreet tones that the viscount was quite well set, had been throwing them together all evening. He handled Lady Derring's meddling and patent maneuverings with such good grace that Meredith admired his temperance. Still, he did seem callow and his conversation a bit limited. His frequent references to *Mother* were a touch alarming. Hopefully, he wasn't a man tied to his mother's skirts.

"He's twenty-six. How old are you?"

"Twenty-five."

"Then there should be no concern on that account. He's a good age for you." Portia's eyes widened. "Unless you're angling for a husband with one foot in the grave?" She tapped her lip thoughtfully. "Now there's an idea with merit. Then you would soon be free again. Although best make sure his pockets are deep or you'll be right back on the auction block." Portia nodded her head in sudden decision. "You're quite right, Meredith," she announced, as if Meredith had voiced agreement. "I think I shall look to some of our elderly gentlemen. That way I should only have to suffer the shackles of marriage for a short duration."

Meredith slapped Portia's arm lightly with her fan. "I would rethink that plan. He'll probably live to a hundred and you'll waste your youth nursing him."

Portia wrinkled her nose, the action jiggling her spectacles. "With my luck, you're right."

Conversation ceased as Lady Derring arrived, the young man in tow. "Meredith, Lord Havernautt is a marvel at the keys. You must join him in a duet."

Meredith cringed, certain that caterwauling in front of so many respected members of the *ton* would do nothing to further her matrimonial goals. "I am really not an accomplished vocalist. Even my father, upon hearing my voice, forbade me joining the church choir for fear it would deter attendance."

Lord Havernautt laughed heartily at her anecdote.

Lady Derring didn't so much as crack a smile. "Nonsense." She beat her cane on the floor authoritatively. "I was just telling Lord Havernautt what an accomplished young lady you are. Besides, some musical diversion before dinner is just the thing to prepare the palette."

More likely her voice would sour stomachs to food permanently. Meredith took one look at the dowager's implacable expression and knew arguing was pointless. With doom settling heavily on her chest, she accepted Lord Havernautt's arm and shot one last helpless glance over her shoulder at Portia.

With as much grace as she could marshal, Meredith accompanied Lord Havernautt to the pianoforte, feeling curious eyes already trained on her. Lady Derring banged her cane. "Attention! Lord Havernautt and Lady Brookshire have chosen to honor us with a duet."

From across the room, Aunt Eleanor's eyes met hers in startled dismay, her face quite pale at the prospect of Meredith breaking into song. Meredith tried not to groan as the elegantly clad men and women assembled closer to the pianoforte, breaking out in a smattering of polite applause. Their faces reflected courteous anticipation. The doom in her chest grew heavier as she stood beside Lord Havernautt. Together they perused the available selections of sheet music. She didn't recognize the selections and guessed them to be more modern, popular songs that had not reached Attingham. Finding no familiar hymns, they settled upon an old country ballad Meredith vaguely recognized.

Lord Havernautt began to play, his fingers moving over the keys with smooth expertise. She missed her start. Polite enough not to comment, he simply trilled back to the beginning. Finally, she gathered her nerve and opened her mouth.

Her voice wavered and trembled uncertainly, wobbling and cracking on the air until she launched herself into song. She sang with aplomb, if not skill, shattering the high notes and strangling the low ones until she mercifully reached the end. Face flaming, she executed a curtsy for the obligatory applause. Meredith avoided eye contact with anyone, knowing she sang wretchedly but could do without seeing the ridicule in everyone's eyes. She dared a glance at Lady Derring. The old woman looked positively sick, a greenish tint to her features. She had tried to warn her. Perhaps the old dragon would heed her in the future.

"Bravely done." Lord Havernautt gave her arm an encouraging squeeze as they made their way back into the crowd.

She smiled in gratitude. "I warned you I was truly awful."

He grinned boyishly. "And you certainly were."

They both laughed, and Meredith acknowledged that she could *befriend* him. A novel thought. She had never befriended a gentleman. Perhaps marrying a friend marked the best way to achieve matrimonial accord. She would never mistake herself in love, never be fool enough to risk her heart. Furtively, she slid him a considering glance.

He was young, yes—and his weak chin disappeared into his neck—but he appeared affable and even-tempered. *Safe.* She suspected he would be easy to manage and not demand too much of her, namely her love and obedience. Could Lord Havernautt be the husband she sought? Could she have found a suitable candidate the first evening out? She supposed the only way to find out was to put him to the paces and test him with her list of criteria.

Unbidden, the memory of Nick emerged. Her face grew hot as all thoughts of *friendship* fled. There was nothing safe about him. The memory of his kiss never loomed far—in fact kept her awake at night. He had awakened desires and yearnings she never knew existed. Too bad friends did not inspire those kinds of feelings. Yet introducing desire into a marriage was in direct opposition to her criteria. Criteria she had set forth for the express purpose of protecting her heart.

"May I escort you to dinner, Lady Brookshire?"

"That would be lovely." As guests began to file into the dining room, she searched for Portia, curious which escort Lady Derring had foisted upon her. Meredith scowled when she finally caught sight of the girl . . . and her companion.

What was he doing here?

Given his lack of reply to Lady Derring's invitation, it had been assumed Nick would not attend. Butterflies danced in her belly. She had not seen him since he had stormed into her bedchamber and stopped Henrietta from dyeing her hair. Since that shattering kiss, she had vacillated between longing to see him again and apprehension that she might.

With Portia draped over his arm, the bright blues of her gown were a stark contrast to Nick's black evening attire. The feminine whispers and tittering indicated that his arrival had been duly noted. The women drank in his arresting good looks with bright, feral eyes. Meredith felt strangely bothered by the lascivious nature of their gazes. The insane urge to stand upon a chair and announce his disinterest in *Good Society* and gently bred ladies seized her.

Portia and Nick drew alongside her and Lord Havernautt, at ease in each other's company. Nick's eyes raked her body with a thoroughness that made Meredith's face flame. Her hand itched to cover the expanse of bosom the low-cut gown revealed, but she held her ground. Until that moment she had felt almost pretty. She resented that his arrival reduced her confidence to nothing.

His mouth twisted in a mocking smile. "That was atrocious singing, Meredith."

Portia covered her lips with a gloved hand. Her girlish giggle escaped nonetheless. "She tried to beg off, but Grandmother would not hear of it," Portia offered in Meredith's defense, her blue eyes twinkling.

"Well, Lady Derring won't make that mistake again," Nick murmured.

Meredith flushed. Knowing Nick had witnessed her performance and suffered right along with the rest of the guests only heightened her mortification.

Lord Havernautt's arm stiffened beneath her hand and he loftily demanded, "And who might you be, sir?" Meredith knew she should be pleased. His indignation was on her account, but she wished he didn't feel the need to protect her.

Nick sliced Lord Havernautt with a glance before settling his eyes back on Meredith, or more specifically, on her chest. He answered the affronted young man absently. "I am Nick

Caulfield . . . Lord Brookshire. Lady Brookshire's brother-in-law."

It startled her to hear him use his title, the very thing he claimed to repudiate. Did this mean he would take his place as a proper earl? Proper earls joined Society. Proper earls wed proper young debutantes. The idea churned her insides. He met her gaze. His expression turned rueful, and Meredith knew he understood the silent question running through her mind.

"A pleasure, my lord," Lord Havernautt gushed obsequiously, releasing Meredith's arm to execute a smart little bow. "Lady Brookshire has permitted me to escort her to dinner."

Meredith bristled. He need not sound as though he were requesting Nick's permission on top of her own. He did not need Nick's permission on any matter concerning her. No man did. Nick was not her father, or even her guardian. No matter that he treated her like chattel.

"Come, Lord Havernautt." Meredith tugged his arm. "Everyone has gone ahead."

"Yes, of course." He nodded his head deferentially to Nick. Meredith gnashed her teeth and pulled him away from his fawning. Nick and Portia followed at an easy stroll.

Meredith did not swallow a bite of food, despite the elegant fare placed on the great length of table. She snuck covert glances at Nick as he exchanged pleasantries with Portia on his right and the woman on his left—a baroness with rouged cheeks who slid her hand over his arm whilst her husband flirted with another woman at the far end of the dining table. Both spouses appeared indifferent to their bold flirtations. Meredith watched in disgust over the ornate silver candelabras. Such moral laxity was never flaunted in Attingham. Practiced perhaps, but never flaunted.

"Do you not care for partridge?" Lord Havernautt asked solicitously.

"Yes. It's lovely." Meredith wrenched her gaze from Nick and forced a small bite, chewing mechanically, too troubled to even appreciate the partridge pie's flaky crust.

"It's quite acceptable if you don't. Some ladies do not care for game. Mother says it's commoners' fare."

Meredith sipped her wine and spoke thoughtlessly, her mind on the vulgar woman with her hands all over Nick. "And how is it you've escaped Mother for the evening, Lord Havernautt?"

His face reddened, and she chastised herself for being so uncharitable. She had not meant to embarrass him. "I'm sorry," she quickly apologized, setting down her glass and covering his hand with hers. "That was rude of me."

"I do talk of her too much. I can't seem to help it. Mother has been a dominating figure in my life since Father died."

"You're a good son." Meredith smiled consolingly. "No shame in that."

"Perhaps not shame, but it's a little off-setting for prospective wives." He dabbed a linen napkin at the corners of mouth. "Experience has taught me that."

"The right woman would not be deterred."

"Truly?" He reminded her so much of a forlorn little boy, hope burning bright in his eyes, that she gave his hand a little squeeze.

"Of course. If a woman wants to know whether a man would be a kind husband to her, she need look no further than how he treats his mother." Meredith gave his hand a final squeeze before releasing it.

The hairs on her nape tingled with awareness, as though someone watched her. Meredith looked up. Her eyes clashed with Nick's across the table. The anger in his gaze blazed a hole right through her. Baffled, she raised a brow in silent inquiry. In a blink, his anger vanished, leaving nothing behind for her to detect.

He returned his attention to the baroness pawing his arm. To her horror, he fed the woman a berry from his fruit bowl. Heat rushed over her. Meredith snapped her attention to the next course set before her, confusion knitting her brow. The flash of anger in his eyes had not been imagined, but now he appeared totally enamored with his dinner companion and oblivious to her. She watched his flirtation with the baroness with mounting disgust . . . and a tightening in her chest that could only be jealousy.

After dinner a small orchestra set up and began to play at one end of the ballroom. Lady Derring prodded several couples into dancing—Meredith and Lord Havernautt not to be spared. She danced with other gentlemen as well, hoping to expand her search for suitable candidates. After one dance . with a portly gentleman who trod all over her toes and leered down her bodice, and two other dances with gentlemen who plied her with questions on the likelihood of their marriage prospects to this Season's fresh-faced debutantes—in whose ranks she was not included—she desperately craved a respite.

A dull headache throbbed at the backs of her eyes. It had been a long day. A long week, for that matter. Every waking moment had been spent *preparing* her. Her hair had only been the start. New gowns were needed. As were gloves, reticules, slippers, jewelry, all manner of intimate apparel, and more gowns. A consuming endeavor, by all accounts. Greater preparation could not have gone into planning the military stratagems at Waterloo.

She managed to slip out to the terrace and down into the gardens for a much needed moment of privacy while Lord Havernautt danced with Portia. The scent of lilac hung thick in the air, and she inhaled the sweet aroma. She caught a thick, waxy leaf in her hand from a low hanging branch. Rubbing it between her fingers, she strolled down the pebbled path, staring at the night sky and wondering where the stars had gone. Stars littered the sky in Attingham. Here she could see nothing save murky night.

"You shouldn't be out here alone."

She spun around, crushing the leaf in her hand.

Nick leaned against an ivied wall, one hand in his jacket pocket. Her traitorous heart jumped at the sight of him, and she didn't know which of her impulses the strongest. The one urging her to flee? Or the one urging her to close the distance separating them and continue where they had last left off?

Chapter 17

Meredith settled for conversation. By far the safest impulse. "Taken to skulking about gardens, have you?" Her voice spilled out fast and breathless.

He smiled that wolf smile of his—the white flash of his teeth clearly visible in the garden's gloom.

She didn't bother to wait for his response, instead forged ahead with the one question that had nagged her all evening, ever since she first laid eyes on him. "What are you doing here? I thought you left me in Lady Derring's care so you did not have to endure such tiresome functions as this. Have you come to verify that I in fact did not dye my hair?"

"I was invited."

Several lamps dotted the path, but their glow did not reach his eyes. Meredith wished she could see them to better gauge his thoughts.

"I thought you had no intention of playing the noble earl." She stepped closer, but the memory of the last time they were alone flashed in her mind and she halted, moistening her lips nervously, both frightened and strangely stirred.

"Lady Derring insisted I attend."

"So you're here for Lady Derring's sake?" She found that difficult to believe.

"She claims the hovering presence of a wealthy, titled relation will help you land a husband. Make you more appealing."

Meredith snorted, recalling how Lady Derring partnered him with her granddaughter at dinner. "You think that's her true motive?"

"I suspect she has her own agenda. And a granddaughter of marriageable age."

"What are your intentions on that score? The Derrings are prestigious. Marriage to a duke's daughter would be quite a coup."

"For some." He shrugged one broad shoulder. "I have no such ambition. And no intention of marrying. Especially to a girl barely out of the schoolroom."

"You don't plan to *ever* marry?" She could not hide her curiosity.

"I would not make a very good husband," he uttered with a decided lack of remorse.

"No, you would not," she agreed.

His deep chuckle sent a warm ripple of pleasure coursing through her. "For once we are in agreement."

Meredith smiled and contemplated the enigma standing before her. He had been particularly brutish to her since learning of her deceit, but the memory of him comforting her after Sally Finney's death, of his concern for her welfare when he thought her pregnant, lingered. There was depth to him. Compassion. A heart beat beneath that stony exterior.

Shaking off such thoughts, she said, "You are a strange man. Most men would give their soul for what you don't even want."

His rejoinder was fast and brutal. "Or scheme, lie, and cheat, as in your case."

Her smile slipped, replaced with bleak frustration. "You'll never understand why. Have you never done anything wrong in order to protect yourself and others? Never committed a sin or a crime because you felt you had to?"

He didn't answer for some time. She heard his soft exhalation. It was the sigh of a man burdened with the past, and she had her answer. His continued silence confirmed her suspicions as no words could. "I thought so," she answered for him. "Was it a very terrible thing?"

He turned in the direction of the house. The hum of voices played on the air, blending with the distant music. A sudden shaft of light shined down on them from an upstairs window, allowing Meredith to study the strong line of his profile.

One look at his pensive expression and she knew he no longer stood with her in Lady Derring's gardens but at some distant place in his past.

It struck her that she knew very little about him. The whole of his life before they met was a murky chasm. What befell him after his mother died? How had he survived? She had the sneaking suspicion it was an ugly tale.

"For me, it was steal or starve. Beat or be beaten. You have not come close to facing the threats I have."

"Perhaps," she allowed, shrugging and trying to appear unaffected by his troubling words. "But my future was uncertain, and any number of terrible things could have awaited me. How was I to know?"

"No terrible future awaited you," he replied with utter conviction. "Just me."

"You." Meredith smiled without mirth. She spread her arms wide in demonstration. "And here you have me, forcing me to marry—"

"Such a terrible fate," he cut in. "What a monster I am to give you a generous dowry and the freedom to choose your husband. A terrible fate, indeed. Should every woman be so cursed."

Her hand itched to slap the mockery from his face. "I don't see you rushing into matrimony. Most married couples hardly appear to be in a state of wedded bliss. Apparently, you're wise enough to see it's not the most sought after of fates."

"Is that what you expect? Wedded bliss?" His

laugh stirred her insides into a queasy froth. "I fear you're bound for disappointment." His rumbling laughter faded and he asked smugly, as if he already knew the answer, "And your marriage to Edmund? Was it wedded bliss?"

What could she say? She had wanted to love Edmund. If he had given her the chance, she would have loved him with her whole being. "We aren't discussing my marriage."

Her mind searched for a distraction, anything to change the subject from Edmund's rejection. "Why are you really here? I don't believe you came to appease Lady Derring."

He was quiet a long moment, as though weighing whether to accept this change of topic or pursue the matter of her marriage with Edmund. At last he answered her. "Curiosity, I suppose. I wanted to see how you fared on your introduction to the *ton*."

Meredith clucked and stepped forward to flick a piece of imaginary lint from his jacket. "A startling admission from a man sworn to hate me." Her hand lingered on his jacket, one finger lightly tapping the hardness of his chest beneath the fine fabric.

"I never professed to hate you," he replied. His eyes reminded her of a predator glittering down at her in the dark. "I simply don't trust you. You, my lady, are trouble . . . a complication I don't need in my life."

His words stung. Trouble. A complication. Not a person. Merely soiled goods to be dispensed.

Meredith pulled her hand free from where it lingered on his chest and lifted her chin a notch. "Have I passed inspection?" She rubbed her fingertips together as if she could erase the feel of him.

"Could have done without the singing. You won't catch bees with vinegar, you know."

"I had no choice," she grumbled.

His hand reached out to fondle a fat curl draped artfully across her shoulder. "The color of your gown complements your hair. Fortunately, Lady Derring dresses you better than her own granddaughter."

Meredith glanced down at her peach gown of watered silk, pleasure suffusing her at the simple compliment.

As if needing to offset his compliment, he added, "However, the bodice is much too low."

"It's the fashion. And no lower than any other woman's gown tonight," she defended.

"Not every woman here has your charms." He released the curl, the back of his fingers brushing the swell of one breast as he withdrew.

Heat flooded Meredith's cheeks at the innocuous contact, certainly unintentional on his part. Surely only she found it hard to keep her hands to herself. He had made his distaste for her clear. Her gaze darted around, needing to look elsewhere. Anywhere save his face. Unfortunately, her scan of the empty garden only made her more conscious of her surroundings and how very alone they were. The last time alone with him— Her breath caught, and she veered her mind from that titillating memory.

She bit the corner of her bottom lip. "And my conduct? Have you no complaints on that score?"

"Do you need my approval, Meredith?" he asked in all mildness, but the question seemed loaded with danger. "You never seemed to want it before."

"Of course not. I was merely curious." She shrugged, wrapping her arms around herself. Because she was cold. Not because he made her tremble.

"Then to satisfy your curiosity I'll tell you that your conduct does not meet with my approval." His voice rang with unmistakable censure.

Her gaze cut to his face and she dropped her hands to her hips. "I have behaved appropriately," she insisted.

"For a common flirt. Not a respectable widow only just out of mourning."

Meredith sucked a deep breath into her lungs, shaking her head vehemently. "That is untrue. I shouldn't have bothered asking. Your opinion means nothing to me."

She spun around to flee, only he grabbed her arm and forced her to face him.

"You asked, so you will listen. You're moving fast with young Havernautt. Have you already settled on him?"

The sneer in his voice baffled her. She glared from his face to his hand on her arm and back again. Why should he care whose company she kept as long as she found someone to wed?

"We've only just met. It's much too soon to decide anything."

"Then I advise against cozying up to him. The man you eventually marry won't like that you conducted yourself like a hussy with other gentlemen."

"I'm not a hussy," Meredith hissed. "And what business is it of yours how I act as long as I simply catch a husband? That was your *edict*, correct? You said nothing about how I was to behave. Or are you throwing down new rules? If the gentlemen I consider for matrimony need your approval, this is the first I heard of it."

Nick's voice dropped to a gravelly pitch that raised the tiny hairs on the back of her neck. "You held his hand in clear sight of everyone and danced *three times* with him. I was not the only one who noted such forwardness, rest assured. The *ton* feeds on gossip. Do you want your reputation in shreds before the Season officially opens? You'll not gain a proposal that way . . . at least not the type of proposal you're angling for."

Fury flamed her cheeks, scorching her face all the way to her hairline. She found it incredible that he—a veritable social pariah—lectured her on proper behavior when he thrived on offending the sensibilities of others. Then she squashed aside the niggle of doubt his attack on her conduct roused. His opinion lacked all credibility. Why, this very night he had flirted outrageously with a married woman, with no thought to propriety.

"I doubt I earned a great deal of attention. Not

while you and the baroness monopolized everyone's attention. Tomorrow everyone will be talking about Lord Brookshire, the rake with a penchant for married ladies."

"We're discussing your conduct," he replied flatly. "My concern lies with you."

"I don't know why. You're not my father," Meredith snapped, fiercely resenting that he presumed to wield power over her as if he were.

"I bloody well know that," he bit out, his fingers digging into her arm. "But if you would quit being so stubborn, you might hear what I'm saying. Or don't you care what kind of reputation you establish in Town? Perhaps you weren't serious about remarrying. Perhaps you're lying to me. Again."

With a choked breath she reared back, but his hold on her arm kept her close. "Of course I'm not lying. Do you think I wish to be under your thumb all the rest of my days to endure this constant meddling in my life?"

He pulled her closer, and she was instantly, achingly aware of his hard chest pressed against her breasts.

"A gentleman wants a wife above reproach. Whom he toys with is not the one he weds. Even if he wants to, his family would discourage him." Nick pointed toward the house. "And something tells me that boy's family would influence his selection of a bride."

No argument there. Lord Havernautt was clearly tied to his mama's skirts, yet she would perish before admitting such a thing. "Lord Havernautt was not toying with me. *He is a gentleman.*"

"Yes. He did appear quite the doting puppy." Nick's fingers flexed on her arm, the calluses rasping her skin. Sparks of sensation shot up her arm as he pulled her closer yet. "Is that the kind of man you want? A boy that you can lead by the nose?"

"You speak as though I have decided upon him. I have only met him. What exactly is your complaint, my lord? My behavior? Or Lord Havernautt's interest in me?"

Meredith lifted her chin defiantly and pulled back her shoulders as far as his hold on her would allow. The more she thought about it, the more possible it seemed. Her heart lifted, expanded in her chest, inexplicably pleased. A slow grin spread across her face. *Nick was jealous.* She lifted an eyebrow questioningly, awaiting his response.

Nick stared down at her in lengthening silence. His hands still gripped her shoulders. She tapped lightly on his chest and shocked herself by taunting, "This whole marriage matter was your plan, remember? So you best get accustomed to seeing me with other men."

"If you're implying that seeing you with other men troubles me, you're sadly mistaken," he said in an exasperatingly level voice. She wanted to hear the emotion vibrate in his voice. She needed to confirm that he felt *something, anything,* for her. That she was not totally, pathetically astray in accusing him of jealousy. She could not be that big a fool.

Desperation burned to life inside her. Very deliberately she grazed her breasts against his chest in what she hoped to be an innocent gesture—but it was a thin hope given her complete lack of expertise with matters of enticement.

Releasing her shoulders, he grabbed her face in both hands and covered her mouth with his. Satisfaction bubbled up inside her. His kiss was deep and drugging, leaving her so weak in the knees she leaned her entire length against him for support. If not for his hands on her face, she would have collapsed to the ground.

He tore his lips away. She moaned in protest as her eyes fluttered open. His eyes gleamed down at her with dark emotion. She tingled beneath his intense regard. The feel of his callused palms on her cheeks left her giddy.

"Hussy," he hissed before smothering her lips in yet another kiss.

Exhilaration swelled inside her. *A hussy? Yes.* With him she lacked all virtue and became another woman entirely.

He broke away again to mutter, "Remember I already explained that two people don't have to like each other to experience lust." His eyes scanned her face. Even in the darkness she could see the bright flame dancing in their depths, seeming to invalidate his words. The intensity of his expression confirmed that he still wanted her to believe he did not like her.

She forced a serious tone. "A fascinating lesson, to be sure. Perhaps you could instruct me more on these fine points of lust? I'm sure any further instruction would be vastly helpful in hunting for a husband."

She heard his breath catch and watched, riveted, at the sudden ticking in his jaw.

"If you do this with anyone before the actual wedding, I'll throttle you . . . after I shoot him."

He dragged her back and reclaimed her lips. Her hands knotted the fabric of his jacket, wrinkling it beyond repair. And all the while she prayed that this time he wouldn't stop. She kissed him back, matching his fervor, mimicking the thrusts of his tongue. His hands lowered from her face, skimming her back, digging through the soft fabric of her skirts to seize her hips and haul her against him. Her eyes flew wide at the insistent bulge prodding her abdomen. She gasped against his mouth, knowing it signified his desire for her. His need. A need that matched her own.

Ripples of heat washed over her and she wound her arms around his neck, standing on tiptoes and lifting herself higher to fit him more intimately against her. A rush of moisture gathered between her thighs and a moan escaped from deep in her throat as she ground herself against his erection, seeking to alleviate the unbearable ache.

He groaned in response, deepening their kiss.

A woman's shrill laughter floated on the air, a sudden reminder that others roamed nearby.

Apparently all the reminder Nick needed. He set her from him with a sudden jerk. She stumbled, her arms flailing about as she caught her balance. She ached, frustrated, only pride stopping her from begging for more.

He glanced about, his chest lifting with labored breaths. His eyes settled on her, bright and gleaming in the shadowed garden. "Lesson two: never allow a man to get you alone. His only purpose is to take advantage of you."

"I see," she said tightly, trying to still the wild thudding of her heart. "Thank you for the advice. Next time I will better choose who accompanies me into a garden." Gathering her skirts, she attempted to walk past him, but he blocked her path. She lifted her chin to glare at him. "Let me pass."

"So you can find Havernautt to finish what I wouldn't?"

Meredith shook her head and threw up her hands in exasperation. "What is it you want from me? To personally select every gentleman I keep company with?"

"I've made my desires clear. I simply want you to behave yourself."

She jabbed him in the chest. "Like I just did with you?"

"A mistake," he admitted, nodding grimly. "You have the knack for pricking my temper."

"What does rousing one's temper have to do with kissing?"

He crossed his arms over his impressive chest. "Lesson three: provoking a man's temper often provokes his physical passions."

"Interesting," Meredith murmured, only too well understanding his meaning. *Attraction had nothing to do with kissing her.* Her pride suffered a blow for that. She suddenly doubted her earlier assumption that he desired *her*. After all, what did she know of matters between men and women? She had been unable to tempt her husband into consummating their marriage. Why should she think herself able to tempt Nick?

"There seem to be countless ways to attract someone who might normally find you repellent," Meredith said hollowly.

"True," he agreed, his easy agreement further wounding her. "Now, back to the issue at hand. Do I have your promise to behave? Contrary to your implications, I have no qualms in watching other men court you. In fact, I greatly anticipate seeing you wed. I will heave a great sigh of relief on that day. But in the meantime, I would hope you conduct yourself with proper modesty."

"I can't promise that I'll conduct myself to meet your approval, and I won't explain my actions to you on every occasion. If you disapprove of my behavior and have qualms about the gentlemen I entertain, then perhaps you should keep your distance."

Nick sighed and looked out at the shadowed garden. After a long moment he nodded and startled her by saying, "Very well. Perhaps that is best. I'll let you go about your husband hunt your own way."

Disappointment rushed over her. She had not expected such willing agreement. Did that mean she would not see him anymore? The possibility gave her a pang of regret.

"I'll stay away. Just see that you've found yourself a groom by the end of the Season." He nodded, as though quite decided. "Yes, that way you'll be sure not to prick my temper, and we will not have any more of these unfortunate lessons."

Unfortunate. Is that really how he viewed kissing her? Meredith swallowed past the knot in her throat. "Have no worry. I'll find a husband." An unexciting, peaceful man. Someone safe. Someone totally unlike Nick.

An awkward silence hung between them before he suggested, "You best get back before you're missed."

"What of you?"

He waved a hand aimlessly. "Oh, I'll find my way out through the gardens." He craned his head as though searching for a hidden gate.

"Shouldn't you make your farewells? It is bad form to just sneak off."

His expression turned indulgent. "Ah, Meredith, always expecting me to conform. Do you really think I care? Before tonight most of these people never knew I existed. My absence will hardly be noted."

But they all knew now. Every woman inside

would mourn his disappearance. By tomorrow his name would be on the tongue of every matchmaking mama and papa. Handsome, titled, rich: an irresistible catch. At least with his departure she could stop making a fool of herself over a man who viewed her as an irksome rash—something he would rather ignore but felt compelled to carefully mind.

His tall figure merged into the darkness until she could no longer make out his shape. The clang of a gate soon sounded, echoing in her heart. She lingered a few moments, trying to rid her mind of him before heading back inside, to the string of dance partners Lady Derring doubtlessly had waiting for her.

A visit to a lending library had seemed a splendid idea. Certainly it would be an excellent reprieve from the endless shopping trips Lady Derring dragged her on throughout Town. How many reticules and gloves could one woman need? Meredith refused to accept that a lady must possess one for every gown.

The escape from yet another excursion to Bond Street—and Lady Derring's constant harpings—presented itself in the form of Lord Havernautt. Since Lady Derring's party, he never strayed far. If on any given day he did not appear, a bouquet of hothouse roses arrived in his stead. Slowly but surely, she had put the unsuspecting gentleman to the test. So far he seemed to satisfy all her criteria. Her feelings for him, though kindly disposed, did not run to love or even remotely close to the blood-singing attraction she felt for one particular man. From all appearances, and with Lady Derring's assurances, Lord Havernautt was quite well set and would have no problem maintaining her and her family, should he be inclined to make an offer. As to the matter of his willingness to father children, he had made a few casual remarks that led her to conclude he desired offspring. All things considered, it appeared to Meredith that she had found her man.

"I do believe he is quite taken with you, Meredith," Lady Derring had announced upon the arrival of the third bouquet, glowing with such satisfaction one would think she had accomplished some great personal feat. Yet her triumph was only momentary.

Remembering her primary charge, she had soon shifted her attention to Portia and subjected her to a withering glare. "If only getting *you* wed would prove as easy." As always, that complaint inevitably led to the next. "Where has Brookshire got off to lately? Incredibly rude of the man not to accept any of my invitations."

Had she been so disposed, Meredith could have informed Her Grace that Nick was not likely to appear at any more of this Season's functions. For all that he vexed her, longing ripped through her. She could not deny that she craved the sight of him, that she missed the taste of his mouth on hers. It had been a fortnight since their last encounter, and she suspected he meant to keep his promise and stay away. Only she could not forget him, spent far too much of her time daydreaming over him. Meredith pressed the backs of her fingers against her heated cheeks, well imagining the twin spots of pink staining her face as she stood amid aisles of books, fantasizing about the very man whose sole goal was to get rid of her.

"There is a charming café next door." Lord Havernautt's voice intruded on her wonderings. "Would you care to stop in for tea? If it's no longer drizzling we may sit beneath the portico and watch passersby for anyone we know." She dropped her hands from her face and smiled brightly, perhaps too brightly—anything to distract her from her guilty thoughts. With a willing nod, she placed the book she had blindly been thumbing back on the shelf.

"Yes, let's find Portia."

In their search for the young lady, Meredith came face-to-face with Adam Tremble.

"Lady Brookshire." His hand fluttered to his throat, mirroring her surprise. Those knowing eyes of his raked her elegant day dress of dark green muslin, staring overlong at her middle, taking in the absence of a protruding belly. He fingered his yellow and peach cravat, and she blinked, momentarily distracted by the striped pattern.

"Mr. Tremble," she greeted, acutely conscious of Lord Havernautt hovering close at her side, waiting for an introduction. She stifled a sigh and forged ahead with the unavoidable. "Lord

Havernautt, this is Mr. Tremble, a dear friend of my late husband's."

"A pleasure, sir." Lord Havernautt inclined his head.

"Indeed." Mr. Tremble's lips flattened into a thin line. "You appear in fine form, my lady, though the last time we met you were in a decidedly delicate way." He let the statement hang between them, lifting a brow, clearly awaiting an explanation.

Meredith had hoped her lie would not follow her to London. Foolish perhaps, but other than Lady Derring, no one appeared to know of her alleged pregnancy. Now here stood Adam Tremble, armed with the knowledge of her lie, once again proving a nuisance.

Biting her bottom lip, she glanced at Lord Havernautt's face. Only curious surprise there. Well, she supposed it premature for him to make any judgments from what little Tremble had revealed. Satisfied that he did not appear dismayed, she turned to address Tremble and award him the information he clearly sought. He was either ignorant of the fact that such subjects were not discussed among mixed company or chose to disregard etiquette in the hopes of discrediting her before her companion. From the haughty flare of his nostrils, Meredith suspected the latter. "Unfortunately I am no longer *enceinte*."

Tremble's lips twitched as though tempted to smile. "A truly dreadful loss." He spoke the proper words. Only her ears detected the gratification in his dulcet tones.

"Indeed, Lady Brookshire," Lord Havernautt said, quickly contributing his sympathies. "I had no idea the extent of your grief. How have you borne it?" He clasped her hand in his, adding, "Poor, sweet lady." His heartfelt, anxious gaze made her feel the veriest of wretches, especially in front of Adam Tremble, who knew full well of her deceit.

"Oh, you need not pity Lady Brookshire," Tremble inserted. "She is always a woman to land on her feet." From his pointed look at the two of them, he clearly thought she had found a plump pigeon to pluck. With Lord Havernautt holding her hand, they probably appeared quite the cozy couple. She extricated her hand and looped her arm through Lord Havernautt's.

"It was lovely to see you again, Mr. Tremble," she lied, urging Lord Havernautt along.

They located Portia in the nether regions of the library, her nose buried in a dog-eared copy of *The Rights of Women in the British Empire*, and coaxed her next door with them.

There, taking a sip of tepid tea, Meredith fidgeted under Lord Havernautt's worshipful appraisal. Apparently she had just been elevated in his eyes. He gazed at her as though she were a hero newly returned from war. Blast it, why did she have to bump into Adam Tremble with Lord Havernautt, of all people? If she did wed him, that lie would stand forever between them. Lies were a sticky business. One always led to another, then another . . .

Thankfully, Portia kept the conversation lively, chattering all the way back to Lady Derring's about the books piled high on her lap, allowing Meredith to mull in silence beside Lord Havernautt.

Finch was waiting for them in the foyer. "Lady Derring is holding tea," he told them.

The moment before they entered the drawing room, Lord Havernautt grasped her elbow to keep her from following Portia. Meredith lifted her face inquiringly.

"Are you well, my lady? You have been withdrawn ever since meeting with that Tremble fellow. I hope painful reminders did not spoil your day," he murmured.

His kindness increased her discomfort. She twisted the fingertips of her gloves, stretching the fabric until the fine meshed cotton was translucent. "No, I enjoyed our outing."

He looked beyond her to the drawing room where Portia and Lady Derring waited. The two women made a show of focusing their attention elsewhere: the tea set, the carpet, the vaulted ceiling. Yet it was clear where their attention truly lay, and that they were listening to every word. In spite of their audience, Lord Havernautt inhaled a deep breath and hastily confessed, "I hope I am not too sudden in saying that I have come to much prize your company, and I hope to become even better acquainted with you."

Meredith played with the fringe of her reticule, unsure how much more time they could spend together without offending propriety.

"I should like for you to join me at the family estate in Cumberland so that you might meet Mother. Perhaps after your presentation at court? I realize it is bad form to drag you away at the start of the Season, but Mother does not care for Town and I so want her to meet you." He looked so hopeful that she could not have refused him if she wished. And from Lady Derring's vehement nods, it appeared to Meredith that she did not have a choice anyway.

"I should like that very much, my lord."

"Teddy. Please call me Teddy."

"Teddy," she allowed, inclining her head.

He grinned like a child awarded a treat. "Shall I call you Meredith, then? Would that be acceptable?"

Nick's bold use of her name flashed in her head. He had never asked permission. She scolded herself for even comparing the two men. A good thing Teddy was not like Nick. A very good thing. If he were, he would not meet her criteria.

"Of course . . . Teddy."

"Brilliant!" In his pleasure, he grabbed her hand and placed a wet, fervent kiss to the back of it. "I count myself lucky to have found you so early in the Season and to have escaped another round of simpering debs. Your maturity and grace are very calming. You have borne experiences that make you all the more enchanting, the mark of a true woman, no green girl."

His words caused her no small amount of alarm. She was older than the average debutante, but not necessarily more experienced. Tucked away in the country for so long, she sorely lacked a repertoire of experience . . . most notably in the bedroom. In that regard, she was most certainly a girl. How could she convince him she was a matron of seven years who had suffered a miscarriage? She gnashed her teeth until her jaw ached. How had her life become so complicated? How could one single fib have escalated until she found herself mired in a whole web of them? She felt like stamping her foot in childish pique. If it weren't for Nick, she would not be in this predicament. He was the one insisting she acquire a husband. Due to him, she faced the problem of explaining her virginity to her future husband.

Meredith had heard the whispers. She knew a virgin experienced pain her first time. And there was blood. A widow wouldn't bleed. How could she explain the blood? She wasn't certain what would be worse: telling Teddy that Edmund had found the notion of consummating their marriage distasteful, or explaining how she invented a pregnancy and subsequent miscarriage. In either case, he would probably have their marriage annulled at the first opportunity.

Nick was a worldly man. He should have foreseen this problem. After all, he was the one *insisting* she remarry. Yes, she would go to him and lay this dilemma at his feet. Certainly he would see that she could not go through with this marriage now.

Meredith returned Teddy's smile with a shaky one of her own and accepted his arm. As he escorted her into the drawing room, she told herself that her suddenly churning stomach had nothing to do with facing Nick again, that she only sought an audience, only needed to explain that she could not wed someone under a cloud of lies. She was sick to death of lies. No more.

Wanting Nick with every breath in her body had nothing whatsoever to do with her desire to see him again.

Chapter 18

The hired hack waited at the corner at half past eleven just as Meredith had instructed her maid to arrange. Her slippered feet carried her down the sidewalk in a combination of haste and caution. She tried to hurry, wanting to put as much distance between herself and Lady Derring's mansion, but the lack of visibility made her step cautiously. The fog hugged her like smoke and shrouded the hack from view until she nearly smacked into it. Its dark outline materialized suddenly, a slumbering beast lying in wait.

She paused to issue instructions to the driver before ascending unassisted into the coach. Devising an excuse to stay home had been relatively easy. Her complaint of a headache had been readily accepted as the others prepared for an evening out. In truth, Lady Derring's managing ways had subsided, at least in regard to her. All due to Teddy.

She'd had a momentary spurt of panic when Aunt Eleanor insisted on staying behind to take care of her. Fortunately, Lady Derring added her voice to Meredith's protests, saying she needed a good night's rest to cure her ails and Aunt Eleanor need not miss the musicale.

Pushing thoughts of her aunt and Lady Derring to the back of her mind, Meredith marveled at her boldness as the hack crawled sedately through the fog-filled streets of London. She knew that Nick resided at his gaming establishment, the Lucky Lady. She saw it as a fortuitous circumstance, increasing his availability. If he had not yet retired for the night, she need only wait for his appearance.

On the morrow she would be presented at court. After that she would depart for Cumberland, Lady Derring, Portia, and Aunt Eleanor in tow. If Lady Derring was to be relied upon, she would be betrothed at the end of the house party. She had to see Nick tonight.

The hack came to an abrupt halt, rocking her from side to side on the squabs. Steadying herself, she parted the curtains and peered out. The Lucky Lady stood before her, several stories high, lights blazing from its stone and oak facade. The structure resembled an Elizabethan playhouse of old, with Tudor style windows and heavy oak beams crisscrossing the front. It looked more like a grand home than a business. A smile touched her lips. It reminded her a little of Oak Run. Perhaps Nick missed his former home more than he knew.

"Getting out?" the driver barked from his perch.

She hopped down, fished a coin out of her reticule, and tossed it to him. The hack clattered away, leaving her alone. She pulled the hood of her black cloak over her head, her fingers luxuriating in the gray ermine fur trimming the edges. Another one of the elegant purchases Lady Derring had insisted upon. She gathered the folds of her cloak about her, self-conscious of the provocative gown beneath. Like most of her new gowns, the green silk exposed vast amounts of shoulders and cleavage.

Upon entering the Lucky Lady, she hovered uncertainly on the raised dais, not yet taking the Italian marble steps that descended into the large room abuzz with activity. Several heads lifted to note her arrival. Tables dotted the room, occupied by gentlemen—even the occasional woman. Whirring roulette wheels added their volume to the steady drone of conversation. Liveried servants wove about the room carrying gleaming silver trays laden with drinks, food, and cigars.

A woman seemed to be directing these servers, snapping her fingers at one footman, directing him to offer cigars to several gentlemen playing at a nearby table. She caught Meredith's notice primarily because of her unbelievably red hair, but also because of the air of ownership and authority about her. She was striking, despite her gaudy dress and hair. Meredith immediately wondered at her relationship with Nick. Was she an employee or more? Her air of command marked her as no one's servant.

Meredith's stomach heaved when she spotted a few familiar faces among the crowd. Until now she had not appreciated the fact that gentlemen of the *ton*—primarily gentlemen of her newfound acquaintance—frequented Nick's establishment. If recognized, she would be ruined, all hope for a match gone. Her chances with Lord Havernautt would be forever lost, despite his apparent attachment for her.

One face in particular stood out. Bertram, Portia's errant older brother, sat among the crowd. He lifted his head from his cards and took a fortifying drink from the glass in front of him. She clutched at her hood and staggered back several steps, her resolve crumbling. Suddenly, her adventure did not seem so thrilling—the need to talk with Nick not nearly that important. Not if it led to discovery and ruin.

Whirling around, her panicked retreat was brought to a swift halt when she smacked into another body.

A grunt of pain preceded a coarse, "Watch where the hell you're going."

"My pardon, sir, I'm terribly sorry."

The sight of a sneering, pockmarked face did

little to soothe her already frayed nerves. "Bloody right you are." Pale eyes inspected her face and fine cloak with insulting thoroughness, as though she were a piece of horseflesh. "A right fine piece you are. Look like a regular lady. Talk like one too." Hard fingers took hold of her arm as he thrust his face closer to hers. "You already belong to someone, lovey?" His shifty eyes looked over her shoulder, as if to satisfy himself that she was indeed alone and unprotected. When he looked back to her, the glitter in his pale eyes chilled her to the bones. Thin lips stretched over an uneven row of rotting teeth. "A pretty girl like you shouldn't be out alone. There's all kinds of danger for a girl without a protector. Why don't you come with ol' Skelly and let him look after you?"

She assured herself that he could not simply drag her off. Not in front of so many witnesses. Not if she protested. Not if she cried for help. She bit her lip in consternation, her quandary clear. Should she cry for help and alert everyone in the Lucky Lady to her presence, her identity? Certainly not. Surely she could handle this matter herself without creating a scene.

Skelly, as he had identified himself, began dragging her toward the front door. She dug her heels in and shook her head, striving for a calm she did not feel as the soles of her slippers slid with frightening speed along the marble floor.

"I'm waiting for someone," she hissed, still unwilling to draw attention to herself. "I'll thank you to release me so that I can make my own way."

"Any bloke keeping a fine piece like you waiting simply don't deserve you. I'll set you up like a princess. You won't have to lift a finger . . . just your skirts." He chortled, amused by his own quip.

She gasped. He could not be serious. Her reticence vanished at once. He almost had her to the door. Reputation be hanged. She could not allow this man to abduct her.

She spoke through gritted teeth, deciding to give him one last chance. "Release me."

His hold on her arm did not ease in the slightest. "Don't be skittish—"

She cocked back her arm. With her elbow pressed close to her side and her thumb tucked carefully under her fingers, as Nels had taught her, she jabbed him with her fist. She hardly noted the pain in her hand as her fist made contact with his face. The satisfaction in seeing blood spurt from his nose eclipsed all discomfort.

"Little bitch, you mashed my nose in." Even with his hands clutched over his nose, his muffled words were clear enough to understand. Blood seeped between his fingers in a steady stream of crimson. Instead of taking the opportunity to flee, she could only watch in fascinated horror at the damage she had wrought, looking back and forth between her fisted hand and his bleeding face.

"What's going on here?" The brassy, red-haired woman approached. Hands on her hips, she glared first at Meredith, then Skelly. "You know Nick told you not to step foot in here again." She jerked her head in Meredith's direction. "She one of your girls? Nick won't have you working over one of your girls in his place—"

"I am *not* one of his girls," Meredith inserted indignantly, having a good idea what that distinction implied. "He tried to force me to leave with him."

"That so?" The woman dipped her head to gain a better look at her shadowed features. "Well, looks like you handled him." She turned her attention back to Skelly, who was mopping at his face with a dingy-looking handkerchief. "If I were you, I would leave before Nick sees you."

"See who, Bess?"

Never had she experienced joy and dread simultaneously. Nick sauntered forward, looking splendid in a black jacket and silvery gray waistcoat. Her heart beat wildly in her chest. He was magnificent. More so than she remembered. Her face flushed. Dread reasserted itself. She was sure to receive a tongue-lashing as only he knew how to deliver for venturing out unescorted.

Hovering there, waiting for him to notice her, she realized how foolhardy her actions. Good Lord, look what nearly happened to her. Her breath trapped in her chest as she braced herself for the moment he recognized her.

"Skelly has taken to accosting our guests," Bess informed Nick.

"That's Mr. Fairbanks to you." Skelly patted his bloodied nose, his voice muffled by the handkerchief. "And I didn't accost anyone. That bitch hit me."

Nick finally looked at her. The concern and sympathy ready for one of his patrons immediately vanished from his face.

"What in hell are you doing here?" he growled, taking a threatening step toward her.

"You know her?" Bess asked sharply, the arms crossed over her chest falling to her sides.

Nick ignored her question, either unaware of it or indifferent. "What are you doing here?" he repeated.

Meredith darted a wary glance to Bess's and Skelly's rapt faces. Skelly held his handkerchief midair, suddenly forgetting his bloody nose. Bess scowled darkly.

"I needed to speak with you." She hated the telling tremor in her voice.

"You couldn't have sent a message?" He grabbed hold of her shoulder and gave it a shake. "This is no place for you. What were you thinking?"

"Why is this no place for *her*?" Bess demanded, stepping forward to stand side by side with Nick.

Meredith held her hands up in supplication. "I needed to speak with you privately. This seemed the best way. I realize now that I should have sent word that I was coming." She glanced uneasily between Bess and Nick. Both glared at her with equal expressions of hostility, and Meredith was unsure which one posed the greatest threat to her at the moment.

"You should not have come at all." As if suddenly remembering what had happened to her, he abruptly released her shoulder and wheeled around, grabbing Skelly by the throat. "You touched her?"

"She was alone!" Skelly scratched at Nick's fingers with an animal-like frenzy, wheezing, "I didn't know she was yours. I didn't hurt her. She mashed my nose—I'm the one bleeding like a stuck pig."

"And I can imagine just what you did to warrant that." Nick's knuckles were white around Skelly's throat, and Meredith placed a restraining hand on his bicep. The muscle hummed with tension beneath her fingers.

"Nick." She spoke his name softly, trying to reach past his anger. He looked down at her hand on his arm as Skelly continued thrashing against his hold. Her voice beseeched him. "Let him go. He's not worth it."

"Nick," Bess interrupted, her angry gaze scouring Meredith. "People are watching." Her eyes swept Meredith and Skelly in mutual contempt. Indeed, several people were beginning to gather around them, inching up the steps to the dais. Meredith dropped her hand and tried to disappear even farther into the confines of her cloak.

Nick hesitated for the briefest moment, a tumult of emotions flickering over his face—his desire to continue choking the life out Skelly the most apparent. At last he shoved the man away. "I warned you to stay out of here. There won't be a next time."

Skelly nodded, rubbing the angry red flesh of

his throat. "I hear you." He spared one last venomous glare for Meredith before stalking out the front doors.

Nick looked back at her, fists closing and opening at his sides, his expression as dark and forbidding as when he had looked at Skelly. Did he want to choke her too? If possible, she shrank even farther into her cloak. He tore his eyes from her to take in the curious faces around them, realizing, just as she did, that they hovered on the brink of scandal. His jaw tensed in grim acknowledgment of the crowd drawing ever closer.

Bess stepped in front of Meredith. "It's time you leave. You've caused enough trouble."

Meredith tried to peer around the woman to catch a glimpse of Nick. She waited the span of a few breaths, enough time for him to stop her if he were inclined. With a curt nod of acceptance, she veered for the door.

Meredith managed only two steps before Nick grabbed hold of her wrist and walked her straight out the door with swift, purposeful strides.

"Nick!" Bess cried behind them. "Nick!"

A ridiculous rush of triumph surged through Meredith. For whatever reason, he had not let her walk out the door alone. She tried to look over her shoulder to see if Bess's expression matched the fury in her voice, but Nick moved too quickly.

His voice reached her ears in a fast and furious growl. "I'll see you home, but I suggest you shut your mouth on the ride there or I might do something we'll both regret. I used up all my charity letting that bastard go. I don't have much left over for you."

She nodded dumbly. Nick pulled her along, her smaller strides three for every one of his. He hailed a hack. Barking the address, he yanked the door open with such violence she cringed. She tried to get in without his assistance, but he had no patience for that. With an angry snarl, he grabbed her by the waist and tossed her up before him. She scurried to the far corner of her seat, away from him and his frightening anger.

He settled his long frame on the opposite seat as the hack began its crawl to Berkeley Square. For several minutes he ignored her, staring out the small slit in the curtains as if he saw something of interest in the impenetrable fog.

At last he broke the silence to ask, "Were you recognized?" He continued to look out the window as though he could not tolerate the sight of her.

Clutching her cloak with damp palms, she wet her lips and replied, "No. At least I don't believe so."

"Well, we will know by tomorrow if your stupidity has brought ruin on your head."

His words were a stinging slap, and her defenses stirred. She had never been one to take insults kindly, and he continually cast more than his share upon her person.

"I'm *not* stupid—"

The blistering stare he turned on her silenced

the rest of her argument. "No? How would you describe your actions? Endangering your reputation and placing yourself in the path of Skelly Fairbanks is certainly not the mark of an intelligent woman. I suppose I can now add foolish to the list along with greedy and scheming."

Her hands tangled in the folds of her cloak and she beat them in her lap. "Am I forever the villain to you?" Foolish tears burned at the backs of her eyes. Had she ever truly thought him kind? Where was the man that had held her so tenderly the night of Sally Finney's death? "I don't know why I even bothered coming."

"Indeed, why? You said it was important." He frowned.

It was her turn to look out the window. She crossed her arms, determined not to utter another word. She'd be damned before she confessed her reason for venturing out tonight was to lay the issue of her virginity at his feet. To beg him to reconsider forcing her to marry, thereby forcing her to enter into yet another pretense. At the moment, marriage did not seem so distasteful if it removed her from his maddening control. She would not lower herself by asking him for anything.

"What was so important to risk putting yourself in Fairbanks's clutches? Do you even know what type of man he is?"

She snorted indelicately. Skelly Fairbanks had revealed exactly what kind of man he was in their brief encounter. She continued to gaze out the window, tired of crossing words with Nick, tired of hearing herself sink lower in his estimation, tired of being ten kinds of fool around him. To think she had actually *missed* him.

She heard him move across the coach to sit beside her, and tensed. Hard fingers grasped her chin, forcing her to face him. "He's a pimp. And if you caught his eye, you can bet he had an unpleasant future in mind for you."

She had surmised as much, but to hear him say the words so coldly, so matter of factly . . . a small shudder ran through her.

Forcing a bravado she did not feel, she jerked her chin away from his burning fingers. "I took care of myself, didn't I? At any rate, how was I to know people like him frequent your establishment? What kind of place do you run where it's unsafe to walk through the door?"

Meredith's dig hit her mark. She could tell by the way he started, as though someone had splashed cold water in his face.

Shaking her head, she tried to apologize. "Forgive me—"

"What did you expect of anything connected to me?" he bit out. "I'm no gentleman. No better than Fairbanks."

She shut her eyes against the harsh words, words she refused to believe . . . words she *knew* to be untrue.

He continued, his voice taking on the distant quality of a stranger. "Regardless if you bloodied his nose, you should never have placed yourself in such a situation. Did it occur to you how he might have retaliated had I not come along?"

She spread her arms wide in defeat. "I've said I'm sorry."

His eyes narrowed to where her cloak parted. "What are you wearing?" Before she could stop him he leaned across the seat and flipped her cloak off her shoulders. His eyes widened at the plunging, heart-shaped bodice. "Another of Lady Derring's innovations?"

"It's just a gown." She tried to be nonchalant but felt her face redden with the secret knowledge that she had chosen *this* gown with him in mind. Hot with embarrassment, she grappled to pull her cloak back over her shoulders. With brutal force he whipped it completely free.

"Come, let's see it. You obviously wore it to be noticed. Isn't that what women do? Dress to attract? Let's have a look at what you are advertising."

She made another dive for her cloak. "Give it back. I don't want to offend your sensibilities further," she mocked harshly.

He wadded her cloak into a ball and stuffed it behind his back. "I'm not offended." His husky murmur sent a bolt of heat straight to her core. He pulled her flush against him. "In fact, I'm suddenly anxious to hear why you needed to speak to me." He leaned back, taking her with him, his manner oddly casual considering their far from casual proximity.

"Release me." Her hands fluttered helplessly, having nowhere to land except his chest. Her palms dropped on the firm expanse of muscles.

Unable to resist, her fingers curled into the hardness. She arched her spine to get away but only succeeded in nearly pulling her breasts out of her bodice.

His gaze dipped to where she spilled out of her dress. "You . . . needed me?" She did not miss the double innuendo.

"No," she denied.

"No? Then why are you here?" His hand touched a lock of hair that fell over the curve of one breast, rubbing the strands between his fingers idly.

The flippant quality of his voice set her on edge. As did the way his lazy gaze traveled over her cleavage. He dropped her lock of hair and rubbed the back of his index finger against the sensitive flesh of her breasts. That finger dipped lower, beneath the bodice of her gown, until she felt its friction as it rolled across her nipple. Back and forth, back and forth, each stroke sending the blood roaring to her head.

She whimpered—from frustration or arousal, she could not say. He watched her intently as he pulled her bodice down farther with one effortless yank. Her bare breasts filled his rough palms. It was only that gentle assault that held her, but she could not have pulled away. The low ache in her belly grew with nagging insistency. Her knees slipped down on either side of his hips. She sank onto his lap, both shocked and thrilled at the hard ridge rising to meet that most intimate part of her. His eyes glittered with raw need, stealing her breath. He pinched her nipples, abrading the hard little peaks between the callused pads of his fingers. White-hot pleasure lanced through her and a low, keening moan rose from deep in her throat.

He flung her flat on her back on the coarse velvet seat, nothing save the dark outline of his head visible as he took one nipple into his mouth. She let out a squeak as the wet warmth of his mouth and tongue laved her. He placed a hand at the juncture of her thighs, only the sheer fabric of her dress barring the way. His hand rubbed there, rocking in harmony with the motion of the coach.

Sighing his name, she buried her fingers in his hair and arched against him, pushing more of her breast into his mouth.

He looked up, his eyes dark burning coals. "Say you want this." His desperate request twisted through her belly.

She ran a hand through his hair, tenderly ruffling the locks like so many windblown feathers. *She definitely wanted this. Wanted him.* Perhaps this had been her motive all along. The real reason she had to see him. Heaven knew her thoughts had been filled with him ever since he burst into her life, her body longing for him since his first touch that night outside the nursery.

The desperate need of his gaze shook her. She saw her own beauty reflected there. The awkward vicar's daughter did not exist. Nor did the abandoned bride.

"I want you." Meredith hardly recognized the throatiness of her voice, only knew she wanted him to continue touching her, continue making her feel—for perhaps the first time in her life— that she was worthy. She nodded urgently. "I want you."

He hesitated, a dark cloud falling over the brilliance of his eyes, and she knew instantly that he was remembering who she was and that she had played him false.

"You shouldn't," he announced, then clarified in a firmer voice, "I shouldn't."

Meredith blinked, frustrated. "But you do. We both do."

His hands fell away from her, leaving her bereft and aching. An altogether different fire than that of moments ago began to burn in his eyes. Scorched beneath a gaze that no longer looked at her with appreciation and wonder, she felt like Eve wanting to shield herself in shame.

"Cover yourself."

Those two little words struck her like a slap, and she suddenly felt as she had seven years ago: the naive girl in her freshly pressed nightgown, sitting in a great big bed as she waited for the wedding night of her dreams to arrive. Only it never did. Firelight had flickered off Edmund's flaxen hair, lending it a reddish hue as he loomed over her, his words all the more unbearable for the airiness in which he uttered them. *Darling girl, it would require more than a sour-faced vicar's daughter to tempt me. I only married you to appease my father.*

She shook off the bitter memories and reminded herself that Nick was not Edmund. Nick had kissed her, touched her. *He wanted her.* His hungry gaze swept over her face, taking in the riot of hair tangling about her neck and shoulders, settling at last on her breasts. "I said cover yourself." His voice fell hard and fast, firing her into action.

Fumbling with her dress, she spoke with forced lightness, feigning indifference, wanting to hurt him as his rejection was hurting her. "I had thought you might be up to the task." Her eyes raked his face and body in cold appreciation. Sighing and pretending his rejection was of little account and not a crushing blow, she added, "Since you have not the inclination, I suppose I shall have to wait until my wedding night."

He snatched hold of her wrist, his grip punishing.

Meredith's glare flicked from his face to where he clutched her wrist. In a quiet voice she commanded, "Let me go."

She watched as varying emotions flitted across his face, battling for dominance. At last he gave a curt nod, appearing to reach a decision.

"You want it so badly?" he growled. "I'll give it to you."

Chapter 19

Nick crushed his lips to hers, kissing her so fiercely he knew her lips would be bruised for days to come. A dangerous combination of lust and fury spiraled through him. The lust he understood. She drove him mad with desire—had done so from the start. But the fury he could not. The thought of her with another man had done it. Which he knew was illogical, given that she was only husband hunting at his insistence. He wanted her married, wanted her gone from his life. Nick groaned, both with desire and frustration. He couldn't make sense of it. All he knew was that for now, tonight, he would have her. She would be his. This damnable longing would never depart until he sated himself with her body. Only then could he let her go.

"No backing out now," he warned between kisses, almost as much for him as her. His hands roamed her body. He grasped the edges of her bodice and yanked it back down.

His mouth devoured hers. She matched his kiss, sliding her tongue against his in a sinuous dance. She tasted like honey, and he kissed her long and hard, drinking from her nectar until he grew intoxicated. His anxious hands kneaded her breasts until she moaned in his mouth.

Exultation ripped through him when she buried her hands in his hair and pulled his head to her breasts.

Looking up at her, he flicked his tongue over one nipple and then the other. Her eyes darkened and fire flooded his veins as she squirmed enticingly beneath him.

Still, in the back of his mind was the knowledge that he was making love to the very woman who had tricked and deceived and vexed him to the point of madness. At what point had she become desirable and not just the proverbial fly in the ointment of his life?

As if she could read his thoughts, she frowned and shook her head determinedly. "No more thinking."

Taking his face in both hands, she pulled him back up and kissed him soundly. The sweet feel of her palms on his cheeks stimulated him like the most expert courtesan's touch, obliterating all else from his mind. *Right. No more thinking, just feeling.*

With a groan, he deepened their kiss, digging his fingers in the smooth roundness of her shoulders.

She eased the kiss, murmuring against his lips, "I want to be with you. When I'm an old married lady, I'll have this to remember."

Opening his eyes, he broke their kiss to stare down at her. He brushed the flyaway tendrils at her temples with his thumbs, again disturbed at the thought of her with another man. Then he answered her with another, longer kiss. Right now he did not want to think of her marrying anyone. Like her, he wanted to create a memory—with no phantom husband between them.

He kissed her thoroughly, determined to have no more words. The kiss grew hotter, feverish. He jerked her skirts to her hips. His hands made short work removing her undergarments. His palms skimmed the soft satin of her thighs until his fingers found the center of her and tested her readiness for him. Finding her moist to the touch, he buried one finger into her wet warmth. She lurched against him with a cry, her delicate muscles clenching around him in sweet welcome. His ragged breathing filled the coach, accompanied by the sweet little noises she made in the back of her throat. He worked a second finger inside her, preparing her for him and groaning when her untried muscles flexed around his fingers. He found her tiny nub and circled it with his thumb as he thrust his fingers in and out, in and out, imagining it was his hard length buried in that tight heat.

His thumb worked harder at that little pearl until she cried out. Shudders overtook her entire body as her hips thrust against his hand.

Aching with need, he could wait no longer. His hands trembled in anticipation as he slid his fingers from her slick channel. Freeing himself from his trousers, he guided himself to the apex at her thighs. His eyes met hers as he hovered at her entrance. A feeling like no other seized him as he slid inside her and impaled her beneath him with one smooth thrust. A feeling of rightness, completion, perfection. That everything in his life had led to this moment with this woman. He groaned even as she stiffened beneath the invasion. She jammed her eyes shut against the pain, her breath escaping in a hiss, and he quickly set to work refueling her fire.

Bending his head, he fanned his warm breath against her ear, licking and nipping at the lobe with his teeth until he heard her breath quicken and felt her muscles mold around his manhood like the perfect fit of a glove.

He pulled back and drove into her again. She moaned, her fingers digging into his arms. Gratification filled him and he moved again, faster, pounding her to the seat cushion, inflamed by her rapturous cries and the dig of her fingers on his biceps. She met him thrust for thrust, lurching off the seat and burying her face in his neck as he pumped. Her hard little teeth bit him through his shirt, just above his nipple, inflaming him to move faster, harder. She shrieked with her own release and collapsed back on the seat, a fine sheen of perspiration making her breasts glow in the dim confines of the coach. She moaned low in her throat as he covered her plump mounds with his hands, clutching them in possession as he continued to drive into her, her tight sheath milking him, the tightest, hottest thing he had ever felt. He threw back his head, a primal cry escaping him as he gave one last shuddering thrust.

Nick dropped his head in the crook of her neck, inhaling her woman scent. His manhood still lay buried inside her, and for the life of him he did not want to withdraw.

"That was . . ." She paused, as if searching for the word. She finally arrived at it. "Nice."

"*Nice?*" he muttered against her throat. "If that was *nice*, spectacular would kill me."

"There is no adequate word." Her fingers ran through his hair in luxurious strokes that made his scalp tingle.

With no small amount of alarm, he realized he was in no hurry to leave her arms. His body felt heavy, content, sated . . . the old familiar hollowness nowhere to be found.

He felt full, replete.

And it terrified him almost as much as it thrilled him.

They remained just so, silent and locked together in a sticky union of flesh both were loath to break.

He felt her heavy sigh beneath him. "We have to dress."

He withdrew, not looking at her as he straightened his garments. From the rustling beside him, he knew she did the same. Their timing could not have been better for he felt the carriage rolling to a stop. Parting the curtain, he saw that they were parked across the street from Lady Derring's mansion. Looking back at Meredith, his breath stuck in his throat. She looked lovely—skin flushed, eyes glowing. Like a woman well loved. Her gaze avoided his as she collected her reticule off the seat.

He could think of nothing to say. He had sense enough to refrain from blurting out *Stay*. Even though the thought ricocheted inside his head. She had to return to her world. Where she belonged. Just as he belonged in his.

With one hand on the door latch, she looked back over her shoulder at him. "Good night."

Before he could reconsider, Nick grabbed her arm to stop her from getting out of the hack and hauled her against him, kissing her with all the thoroughness and skill he possessed. He splayed a hand behind her head, anchoring her for his ravaging mouth as he buried his fingers into the mass of her unbound hair, luxuriating in the silken tresses against his roughened palm. Those familiar mewling sounds rose from her throat, firing his blood. Hard and aching again, his hand dove beneath her skirts, his fingers searching out her heat again.

The driver called out something, his uncultured

accents loud and abrasive on the air. Like a frightened bird, Meredith tore her mouth from his, her words spilling forth in a rush, "He'll wake the neighborhood. You have to let me go."

His first impulse was to reply that he didn't *have* to do anything. That the driver could bloody well wake the entire city for all he cared.

Then common sense returned and he nodded. Sliding his hand from beneath her skirts, he pulled back.

With one last unreadable look, Meredith was gone, out the door like a wisp of smoke, leaving him to dwell over all the things he would like to do to her given the proper amount of time.

And a proper bed.

He had the presence of mind to bark out his destination to the driver as he settled back against the seat, determining that he would heed her words and indeed let her go. This time for good.

Nick wrenched his shoulders and arms free of his jacket and flung it on his bed before he realized the large four-poster was occupied. Bess lounged on the damask coverlet, stretched out like an elegant cat, her cheek resting in her palm with an idleness that belied the steady intent of her gaze. Straightening, he crossed his arms over his chest.

"So, Nick." She spoke his name slowly, toying with the beaded threads fringing her low bodice, an expert ploy to attract his attention to her generous breasts, and one that he had seen her use countless times—on him and others. "That's her?"

At his stony silence, she elaborated. "The one you left me for?"

Stifling a sigh, he sat down on a chair and tugged off his boots. Might as well get comfortable if he was to endure an inquisition. "I told you already. I did not leave you for anyone."

"Liar."

He looked up as he yanked his other boot free, one brow raised in warning. "It's late, Bess. We're not doing this now."

"I suppose it's only natural for you to want a proper lady now that you're a fine lord." She sat up on her knees and inched nearer. "She looked like a lady, all ice in her veins, but is that what you want? Some frigid piece of muslin and lace?"

He shook his head, fighting back the recent image of Meredith hot and writhing beneath him. "You don't know what you're talking about."

She slithered off the bed and approached him with a decisive sway to her hips. "You'll never be some Society bloke, Nicky, even if you marry a proper lady. You might blend in with their kind, attend their parties and ape their manners, but that will never change who you really are."

Her words were a douse of cold water, effectively eliminating the calming sense of repletion lingering from his physical union with Meredith. She only spoke the truth. The orphaned urchin would always live inside him. Yet he knew he could no longer deny the other part of him. The earl's son existed too. He was a hybrid, torn between two worlds. Tonight's incident with

Fairbanks made it abundantly clear that he could never shake off his past. It would forever be there. A gently bred woman like Meredith had no place in his life.

"You're from the streets." Bess stopped before him and cupped his face to murmur, "Like me. We're a pair, Nicky. Nothing proper about either of us. I can do things to you no fine lady ever would." She pressed her open mouth against his, but Nick shrugged past her.

"It's over, Bess. Accept it or consider moving on." He pulled open the door to his bedchamber, indicating it was time for her to leave.

"It's her." Bess's lips thinned, nearly disappearing into her face. "You're half in love with her already."

He carefully schooled his expression into one of boredom, masking the jolt her words elicited. "Don't be foolish."

"You're the fool."

He winced at her shrill tone, recalling why he avoided relationships. Always unpleasant to end.

She stormed past him, pausing in the threshold. "You're lying to yourself." Shaking her head, she laughed without mirth. "I hope she breaks your heart."

He shut the door after her and leaned against its hard length for a moment. She was wrong. He was not in love with Meredith. His mother had taught him well what love could do to a person. He would never be that weak. And if he ever did succumb to that weak emotion, Meredith was the last woman upon whom he would lavish such sentiment. To love her would be begging for trouble. He would be damned if he fell prey to love's debilitating thrall.

The sooner Havernautt proposed, the better. His control and good sense would return once Meredith was wed and firmly off limits. Nick gave his head a sure, swift shake. As long as she didn't botch things with Havernautt. A scowl marred his face at the thought. He could be stuck with Meredith indefinitely if that happened, and that was unacceptable.

She needed marriage to some decent, boring nob and exile to the country where the sight of her would never tempt him again. He pushed off the door with a deep sigh. No getting around it. He would have to personally see that it happened.

Meredith hadn't the heart for fox hunting. Or, upon deeper consideration, husband hunting either. Neither of which seemed to matter since she had obliged Portia and joined the hunting party of the very man she had decided met her criteria for a husband.

In truth, she had joined the hunting party so Portia would not be the solitary female in their ranks, and Meredith had not particularly relished staying behind at the house to work on embroidery or pen letters with the other ladies. The chance to ride was incentive enough to set aside her qualms of engaging in the bloodthirsty pursuit of a fox—or so she had told herself.

The racket of baying dogs and pounding hooves, however, prevented her from thoroughly embracing nature. She let her horse lag behind. Teddy, cheeks flushed red with the thrill of the chase, did not notice her falling behind and charged steadily after his hounds.

She pulled on her reins and surveyed the landscape, a small smile playing about her lips as the rest of the riders moved on without her. Her lungs took in great gulps of fresh air. Perhaps no one would notice if she slipped away.

"Come, Meredith."

Apparently, someone had not forgotten her— nor missed her stealthy exit.

"You're falling behind!" Portia shouted, pulling back to look over her shoulder at where Meredith had stopped.

"Go on without me. I only wish to ride."

Portia dutifully trotted over to her, casting one last look of longing at the herd of riders stretching farther and farther away. The thrill of the hunt clearly hummed in her friend's blood, and Meredith idly wondered if one had to be born to the aristocracy to appreciate the mercenary pursuit.

"Truly, Portia, you don't have to accompany me."

"You are certain?" The ring of hope in Portia's voice was undeniable.

Meredith gestured to the party of hunters growing smaller in the distance. "You're losing them. Go."

Grinning, Portia flipped her riding crop across

her horse's flanks and charged off to rejoin the group.

With another cleansing breath, Meredith admired the countryside, briefly closing her eyes against a caressing breeze. She settled into the much needed peace and tranquility of her surroundings, letting it restore her as she prodded her horse along. She turned in the direction of the house, preferring to ride south, where she would be unlikely to meet up with the hunting party. Of course, the fox could take whatever direction it chose, but she would have a better chance for solitude heading in the opposite direction. She passed the house and exited the front gates, thinking to pass through the village she had spied yesterday from their carriage window.

She heard the other rider before sighting him. Rounding the bend, she spotted him just before he pulled his snorting mount in front her.

Her flesh sprang to instant, singing life. "What are you doing here?"

"I was invited." The sun glinted off Nick's dark hair as he reined in his dancing stallion beside her.

Naturally, Teddy would have invited *him*. Teddy viewed Nick as part of her family. What she had not considered was that Nick would actually accept the invitation.

"And you came?" Meredith murmured. Contrary to the calm she presented, her heart hammered in her chest at the sight of him. She had not thought to see him again. At least not so soon. At least not before she was betrothed and well and fully unavailable for future trysts. One thing was clear: her heart was not ready to see him again.

"When it involves you, I find myself doing things typically out of character." His mouth twisted in derision.

Heat flamed her cheeks as certain erotic memories of a carriage ride flooded her mind. Not that such memories ever strayed far.

"I've ceased to wonder why," he added.

She nodded, unsure how to respond, and instead looked to the woods crowding the path around them. The swaying branches, the rustling leaves . . . anywhere but at him. Looking at Nick only brought to mind that night—an unsafe pastime, especially when alone with him like this. It took every ounce of willpower not to reach across the short distance and touch him.

The sound of the dogs could be heard faintly in the distance, serving to remind her of the others nearby. She wet her lips. "You realize you will be subject to Lady Derring's matchmaking again." A breeze whipped the feather of her hat across her face, tickling her nose. Her gloved hand brushed it back.

"I don't mind. There are worse dinner companions than Portia. And how fares Lady Derring's matchmaking with you? Has Havernautt proposed yet?"

He posed the question mildly, but a quick glance at his face revealed his knotted jaw and steely gaze.

"No. Not yet." Looking away, she added, "If he will."

"Oh, he will." He uttered this with such conviction that Meredith risked another glance at him. He sat so tall and imposing on his horse, like an expert cavalryman. She could very well imagine him dashing in a uniform, riding off to battle.

"His mother does not like me," she volunteered. "I do not think I am exactly what she had in mind for a daughter-in-law. And since I suspect my coming here was to garner her good favor, I don't anticipate the posting of banns any time soon."

A horn sounded in the distance, and the baying of dogs grew steadily closer. It appeared the fox was sending the hunters on a merry chase after all. As if sensing the approaching rabble, her horse whinnied and danced sideways, forcing her knee to brush Nick's leg. Even such momentary contact caused butterflies to gather in her belly and liquid heat to pool between her thighs. Would her body forever betray her around him? Even years from now? Married to another man? Could she expect this flood of desire each time they met? Pain pierced her heart. How could she stand such torment?

"He will propose," Nick reiterated with annoying surety.

"How do you know?"

"I have seen the way he looks at you."

Meredith snorted, certain he did not know what he was talking about. "And how is that?"

"Like a child at Christmas, and you're the present he can't wait to unwrap."

Meredith frowned, determined to disagree. She knew Teddy liked her, but he never looked at her in any special way. Did he? It was an uneasy thought that he could desire her the way a man and woman could desire each other—the way she desired Nick. How would Teddy feel when he realized she did not return his ardor? She did not want to disappoint him. For all his insipid ways, he was kind.

"I have done some thinking since we last . . . spoke."

She squirmed in her saddle at his reference to their last meeting. As she recalled, there had been very little talking. The heat in her cheeks rose several degrees. Dropping her gaze, she stared at the leather reins clutched in her gloved hands.

"Since that night I am further convinced of your need to marry—and in all haste. As such, I felt compelled to be here. To assist in whatever way to see you well and quickly wed."

Her eyes cut to his incredulously. "And your presence is required for that?"

"Lady Derring seems to think I am a man of some influence—at least my title and money are." He shrugged. "If my presence will serve in seeing you wed, then so be it."

She felt a steady build of anger. It began in her chest and bloomed, spreading until she felt its burning affect reach the tips of her ears. "How solicitous of you to sacrifice yourself to the pleasures of Society for me."

He pinned her with his gaze and spoke swiftly,

ruthlessly. "Perhaps there is a good reason you have not won his mother's favor. After all, you have never behaved properly."

"I have so," she insisted, hating how petulant and childlike she sounded.

"Indeed?" He tilted his head. The dangerous glint to his eyes warned Meredith the rest of his diatribe would not be to her liking. "Was it when you feigned a pregnancy and lied to the world in order to defraud me? Or when you hied across Town in the middle of the night without an escort and tangled in the entrance of the Lucky Lady with a renowned pimp? Or perhaps when you let me toss your skirts in the back of a hack?"

Hot embarrassment suffused her. The probing bite of each question manifested itself until she felt like she had been cut to ribbons by a lashing whip. That he would even refer to that night so coldly, as if it had all been her doing and something she had subjected him to, made her sick. "You're a beast," she hissed, blinking back the sting of tears. After a deep inhalation she warned, "Don't ever mention that night to me again."

He lifted an eyebrow. "Regretting it?" Despite his cavalier tone, his expression turned guarded.

"No," she whispered, and for a moment their gazes clashed. "I'll never regret it."

However, she feared she would learn to if he continued to debase the memory. And that she could not endure. She had arrived at several conclusions since that night. One of which was that she would do her duty, find a husband and be a good wife—even stomach the required intimacies of the marriage bed with a man other than Nick. What else could she do? He showed no indication of stopping her husband hunt.

And secondly, when life became too dull, or she felt especially lonely in her marriage of convenience, she would pull out the memory of their one night from the far recesses of her heart like an old trinket to be stroked and cherished. Her one night with Nick would be enough. It had to be.

The memory must remain untarnished. No small feat on her part. Especially when he did such an excellent job of being unpleasant. Her best chance lay in avoiding him.

"You might insist on remaining here as my watchdog, but we don't have to keep company. Let's agree to keep our distance, shall we?"

He shifted in his saddle, the leather creaking beneath his weight as he mulled over her suggestion. "It will do more harm than good to present the picture of estranged relations."

She stared back in mutinous silence, her chin set at a stubborn angle even as she acknowledged the truth of his words. Blast him. The thought of Nick trailing her about the place sent a nervous tremor through her. How could she pretend to care for another with the one she truly wanted watching?

Her face must have revealed some of the shock her revelation yielded, because his brow creased in concern. "Meredith, what is it?"

She stared at him dumbly, seeing nothing as her

mind reeled. *She wanted Nick.* And not just in the carnal sense. *She loved him.* Since the night she had met him in the corridor outside the nursery and glimpsed the forsaken boy, her heart had longed for him, had wanted, irrationally, to erase all his hurts. When he had followed her into the fields after Sally Finney's death and taken her into his arms, she had forgotten the dead woman's blood staining her hands. Forgotten everything save him.

"Meredith." He nudged his horse closer and grabbed hold of her wrist as if he expected her to swoon and fall from her mount. "Are you unwell?"

Yes, her mind screamed. Vastly unwell. She would never be well again. Not as long as she was in love with a man who insisted she marry someone else. A man who thought she was the greatest wretch to walk the earth.

She lifted her shoulders in a shrug of calculated indifference to belie the turmoil rolling inside her. "I'm fine," she lied, voice faint.

With a twist of her wrist, she freed herself and wrapped her fingers tightly about her reins, adding in a firmer voice, "Shall we ride back to the house and announce your arrival? The ladies will be pleased. Most of the gentlemen are out hunting. Your presence will be appreciated."

"Very well," he agreed, his eyes studying her doubtfully. Clearly, he didn't think her well. Only Meredith didn't care. He could think whatever he liked as long as he never thought her in love with him.

Chapter 20

The ladies retired to the drawing room after dinner and took up their embroidery or correspondence discarded from earlier in the day. The gentlemen ventured to the library to smoke their cigars and do whatever it was that men did in the absence of women. Meredith busied herself with a letter to Maree at one of the small writing tables, pretending not to feel Lady Havernautt's eyes drilling into her from across the room.

"How long were you married, Lady Brookshire?" Lady Havernautt's blunt question quieted the hum of feminine conversation.

The interrogation had begun. Meredith had been expecting it for some days. The other ladies watched with avid interest as she lifted her head to smile politely at Teddy's mother, a morbidly obese woman who spent her days wedged in a wheelchair specially made for her substantial girth. She was unsure whether Lady Havernautt used the wheelchair for any physical handicap other than being too obese to walk. Upon seeing her physical condition, it was clear why the viscountess no longer traveled to Town. Meredith felt a stab of sympathy. Perhaps she would be equally ill-tempered if she was confined to a chair.

"Seven years."

"And no children?" Lady Havernautt's frown disappeared into the folds of fat lining her chin. "Can you not conceive? A woman is of no value to her husband if she cannot give him a son."

Countless stares swung Meredith's way. Her face grew hot under so much attention. She choked back several retorts, all totally inappropriate. She could not offend her hostess and potential mother-in-law. This she knew. But neither could she submit meekly to the rudeness of her probing questions. It would set an intolerable precedent if in fact she became Lady Havernautt's daughter-in-law.

"And what of a husband's value?" she asked directly. "I find it interesting how one immediately assumes the wife is responsible when a couple does not bear children."

Her comments generated a tittering of scandalized whispers among the ladies present. Lady

Derring nodded approvingly at Meredith from across the room, assuring her that she had not overstepped herself. Portia winked encouragingly.

"And have you any reason to believe your late husband responsible for your lack of offspring?" Lady Havernautt challenged. "How do you know that the failing does not lie in you?"

Meredith longed to astonish them all and confess that she knew, without a doubt, that the fault rested with Edmund, that his unwillingness to consummate their marriage might have something to do with it. Instead, she answered sweetly, "I have no evidence it is my fault, so I will not leap to that conclusion."

"You appear unusually confident that you are not barren," Lady Havernautt accused, a hard glint to her eyes.

"Only another marriage would resolve the speculations on that account," Lady Derring inserted smoothly from across the room, for whatever reason not bringing up her alleged miscarriage. Perhaps because that would not necessarily hearten Lady Havernautt's misgivings. Whatever the case, Meredith was grateful not to have that particular lie bandied about.

The vicountess clearly wanted her son married to a woman capable of producing heirs, and although there were never any guarantees on that score, she knew she would not come across as the strongest candidate with seven years of marriage behind her and no offspring to show for it.

"A grave risk for her next husband, would you not say, Your Grace?" Lady Havernautt demanded, glaring Meredith's way.

Thankfully, the gentlemen chose that moment to rejoin the ladies, carrying with them the faint odor of cigars and a welcome rumble of conversation.

Teddy immediately knelt beside his mother's wheelchair, his voice solicitous as he asked, "Mother? You are not too tired, are you? You have pushed yourself today."

Lady Havernautt adopted a plaintive tone, her hand fluttering weakly in the air, not at all resembling the fierce dragon of a moment ago. "Perhaps I should retire. It has been a trying day."

"Shall I have one of the maids wheel you to your room?"

Lady Havernautt grasped Teddy's hand in one of her pudgy paws. "Why don't you push me to my room and read to me a bit before bed. Your voice always soothes me so."

He looked from his mother to his guests, his expression uncomfortable. Meredith pasted a courteous smile on her face to conceal her incredulity. He could not mean to abandon a score of houseguests in order to read a bedtime story to his smothering mama!

"Very well, Mother." With a deep sigh, Teddy moved behind the wheelchair, granting Lady Havernautt the opportunity to settle a look of triumph on Meredith. *Score one for Mother.*

"Everyone, please entertain yourselves. I will

return shortly." Although he addressed the room at large, Teddy focused an apologetic gaze on her. She gave a brief nod of acknowledgment before he wheeled his mother out.

When they were gone, she scanned the room, catching sight of Nick within a small circle of men. His gaze met and captured hers. Amusement sparkled in the dark depths. That her predicament with Teddy and his dreadful mother was the source of such amusement went without saying. She sniffed and returned her attention to her letter, a little mystified as to why Lord Havernautt's pandering to his insufferable mother did not worry her more. Pinning her matrimonial hopes on a mama's boy should most definitely elicit worry. Strangely, she could not stir herself to care.

"It seems you have been abandoned."

She looked up as Lord Derring dropped inelegantly into the chair across from her. She gestured to the crowded drawing room. "Hardly abandoned, Your Grace."

"Well, can one not be alone in a crowded room?" Lord Derring swirled his glass of port and took a healthy swallow, appearing to be on his way to blissful inebriation. "I find that to be the case," he muttered philosophically as he carelessly waved his glass, its contents sloshing over the rim, spilling down his fingers and dribbling to the floor. Unmindful of the Oriental carpet he stained, he continued, "All these gels without an intelligent thought in their prim little heads. But the ol' dame

says I have to pick one." He nodded to his grandmother reproachfully.

Welcome to the club, Meredith thought with a
decided lack of charity. "There are quite a few accomplished young ladies here, Your Grace."

"Yes," he murmured, his lips hugging the rim
of his glass. "They can all play the pianoforte and
recite their lineage like any well-taught child. But
those aren't exactly the traits I desire in a wife."

And what, she wondered, could those traits be?
The ability to overlook his excessive gambling as
he dragged them into financial ruin? Nick's abso-
lution of Lord Derring's debts would only serve
as a reprieve, not a permanent solution, if his recent presence at the Lucky Lady was any indication. In no time he would be facing debt again.
His family right along with him. Poor Portia. Meredith only hoped the girl married and removed
herself from her brother's damaging sphere before then.

He turned assessing eyes on her. "You're not
like them," he observed, a touch of wonder in his
voice, as though this realization had just occurred
to him. "You have intellect, maturity, confidence.
Must be your state of widowhood."

"Or my advanced years." Sarcasm tinged her
voice.

Lord Derring guffawed. Others swung curious
glances their way.

"That's what I mean. Such wit," Lord Derring
said in too loud tones. She eyed the drink in his
hand suspiciously, suspecting he was already

inebriated. "Too bad your dowry is what it is. I mean it is entirely respectable—I have inquired—but I'm needing more than a respectable sum."

Aside from wondering how the sum of her dowry came to be public knowledge when she herself did not know the amount, she doubted Croesus himself could supply enough money for Lord Derring to gamble away.

"Lady Meredith, would you care to take the air on the veranda with me?"

The voice, that deep, dark slide of velvet, sounded above her head, firing her blood. Her eyes cut upward, noting the hard set of his mouth, the darkness of his gaze, which demanded compliance.

Lord Derring tipped his head back to look up at Nick. "Caulfield, old man, still can't get over you're an earl."

"Likewise," Nick murmured, hardly sparing a glance for the duke as he held out his hand for her.

"Suppose it makes it easier to countenance that I lost so much coin to a peer and not just some commoner." Lord Derring laughed heartily, oblivious that he had gained everyone's notice. From across the room his grandmother's face reddened at his thoughtless remarks. She clearly did not relish her grandson advertising that he had a gambling problem before potential brides, even if it was fairly common knowledge among the *ton*.

"Indeed," Nick replied noncommittally, looking from his outstretched hand to Meredith pointedly.

She could not refuse without appearing ill-mannered. No matter how much her lips wanted to form a denial. Such would generate speculation among the other guests.

Placing her hand in his, she murmured a parting to Lord Derring. Tucking her hand in his elbow, Nick led her out the French doors and onto the far end on the veranda. She barely inhaled the night air before he spoke.

"You should have better care for the company you keep, Meredith. He may be a duke, but he's a reprobate." Nick crossed his arms over his chest in a militant pose, legs braced apart as though he stood at the prow of a rollicking ship.

"I had little to do with it. He sat down beside me."

"What did you say to make him laugh?" Without giving her time to respond, he rushed on, "Flirting with him will not further your reputation."

"Because he laughed, I had to be flirting?" Her snort of disbelief indicated what she thought of that logic.

"It was the way he laughed . . . and the way he looked at you when he laughed."

"Neither of which is in my control."

"I hope you are not foolish enough to consider him if things don't come to fruition with Havernautt. Your dowry does not come close to meeting his needs."

"He's a drunkard. And a chronic gamester. Why would I set my sights on him?"

"He is a duke. It would be quite a coup for any woman."

She turned her back on him and clasped the rail before her, lifting her shoulders in a carelessly affected shrug as she faced the gardens. "I have not given up on Havernautt."

"You may well have to let go of that one." His voice sounded alarmingly close to her ear. Goose bumps sprang up along her neck at the puff of his breath on her nape, at the answering spark of heat that flared to life deep in her core. She stiffened her spine and resisted the overwhelming pull of him at her back that urged her to melt into his broad chest. It took every last ounce of willpower to appear impervious. "His mother will never allow him to marry you."

"It's his decision, not hers."

"You overestimate Havernautt's will—or your wiles. Whichever the case, other suitable gentlemen are present. Extend your attentions to them. Only not Derring."

She had actually tried to further her acquaintance with the other gentlemen present at this house party. Yet her zeal in searching for a husband had dwindled. Especially when her treacherous heart was invested elsewhere.

She fixed her gaze on the shadowy shrubs of hawthorn ahead, unable to turn and face him as she dared to voice the one question burning in her mind. "What happens if I don't become betrothed?" Her hands clenched the stone railing before her.

He inched closer, until the hardness of his chest pressed against her rigid back. She resisted the impulse to lean back, to melt bonelessly against him, to allow his warmth to merge with hers until neither could tell where the other's body began and ended.

"That was not our agreement," he reminded, his voice a growl at her neck.

She couldn't turn around unless she wanted to bury her nose into his chest. And while she might *want* to do that—she could not. So she stayed just so, her back to his chest as she gazed out at the moon-washed garden. "I don't recall any actual agreement between us. I only remember tersely worded commands and decrees."

"Call it whatever you like, we had an understanding. Are you reneging now?" An undeniable desperation hummed beneath the scathing tone of his question, and she wondered at it.

She spoke into the night. "Has it ever occurred to you that I simply may not succeed in gaining a proposal?"

"No. Not unless you deliberately set out to remain unwed." She flinched at the brush of his fingertips against her nape. "Are you trying to back out?" he softly queried. His lips grazed the skin beneath her ear, and her entire body trembled. A lick of heat curled low in her belly.

She twisted around to escape the fiery brand of his mouth on her skin. A mistake. The move forced her flush against him. "Whether Teddy or any man proposes is largely out of my hands.

Things cannot be so easily controlled." The croak of her voice betrayed her, revealed how much his nearness undid her, exactly how *uncontrolled* she felt.

He stared at her for a long moment, his eyes traveling every inch of her face. Her breath hitched when those midnight eyes landed on her mouth. Lips tingling, her hands went behind her to clutch the railing in a death grip. The movement thrust her breasts forward, straining against her bodice.

"You're correct," he growled. "Some things can't be controlled." That said, he grabbed her by the waist and hauled her against him.

His mouth stole hers in a hot, consuming kiss that fired her blood and invaded her soul. Common sense fled. Meredith came off the railing and gripped fistfuls of his jacket. Nick devoured her lips, licking, nipping, sucking. She didn't care that they stood mere feet from a gaping door where members of the *ton* sipped their after dinner drinks. Didn't care that she hovered on the brink of scandal. His kiss obliterated all thoughts of propriety, ignited a deep, soul-singeing recognition within her body that demanded fulfillment.

Nick cupped her breasts through her gown. Her nipples tightened, straining against the thin muslin of her dress, aching to be freed, hungering for the feel of his callused hands, for the wet-velvet rasp of his tongue. He swallowed her moan, drinking it deep in his mouth.

Driven by a wild need to touch, to feel him, she

slid her hands inside his jacket and ran them over his hard chest, across the flat belly and the ridges of muscles that quivered beneath her palms. Desire pounded through her blood, emboldening her. Her hand dropped. She pressed her palm against the hard bulge of his manhood, curled her fingers around its pulsating length. He throbbed in her hand, and heat rushed through her veins, liquefying her bones.

He muttered thickly against her mouth, "Let me come to your room tonight."

His words served as a cold dose of reality. She jerked free and collapsed against the stone railing, inhaling raggedly. "No—this is insanity."

He ruffled his hair with both hands, nodding. After a long moment, he regained his composure enough to mutter, "Clearly your charms are not insubstantial." Looking up, his glittering gaze seared her to the spot. "You're resourceful. Pick a man and get him to bloody well marry you."

A man. But not him. Not the man she wanted. Chin high, she attempted make a dignified departure, but he caught her arm as she tried to move past.

"I'm serious. You have only one Season to make a match. Don't drag this out."

She glared at his fingers on her arm, then up to the hard lines of his face, the thin brackets of tension on either side of his mouth. If she were not in love with him already, she believed she could despise him. Only she knew he was more than this.

More than he would have her see. More than a man desperate to rid her from his life. That's why she loved him.

"Never fear. I'll do as you bid," she vowed, her heart clenching in pain.

He did not immediately release her. His eyes were too busy drinking in the nuances of her face, as if sealing them in his memory. The blood beneath her skin simmered where he held her. Before she had time to reconsider, her emotions got the best of her and she heard herself spit out, "I assure you that however low your opinion of me, you fall far lower on the scales of decency. How can you even stand there and bid me to wed after we . . ." Her voice faded. She was unable and unwilling to make reference to that night. To fling it at him and dirty its place in her heart. She forged ahead, trying to cover her lapse. "You should have stayed in London."

The light from the drawing room illuminated his impassive face. From what she could detect, her words left him unaffected. He appeared as implacable and unmoved as ever.

Meredith turned and faced the French doors, pausing to gain her composure. With her back to him, she held her hands out in front of her and marveled at the way they trembled. If she persisted in wearing her heart on her sleeve, she might as well confess her love. *Dear God*. She pressed a hand to one heated cheek as mortification consumed her. If he stayed much longer, he would see her love for him writ on her face. A woman's laughter floated on the air, incongruous to the moment and somehow firing her sense of desperation.

"Go home. Go back to your life," she whispered, unsure if he even heard her before she rushed inside.

Because her life would be torment as long as he stayed.

Chapter 21

Meredith sat primly in the small boat, parasol angled very correctly over her face to ward off the sun's rays. Teddy steadily rowed them across the lake, slicing smoothly through water as still and silent as glass. The other members of their outing were tiny, barely distinguishable figures along the shore. Some strolled. Others remained sitting on blankets, picking idly from the array of food taken from large straw hampers. The ladies' day dresses were bright dots of color along the green slope of shoreline, reminding Meredith of her gratitude for once again being able to wear color. She smoothed a hand over her dimity skirts. Hopefully, her black gowns would

294

remain in the back of her wardrobe for years to come.

She made out her aunt Eleanor's lavender turban with its purple feather dancing on the breeze. Stationed closely to Lady Havernautt's chair, Aunt Eleanor worked to earn the lady's favor on her behalf. A colossal waste of her time, Meredith thought. Lady Havernautt's icy reserve had not thawed one bit over the past week. When Teddy had suggested taking her out on the lake, the woman stared daggers into her, almost prompting her to refuse. Only Nick's stern look spurred her into accepting. It was a silly exercise in defiance on her part. Especially since time spent with Teddy was time squandered. He would certainly not offer for her without his mother's blessing. A fact that only became clearer each passing day. She hated to admit it, but Nick was right. Her time would be better spent cultivating her associations with other gentlemen.

The early spring wind was stronger out on the lake and buffeted her at every side. She wrapped her pashmina shawl about her, but the fine goat's wool afforded little protection.

"You must forgive my lack of attention this week," Teddy said as he rowed. "But you have borne my neglect with admirable good will."

She suppressed her flash of irritation. Did the man expect her to sit around pining after him? "You have a houseful of guests." How should she have reacted to his neglect? By howling in outrage? "I would not expect you to bestow all your attention on me."

He smiled shamefacedly. "I would accept your pardon if it were the guests that occupied so much of my time."

"You are very attentive to your mother's condition," she allowed, conveniently ignoring the fact that the woman did well enough without him the weeks Teddy spent in Town.

He stopped rowing and laid the oar across his lap to look at her thoughtfully. "You are far more understanding than any other lady of my acquaintance."

She squirmed beneath his approving gaze, wondering how he could still appear interested in her in the face of his mother's blatant disdain.

He continued, "You have been remarkably tolerant of Mother. I realize she has not been her most courteous with you, but you have borne it all . . . which leads me to further believe that you are in fact the woman of my heart."

Because she could abide his mother? Did the man not desire a little more from a wife than such an idiotic qualification? What if the day arrived and she had enough of his mother and snapped? Would he then lose all regard for her?

Despite the wintry air, her palms began to sweat, her hold on her parasol growing slippery. Apparently, both she and Nick had misread the situation, and Teddy did not necessarily need his mother's approval to pursue her. From the way he steadily regarded her, adulation brimming in his eyes, she feared he was about to proclaim himself.

She began gently, hoping to dissuade him. "I would hate for you to displease your mother by paying me court—"

He cut her off with a wave of his hand. "Mother has objected to every lady I've brought around. That is nothing new. I am confident she will soon see that you—a mature woman of advanced years—are just the thing she needs in a daughter-in-law. Some young debutante would be far too flighty and capricious of nature to handle Mother's moods and demands."

She felt the color drain from her face. The biting wind at her cheeks did not chill her quite so much as his words.

Advanced years?

If not stuck in a boat with the dreadful man, she was certain she would find a way to excuse herself. As it were, she sat there and listened to Teddy pontificate on how very well suited she was to serve as a daughter-in-law to his estimable mother.

"Mother can be difficult and demanding, but you're just the sort to dance attendance on her . . ."

Dance attendance? Did he want a wife or a companion for his mother? Her burning indignation delayed the rest of his words from registering. But when she did hear him, her indignation only escalated.

"You have such a forbearing and biddable nature. I know for certain Mother will grow to appreciate you."

Forbearing? Biddable? *Who was he talking about?* Certainly not her.

Even though no formal proposal had been issued, Meredith felt a lasting and deadly noose settle about her neck. Unless, that is, she found some way out of this dilemma.

She looked helplessly at the distant shoreline, wishing it were closer, that she was anywhere but trapped on this boat. Among the figures dotting the land, one seemed to materialize and separate from the others. She identified the black Hessians and buff-colored breeches and knew instantly it was Nick. The hard line of his body faced the water, and she knew he watched their little boat. She could not help thinking how pleased he would be to learn that Teddy was still very much in pursuit of her. That he in fact seemed on the verge of a proposal.

"Meredith? Are you well?"

Teddy leaned forward in the boat and sent it rocking unsteadily. She clutched the sides, sniffing back the ridiculous urge to weep.

"Ah," he murmured knowingly. "You are moved, I can see . . ."

She shook her head doggedly from side to side, watching in horror as Teddy's eyes drifted shut and his head dipped her way. She lurched back from the impending kiss, so intent on dodging his puckered lips that she barely registered the increased rollicking of the boat. Until it was too late. She simply sought to avoid his kiss. Still, she had no time to consider that a capsized boat might mean more than a soak but a likely drowning. Even without the burdensome weight of her dress, she was only a fair swimmer.

With a shriek, she plunged into the icy water, her open mouth swallowing a lungful of water. Her legs kicked at the heavy, sucking weight of her skirts. She broke the water's surface for a moment, just long enough to hear Teddy wailing her name before her skirts dragged her back down. She sank deep enough for her feet to brush the muddy bottom of the lake. Fighting the tangle of skirts and petticoats, she tried to push off the bottom, to propel herself upward, but could gain no purchase.

The burning in her lungs increased to dizzying proportions. Her mind drifted in a dreamlike haze. A face emerged. *Nick.* With renewed vigor she clawed at the water, determined that she would see him again. She would not die this way.

And in that bleak life or death moment, she realized how foolish she had been to consider marrying another man when her heart belonged to him.

Nick's arms sliced through the water in smooth, swift strokes until he reached the boat. It floated upside down with an idleness that mocked his heart-stopping panic. Havernautt slapped the lake's surface, treading water and calling Meredith's name in frantic tones.

Nick wasted no time in such a helpless endeavor, instead disappearing beneath the water's surface with one great gulp of air. Thankfully, the lake wasn't that deep, and he was able to make a general sweep of the area beneath the boat. His eyes could see nothing in the murky water but they strained nonetheless, searching for a glimpse of dress. Seconds ticked past. He thought his heart might explode from his chest. Possibly from lack of air, but he suspected more from panic. Panic and something else he could not quite name.

A lifetime passed before his hand grasped material so soft and lissom it could only be the wet fabric of Meredith's gown. He yanked hard and was awarded the solid feel of her body tumbling into his arms. Nick kicked off the lake's bottom and sent them both surging to the surface. He clamped one arm under her breasts and swam for shore, not giving a thought to Havernautt, who struggled to climb inside the boat he had finally managed to right.

They were swarmed the moment they reached shore. Meredith coughed in his arms, the sound music to his ears. It meant she was breathing. She lived. He broke through the mob and laid her on one of the blankets. Aunt Eleanor hovered close, wringing her hands as he rolled Meredith on her side and pounded her back, forcing her to cough up any residue from her lungs.

"Where is my son?" Lady Havernautt ranted from her chair.

"Rowing back in the boat," Lady Derring replied, her snort of disgust undisguised.

"Coward," Portia muttered in a voice that, while

failing to meet Lady Havernautt's ears, succeeded in reaching others.

Nick felt his temper boil as he glanced out at the lake where Havernautt rowed at crawling pace to shore. If he hadn't been here today, she would have drowned. To think he had almost stayed in London.

She ceased coughing but her chest still rose and fell with labored breaths. Her bleary eyes blinked up at him from her ashen face. He caressed one cheek, sweet relief flooding him.

"You need to take her to the house," Aunt Eleanor directed. "Her teeth are chattering."

He nodded. Without a word, he swept her into his arms. In seconds he secured her beside him in the sole carriage that had delivered Lady Havernautt to their lakeside picnic. The rest of them had walked the short distance from the house.

Lady Havernautt squawked from her chair at this acquisition of her transportation. "That's my carriage!"

"I'll have it returned," he called out, indicating to the driver that he should proceed. The driver looked uncertainly from Nick to his clearly displeased employer, the reins lax in his hands.

"Drive," Nick barked. The driver took one look at his hard face, forgot about the squawking Lady Havernautt, and slapped the reins.

Meredith rested her head against his shoulder on the brief drive to the house, saying nothing. Her eyes drifted shut. Spiky wet lashes cast crescent-shaped shadows on her cheeks. He rubbed her arms briskly, trying to infuse some warmth into her, hoping to see even a touch of color return to her cheeks.

When they arrived at the house, Nick commanded the wide-eyed housekeeper to fetch a hot bath to Meredith's room. He then guided her upstairs. Once in her room, he closed the door and began removing her sodden clothes without a single thought to propriety. All that mattered was getting her warm.

At this, she revived herself enough to exclaim, "What are you doing?"

"Getting you out of these wet clothes."

"You musn't." She slapped weakly at his hands.

He grabbed her wrists and looked her in the eyes. "It is nothing I haven't seen before."

A charming flush of color returned to her face at that reminder. He added in a softer, coaxing voice, "You need to get dry and warm yourself before you take ill. Now be a good girl and stand still."

After a moment's hesitation, her hands dropped to her sides. He made short work of undressing her, trying not to let his eyes stray to the curves each removed article of clothing revealed. He grabbed a dressing gown tossed over the screen and quickly wrapped it around her. Sitting on the bed, he pulled her down with him so he could rub warmth back into her limbs.

As he blew hot air on her chilled palms she pointed out, "You're wet."

He paused, realizing for the first time that he

was in fact quite wet. Funny, he had not noticed in his concern for her. He shrugged. "I'm not cold."

"You must be freezing," she countered.

"We need to warm you up first." He resumed his ministrations, shifting his attention to her blue-tinged legs. A curse erupted from his mouth as he tried to chafe color back into her cold flesh, "Goddamn Havernautt."

"It wasn't his fault," Meredith defended in a small voice. "I overturned the boat."

Nick looked up, his hands stilling on her calves.

Meredith dropped her eyes and plucked at the ruffled edge of her dressing gown. "He was trying to kiss me. I leaned back and—"

"He tried to kiss you," Nick echoed, feeling her words as thoroughly as a punch to the gut.

His impulse was instinctive, primal. *Kill Havernautt.*

And his thinking was just as irrational. *No man touches what is mine.*

Clearly, his one night with Meredith had left him greatly confused. He was reacting as if she meant something to him. As if he . . . Nick shook his head, reason asserting itself before he dared examine his feelings for her further. His objective was unchanged. *Get rid of her.*

He asked woodenly, "Does he still want to marry you?"

With a searching look of her own, she slowly answered, "My forbearance of his mother has raised me in his estimation. He all but proposed to me right there on the lake." Her brow puckered in perplexity.

He battled an illogical spurt of jealousy. He had no right to feel possessive. She was doing what he told her. Finding a husband. Removing herself from his life.

He slid his hand from her leg and stood. She looked up at him with wide questioning eyes. The brown spattering of freckles stood out against the pallor of her face, and he fought down the impulse to trace a finger across the bridge of her slim nose.

"Good," he said, a decisive ring of finality in his voice.

Just then the door opened and several servants entered bearing steaming buckets of water. Nick watched unseeingly as they dragged the tub from behind the screen and began to pour.

He faced her, murmuring with deceptive mildness, "Heed my advice. When you're wed to Havernautt, steer clear of the lake. Next time I may not be around to save you."

Turning on his heels, he strode out of her room, as far from her as he could get before he did or said something truly regrettable.

Nick waited in a wing-backed chair. Positioned in the corner of the room, it was safely shrouded in shadows. He wanted the opportunity to see her face the precise moment she entered the room. Before she had the chance to see him and wonder at his presence.

When she entered the room, his breath caught tight in his chest. Without sparing a glance for Havernautt at her side, he studied her over steepled fingers, a heavy sense of foreboding sinking him farther into the well-padded chair. He could not shake the ominous feeling. He knew the purpose behind this little meeting.

As if sensing his presence, she pulled up short. Her eyes searched the room's dark paneled walls until they alighted on him tucked discreetly in his corner. His nostrils flared like a stallion scenting a mare. Was it his imagination? Or memory? But he thought he could smell her across the room. Waves of awareness vibrated between them. Her glittering gaze reached across the distance to him and flicked away, discounting him as if he were something to be scraped off the sole of her shoe. Essentially the same look she had bestowed upon him all week. Ever since he had saved her from drowning and deposited her in her bedroom.

Sitting with an ankle crossed over his knee, Nick braced himself, trying to present the image of a reposing, unaffected gentleman.

"Meredith, have a seat." Teddy pulled her down beside him on the sofa, folding her hand in his. Nick's gut cramped at the sight of those slender digits disappearing into Havernautt's fist. How could she still encourage Havernautt? The bastard let her drown. Was that the kind of man she wanted by her side for the rest of her life?

"I hope you don't mind, but I asked Lord

Brookshire to join us." Havernautt's voice penetrated Nick's mental grumblings.

She darted a quick resentful glance at where he sat, and Nick read the question in her eyes. In response, he lifted his shoulders in a slight, bored shrug that belied the tension coursing his blood.

Havernautt continued, "I felt that as your guardian—"

"He's not my guardian," she wasted no time correcting. "I am of age."

Nick could have guessed she would set to rights that misapprehension. He smiled, then scowled. Why must he know her so well?

"Well . . . yes," Havernautt floundered, his eyes flitting back and forth between Nick and Meredith. "But he is your only male relation—"

"There is my father," she corrected once again.

"Er, yes, of course." Teddy tugged at his cravat miserably, and Nick almost felt sorry for the bastard. But not quite. "I was given the impression that he is not, er, in prime health. . . ."

Her face flushed, and Nick knew she was embarrassed and defensive all at once, no doubt wondering what gossip Havernautt had heard about her father. It could not have been complimentary. Gossip never was.

He decided to spare them all by hurrying things along. If permitted, Havernautt would drag this out until tomorrow. "Get to the point, Havernautt. What is this about?"

A flicker of annoyance crossed Teddy's face, then disappeared in a flash. He squared his shoulders, and with a faint cracking of his knees, knelt before Meredith. "Lady Meredith, will you honor me by becoming my wife?"

Nick found himself leaning forward, hands braced on the arms of his chair, straining to hear her answer.

She bowed her head, the line of her profile elegant and graceful in the dimly lit study. With his breath held tightly in his chest, he studied the sweep of lashes veiling her downcast eyes. Her gaze fixed on the hands holding hers. He watched as she turned her palms over, considering Havernautt's hands as if she would find the answer carved on his flesh.

Noise roared through his head with the increasing fury of a storm. His scrutiny of her at first distracted him from realizing the noise was a single word reverberating through his mind, repeating over and over again, speeding together like so many droplets of water in a rushing stream until indistinguishable. *No, no, no, no . . .*

He didn't want her to wed Havernautt. Or anyone else for that matter. After all his pushing and prodding and bullying, he wanted to hear her refuse. He wanted her to tell Havernautt he could take his proposal and stick—

The soft sound of Meredith's voice slipped past the roaring in his head. "Yes."

Yes? She actually said yes?

He *should* have been relieved. The bloody husband hunt was at an end. As well as his forced mingling and socializing with the *ton*. In more ways than one, he was free again. Free to resume his normal life. Free of one deceitful, scheming woman. *Free to forget her.* But no sigh of relief was forthcoming. Only fury. Fury and desperation. The sight of Havernautt pulling her into his arms jarred Nick. He lurched from his seat, hands fisted at his sides like a rigid tin soldier.

Havernautt detached himself from her while still keeping a proprietary arm looped around her waist. He faced Nick with a stupid grin on his face. "I requested your presence, my lord, in order to ask your blessing."

Nick looked only at her.

She stared back in cold silence. Not a warm expression, by any means. Nothing in her look suggested she felt anything for him at all.

"My lord . . ." Havernautt's voice cut through the silence, a touch of anxiety in his voice. "Do we have your blessing?"

Nick opened his mouth, ready to give his blessing, but no sound would come forth.

"Come now, Teddy." She touched Havernautt's arm. "It's silly to ask for the earl's blessing." She released a thin, vacant laugh, continuing to stare at Nick in that cold, infuriating way. "He is no blood kin to me."

"It is not silliness to me," Havernautt replied in haughty tones, eyes still on Nick, waiting.

"But of course he approves," she sighed, and gave Nick a quelling look. When he still said nothing, she cut her gaze to Havernautt. "He is no doubt ecstatic you offered. He has encouraged our courtship from the start. Is that not so, my lord?"

To put it mildly.

Nick found himself speaking, but the words seemed to come from somewhere buried deep inside because his brain marveled to hear himself say, "Sorry, Havernautt, but I cannot give my blessing." As he delivered this announcement, he could swear he saw a flash of relief cross her face before indignation took over.

"What?" she demanded in affronted tones.

Havernautt shrugged past her and advanced on Nick, hands lifted in supplication. "I don't understand, my lord. Have I done something to offend you?"

Before he had a chance, Meredith answered for him. "You have done nothing wrong, Teddy." She shot an angry, bewildered glare at Nick, hissing none too discreetly, "What are you doing? This is what you wanted."

"I thought so." He nodded in agreement, tension surging through him. "But I find I cannot let you go through with this."

She stepped past an astonished Havernautt, disregarding him to jab Nick in the chest with her index finger. "Well, I find that I'm tired of living my life at your whim."

"Pardon me for saying so, my lord," Havernautt interjected with a surprising degree of spirit, "but if you cannot give me a single valid reason for protesting this match, then I am afraid your lack of blessing won't matter."

"Is that so?" Nick asked, feeling his mood take a sudden, dangerous shift.

Meredith's eyes widened at his menacing tone and she stumbled back a step.

Nick continued in that lethal voice, "Would the fact that I have compromised the lady be a valid enough reason?"

She covered her face with her hands and would have fled the room if Nick had not grabbed her hand and forced her to his side. Satisfaction swelled inside him at Havernautt's stunned expression. A deep, primal satisfaction.

Until the bastard turned his shock and contempt on Meredith.

"Whore," he hissed, face twisting into ugly loathing.

Nick left her side in a flash, sending his fist flying into Havernautt's face with a resounding smack of bone against bone. Havernautt crumpled to the carpet. Nick flung his arm back for another go, but Meredith grabbed hold of it. "Nick! No!"

He tried to shrug her off, but she clung tenaciously. "Nick, can you blame him? After what you just said? Leave him be."

He turned to look at her flushed face, his arm lowering a bit, the wild desire to finish Havernautt off thrumming in his blood.

"Get up." Nick kicked Havernautt's boot.

Glaring balefully from his bloodied face, Havernautt shook his head and scuttled farther away.

"I'm marrying her," Nick ground out before he

had time to consider what he was saying. "Understand? One word, one slur against my wife, and I'll finish this."

Meredith still clung to his arm. Nick followed the sight of her pale, slender fingers up to her equally pale face.

It was done. She was his. He had seen to that.

"Pack your things and meet me downstairs in five minutes."

Chapter 22

Nothing will change. His life would go on as before. He glanced across him at the woman he had claimed for himself only a short while ago. *Nothing will change,* he repeated. Nothing except that Meredith would now occupy a permanent place in his life, in his bed.

Several hours had passed since she met him in the foyer, and still she had not uttered a word. Her silence unnerved him. She had come along willingly enough, but her mutinous silence made Nick feel as though he were kidnapping her. He was *not* a kidnapper. And she didn't have to sit there wringing her hands and biting her lip like a bloody hostage.

"Did you really intend to marry that worthless fool?"

Color flooded her face at his ruthless words. Perhaps not the best way to broach a conversation, but her acceptance of Havernautt's proposal—ridiculous as it seemed, given his ultimatum that she find a husband—rubbed him the wrong way. He simply could not let her go through with it. Perhaps if she had chosen someone else . . . someone with a measure of backbone. Nick shook his head. No. The bloody king himself could have proposed and he would have stopped her.

"Do you stop every woman you've bedded from marrying another?" she countered.

"No," he answered drolly. "Quite a few are married with a brood of children by now."

"Then why me?"

An excellent question. And one he was unprepared to answer. At least not without delving into emotions he had no wish to examine.

"Answer me, Nick. Why couldn't you let me marry Teddy?"

Rather than answer her question, he looked out the window at the countryside and asked mildly, "Aren't you interested in where we're going?"

Crossing her arms over her chest, she grudgingly said, "Very well. Where are we going?"

"Gretna Green."

"Scotland?" Her eyes narrowed to wary slits. "Whatever for?"

He thought the reason clear enough but obliged her by explaining anyway. "Despite what you may think, I didn't intend to propose to you when I entered that study."

She leaned forward, her eyes conveying a decided lack of delight as she said bitterly, "Was that a proposal? I could not tell. You were addressing Teddy when you *declared* that you were going to marry me. Of course, you can't have been sincere."

He frowned. "Men never lie about such subjects. Trust me."

Her eyes flared wide, as vivid a green as the hills rolling past them. "I certainly won't hold you to your . . . proposal." She uttered the word proposal like it was obscene.

"I would not have confessed to compromising you unless I was prepared to marry you," he explained with a sigh.

"Yes, while we are on the subject, how dare you blurt out that we . . . we . . . how dare you humiliate me! I won't ever forgive you for that."

He shrugged. "Whatever the case, I did tell him. It's done, and since we don't have a wedding license, to Gretna we go."

Her chin jutted out at an obstinate angle. "I don't see the wisdom behind compounding this debacle by rushing into marriage. Rest assured, you need feel no obligation to marry me."

"I told Havernautt I bedded you. Then whisked you away before a house full of London elite. We are getting married." His voice rang flat with finality. "There's no other choice."

"I disagree." She glared at him in defiance.

"Look," he began, "unless you want to become a social pariah, we must."

Her green eyes blazed brighter. "The only reason I face becoming a social pariah is because you told Teddy—"

"Yes. We've already gone over that," he snapped. "Move on. It's done. The point is that you are ruined unless we wed."

Arms crossed tightly over her chest, she quivered with suppressed fury, snarling like an angry cat, "You might as well instruct the driver to turn this coach around. You can't force me. I'll take being ruined over marrying you." That said, she averted her face to look out the window, signaling the conversation's end.

He steadied his own rising temper with a deep breath. The little minx could resist all she liked, but she would marry him. He could never release her to another man's bed. That much he knew. Perhaps no more than that. He could never love her. Never love anyone. His mother had taught him that. Taught him that love made one weak and pathetic. Even in death his mother had called for his father, the very man who brought her low. His father—*love*—had heaped only pain and degradation upon her.

Still, there was no denying he wanted Meredith. And it might be selfish, but he was keeping her. His blood warmed as he studied her, from the elegant line of her nose with its charming spattering of freckles, to the generous curve of her bosom. He had been deluding himself. One night with her would never be enough. At least their marriage would have those rewards. Because physical attraction aside, it would be less than idyllic. She was grasping and untrustworthy, but then, his unsavory past made him unfit for any gently bred woman. Perhaps that made them a good match after all.

"In fact, I can."

She faced him, one brow lifted in haughty regard. "Can what?"

"Force you to marry me," he clarified.

The chilly, denigrating smile she bestowed upon him grated. "You forget, my father was a vicar. I know full well a clergyman cannot marry a couple without their mutual consent. You cannot *make* me do anything."

"The right amount of coin should convince some less than ethical priest to ignore your protests." He watched smugly as her superior smile slipped, adding, "It is really a simple matter. Especially in Gretna Green where blacksmiths perform nuptial rites."

"You wouldn't dare."

"If you fail to see reason, yes, I will." At her bleak expression, he explained carefully, "I won't be responsible for your social ostracism. And that is exactly what you face if I don't marry you. I know you think you can cope, but that's only because you don't know. You can't imagine the loss of your good name. It will touch every facet of your life. I won't let it happen to you."

Some of the fire slipped from her gaze and he

sensed her temper waning as she searched his face, asking softly, "Your mother?"

After a pause he nodded, unwilling to elaborate further.

She sighed and looked out the window again. A moment later she relented with a small jerk of her head. It was all the agreement he needed.

A misty Scottish dusk lingered on the air as their coach rolled into Gretna Green, the first village on the Scottish side of the border, thereby making it the most natural destination for English couples requiring a hasty wedding. The village was notorious for rushed and often dubious nuptial ceremonies that took place in public meeting rooms and inns seconds before outraged papas stormed onto the scene.

Their coach stopped at a five-road junction where several such inns littered the quiet crossroad. Meredith waited while Nick exchanged words with the driver before escorting her across the road to a blacksmith's. She lifted her gown, careful not to soil the hem as they stopped beneath a large jutting portico extending from the barnlike building.

The clanging of metal to anvil reverberated from within the barn's shadowy interior. She looked to Nick expectantly, wondering if something was wrong with the horses that required the services of a blacksmith.

He ignored her and called out loud enough to be heard over the racket. "Robert Elliot?" The noise stopped. A tall, dour-faced man in a leather blacksmith apron appeared, wiping the sweat from his brow with the back of his hand.

"Yes. How can I be of help?" The man took in the finery of their clothes. "You'll be needing the services of a priest, sir?"

"Yes," Nick answered.

"How soon?" Robert Elliot jerked his thumb behind him. "I'd like to finish forging a couple shoes, but if you've an angry da on your heels, I can ferret up two witnesses and we'll wed you in the blink."

She gasped, glaring at Nick with the indignation that only a vicar's daughter could feel. "In a blacksmith shop? With a blacksmith officiating? You weren't jesting?"

Robert Elliot grinned as he used his leather apron to wipe the grime from his hands. "I do it all the time, miss. Married thousands right proper and legal."

"Well, do not rush to add me to that impressive number, Mr. Elliot." She spun around to leave, her earlier anger not so forgotten that it couldn't be revived at this indignity. Nick halted her with a firm hold on her arm.

He addressed the blacksmith. "We're in no rush. Can you meet us at your convenience?"

"Aye. Just give me an hour to finish up here. The Heart's Cross be the best inn," the blacksmith advised, pointing to one of the coaching inns.

"Thank you," Nick said before pulling her toward it.

Her feet flew to keep pace with his longer strides. "Did you not hear me? I will not be wed by a blacksmith. I don't know what you can be thinking." Nick continued to ignore her, the only indication he had even heard the slight twitching of his lips. "Did you take leave of your hearing along with your senses?" she demanded.

He skirted the ruts in the road left by carriage wheels, clasping her close when she stumbled, still not answering her as they entered the inn. Greeting the innkeeper, he arranged for a room to be prepared for the night. "Is there someplace we may conduct our nuptials away from the rest of your patrons?"

"Of course, my lord. I can set the back parlor aside for your privacy." The red-cheeked innkeeper bobbed his head obligingly.

"Mr. Elliot should be joining us within the hour, if you would be so good as to escort him to the parlor."

"Yes, of course."

"Is he really a priest?" Meredith interjected, voice thick with doubt.

The innkeeper's eyes widened. "Robert? Oh yes, miss. Have you never heard of an anvil priest before?"

She shook her head, wondering if she had entered another world when they crossed the border into Scotland. Next she would learn that elves prepared their food in the kitchen.

"Would you like to wait in the parlor until Robert arrives?" the innkeeper asked. "I can have the missus bring you and your young lady refreshments."

"That would be fine, thank you," Nick replied, ushering her along as they were led into a shabby yet comfortable parlor.

Her lips thinned in silence while they waited for refreshments. A mantel clock ticked in the still air as she struggled with the notion that a blacksmith would bind her in holy matrimony to the man sitting across from her. The innkeeper's wife rolled in a tea service loaded with all kinds of appetizing fare, and departed quickly when her lively chatter could not lure Meredith into conversation. Meredith nibbled a dry biscuit. Nick appeared content with her self-imposed silence and picked up a newspaper to read, as if it were any other day and not minutes until they were bound for life.

Unable to stand it anymore, she exclaimed, "You really mean for us to be wed by a blacksmith?"

He lowered his paper with a beleaguered sigh. "I assure you that this marriage will be real in every sense. Our wedding may not meet the standards of a vicar's daughter, or compare to the grandness of a wedding at St. Paul's, but our marriage will be no less legitimate in the eyes of God and the law."

"God?" She tilted her head, voice ringing as she demanded, "Since when do you recognize God's law?"

His lips flattened into a line of displeasure. "I

don't, but you do. That British law will recognize our union is sufficient enough for me."

She found herself asking the question that had been burning in her mind since she accepted their marrying. "And after we're married? What then?"

He looked back to his paper and answered carelessly, "I have not given much consideration beyond today."

Not good enough. She wanted to know. She had to know. Never again could she tolerate the ground being ripped out from under her. This time around she would arm herself with knowledge rather than risk disappointment later. Matters needed to be discussed and settled before the final vows were uttered. Before tonight.

Leaning back in her chair, she regarded him through narrowed eyes. "I would prefer to return to Oak Run. You, I assume, wish to remain in London where your business keeps you."

He dropped his paper again, but this time his voice was anything but careless. "Let me inform you exactly what kind of marriage awaits us."

She straightened in her chair.

"Have no misapprehensions about love," Nick began, his voice reminiscent of her father's when he had orated from the pulpit. "Love is not part of the arrangement. My parents' marriage began as a love match and ended with misery. Hear me now—I won't ever love you. Sorry if I offend you, but I shall be blunt to avoid potential confusion."

It was a long moment before Meredith recovered

her voice enough to lie through her teeth. "And I won't love you."

As if she hadn't spoken, he continued, "I will endeavor to forget your penchant for dishonesty and treat you with respect. Mutual respect is better than what most marriages possess. I'll lead my own life. You may lead yours. But I see no reason why we can't share each other's bed on occasion." He paused to let his eyes rake her. "We found it pleasurable the last time."

"You arrogant—" She struggled for a word foul enough. "Peacock!"

He made a clucking noise. "Meredith, I don't believe I have ever heard such language from you. I would think you pleased. You're getting more out of this union than the last time. At least now you have the benefit of a man in your bed."

That barb hurt more than she would ever let on. And it shocked her too. She didn't think him callous enough to fling Edmund's rejection in her face. "It would be a benefit if the man was anyone other than you."

"Still have that nasty lying habit, I see. Would you care for me to prove our attraction?" He pushed himself up.

She held up a hand to ward him off, grasping desperately for words to distract him. "Why must we be intimate? You said we are not to love—"

"Don't be like so many tiresome females who mistake intimacy for love. Sex is not love." He grinned in a mocking manner, flashing her his wolf's smile. "It's purely a physical need, and one that annoyingly surfaces whenever you're around. I don't quite understand it myself."

His eyes bored into her with the relentlessness of a hammer. "I am sure this desire will grow cold with time. It always does. But for now sex is a stipulation I insist upon."

She shook her head. "No. Edmund did not require that from me and—"

"To hell with Edmund." His grin vanished. "How can you compare me to him? My needs are quite different from his, as you very well know. Or did our night together not convince you of that?"

She felt her brow knit with confusion. What was he talking about?

After a moment his irritated expression altered to one of speculation. "Meredith . . ." He dragged out her name slowly.

Her tongue darted out to wet her lips. "Why are you looking at me that way?"

He studied her as if he had never seen her before. He leaned forward to examine her face closely, as though he might see the truth etched there. "You do know why Edmund never laid a hand on you, don't you?"

She flinched. "Of course. He explained it quite clearly to me on our wedding night." She tried for a tone of indifference, but couldn't hide the pain in her voice, belying her pretense. Nick didn't need to know about the hurt she buried inside. He knew too much already. She preferred to keep her shame to herself.

"I don't think you do," he murmured in awed tones.

"Yes, I do," she said, her hands clenched at her sides. Blast him. Did she have to spell it out? "Do I need to say it? Fine. He had no interest in me. On that point he was quite clear. He found me undesirable." She giggled. A shrill, humorless laugh rife with pain.

"Meredith, your self-image cannot be that skewed." He watched her in blinking silence for several moments. "Is that what you thought all these years? That Edmund didn't want you because he found you lacking?"

She scowled and crossed her arms. "I'm so pleased my shame is a topic of interest to you."

"Shame?" His eyes scoured her face. "Dear girl, Edmund did not desire you because he *could* not. No hot-blooded man with healthy appetites would leave their marriage to you unconsummated." His meaningful look was not lost on her. At the bewildered shake of her head, he clearly decided bluntness was in order. "He could not desire you because he preferred men."

Her arms dropped limply to her sides. Myriad thoughts raced through her mind, the governing one being disbelief. "That is preposterous. I have never heard such a thing. It cannot be—"

"My sweet, naive girl, it is true. Trust me."

She splayed a hand to her bosom. "Then it was not me Edmund found objectionable?"

He smiled wryly. "It would have been the female

population as a whole that my brother found undesirable."

"All these years I thought it me." She pressed her fingertips to her lips and averted her face to shield the springing of hot tears.

"Look at me," he commanded.

She shook her head vehemently, pitching forward to bury her face in her hands, too embarrassed and overcome by his revelation to face him. She was unaware he had moved until he grasped her by the shoulders. "You've suffered enough. Needlessly. No more. You are desirable. I only have to look at you to want you." His voice grew husky. "Hell, we've been arguing because of that very thing. I want you, Meredith. Badly. And I won't accept a name-only marriage."

He tilted her face up and ran the rough pad of his thumb over her moist cheeks. Lowering his head, his intention became clear. He meant to kiss her.

Slippery as a fish, she wiggled out of her chair and stood several feet away. "We cannot," she stammered.

"Cannot?" he echoed. His hands fell, looking strangely bereft at his sides. If she hadn't moved, she would have those hands on her right now.

"Perhaps I can't separate intimacy from love," she cried out desperately, inching behind her chair. "You don't want that, and I certainly don't either."

He paused, clearly thrown off at her confession.

"You don't want love, Meredith. Love makes people weak and vulnerable. It brings only suffering." He said this so matter of fact, she knew he believed it.

"Perhaps. But I can't say I won't fall prey to it." She took a deep breath, adding, "Or that I won't come to want it from you."

His face hardened with resolve, and that familiar steel returned to his eyes. "I'm hardly the type of man to marry a beautiful woman and not lay a hand on her. Especially after I've already had a taste. Just keep reminding yourself what a bastard I am and you'll be incapable of loving me."

She shook her head stubbornly and ignored the part about being beautiful. Now was not the time to let his words muddle her head. "You're marrying me out of some misplaced sense of responsibility," she insisted. "I don't think it ethical to share each other's bed when we have no intention of being a true spouse to each other. Just because we did it once doesn't make it right."

His hands opened and closed at his sides, and she sensed him battle the urge to shake her senseless. Her eyes dropped nervously to the worn carpet at her feet, avoiding his reproachful gaze.

"Think whatever you like. But tonight we will consummate our vows. And I doubt very much that your ethics will lodge much of a protest. As I recall, you found it quite enjoyable before."

His words galled her. Mostly because of their truth. If he waged a campaign of seduction against her, she did not stand a chance. Despair washed over her. From that first night when she stumbled upon him outside the nursery, her heart had begun its descent. But she had to try. Pride demanded it. The crush of Edmund's rejection wouldn't compare to what this man could do to her heart. A lifetime tied to a man who could not return her love would be hell. Every moment spent praying that he never realized her heart was irrevocably bound to him would be agonizing. Just being near him day after day, suffering his apathy in the face of her love would slowly destroy her.

Mr. Elliot, hair wet and molded to his head like a helmet from a fresh washing, chose that moment to arrive. The innkeeper and his wife stood in as witnesses. The jolly-faced woman plucked some flowers from a vase and thrust them into Meredith's hands. Clutching the sticky wet stems in her palms, she numbly listened to the words binding her in marriage for a second time.

"Do you, Nicholas, plight your troth to this woman before God and these witnesses?"

"I do," Nick replied, voice cool, calm.

Mr. Elliot turned to her and repeated the same question. She tried to absorb the moment so she could later recall it for dissection, but it passed in a blur. She must have answered satisfactorily, for Mr. Elliot pronounced them husband and wife and Nick's hands were on her shoulders turning her to accept his kiss. His lips merely grazed hers. One second she felt their light pressure, then she was spun about and hugged by the innkeeper's wife, the woman chatting as happily as if she had not stood witness to hundreds of weddings in her back parlor.

And just like that, it was done.

She was wed to the very man who had vowed to be rid of her.

Chapter 23

They dined at a small linen-covered table in their room. She didn't know whether the innkeeper had assumed they wanted privacy or if Nick had requested the arrangement, but she could have done without the strained silence.

The bed wasn't nearly as large as hers at Oak Run, but her eyes continually strayed to its hovering presence, a constant reminder of what was to come, of the wedding night that awaited consummation. The two of them would barely fit in its tight space. They would have to sleep pressed against each other—or on top of each other. A blush heated her face at that image. She took a small sip of her claret, forcing her eyes away from the bed.

"You don't like the food?"

"It's fine." She stabbed a piece of roast chicken in an effort to appear hungry, her mind still grappling with Nick's earlier revelation. *Edmund had not desired her because he preferred men.* Not because he found her personally objectionable. Her entire measure of herself for the last seven years had been based upon that stinging rejection. Now she didn't know what to think. She was a stranger to herself. Everything she had known, everything she thought, had been based upon . . . a misunderstanding.

"If you're finished, I can call for them to clear the plates." He leaned back and patted his trim stomach. "I'm stuffed." She noted his plate had indeed been picked clean. While she silently tortured herself, he had enjoyed his dinner.

"You might as well," she sighed, belatedly realizing that brought her closer to the moment of reckoning. She should have delayed dinner as long as possible. Perhaps until daybreak. Anything to postpone climbing into that bed.

"Would you care for a bath? I can have one sent up." He set his napkin on the table.

Leaping at the chance for another delay, she nodded. "Yes, please."

When Nick departed to make the arrangements, she proceeded to unpack her wrinkled clothing from the valise. Shaking out a day dress, she hoped the wrinkles might be gone by morning.

Nick soon returned with a maid who quickly cleared away the dishes. Two boys arrived with steaming buckets. They dragged a hip bath to the center of the room and emptied the buckets into the gleaming copper tub. When the last boy departed, she looked expectantly at Nick, waiting for him to take his leave. Instead, he shut the door, sat on the bed and proceeded to tug off his boots.

"What are you doing?" she demanded, strangling the nightgown clutched in her hands.

"Undressing," he answered as if it were obvious.

"Here? In front of me?" She looked around frantically as if there might be someplace to hide. She spied the screen and pointed to it. "Use the screen."

He arched a brow superciliously. "Meredith, we're married. And we have already seen each other naked. You hardly need act the affronted maiden." His first boot clunked to the floor, quickly followed by the second.

"We've not seen *all* of each other," she hotly reminded.

He paused thoughtfully before smiling dazzlingly. "True. We'll have to set that matter to rights, won't we?"

She scowled and tried another tactic. "I thought you were going to let me bathe."

"I am."

"So why are you undressing, then?"

"I intend to wash after you." Shrugging out of his waistcoat, he motioned to the tub. "Don't let the water grow cold. Get in."

"With you in the room? No, thank you." She

flung her nightgown on the bed and crossed her arms.

"Take a bath," he snapped as if she were a wayward child and he the afflicted parent. "I assure you I won't ogle. I've seen naked women before, even at their baths. And since we are properly wed, I certainly don't intend to humor your modesty. You wanted a bath. Get in." He loosened his cravat and sent it fluttering to the bed.

"Your presence during my bath *offends* me," she ground out, dropping her hands to her hips. It took all her control not to stamp her feet. "I would like my privacy."

"Too bad." He yanked his shirt from his waistband. She tried not to appreciate the muscle and sinew rippling beneath the sheer linen of his shirt with that angry motion.

"You're being very ungracious. I simply cannot bathe if you insist on staying in the room." She grit her teeth, waiting for him to relent and leave.

"Very well. Don't," he replied, pulling his shirt over his head. "But there's no sense letting the water grow cold." His white shirt landed on the floor like a descending dove. Her jaw went slack and she salivated at the sight of his naked chest. A white-ridged scar rippled across his ribs with every movement, emphasizing his tanned skin. Her fingers itched to trace its outline.

His hands were on the buttons of his breeches, and before she had time to look away, those breeches slid down his narrow hips. She spun around but not before catching an eyeful. His low chuckle raised the tiny hairs at her nape. The mental picture of him sliding those breeches down his hips stayed with her, tormenting her as she heard a splash of water followed by his low groan of pleasure.

"Meredith, you don't know what you're missing," he called. Somehow she knew he wasn't referring entirely to the bath.

Careful not to look in the direction of the tub, she grabbed her nightgown off the bed and moved behind the screen to change, doing her best to ignore the sounds of him bathing. Unable to resist, she peeked carefully around the screen and admired his smooth, broad back. Satisfied he was concealed from the waist down, she emerged, planning to be asleep before he joined her in bed. Or at least feigning sleep.

He stopped lathering soap to stare at her as she hurried past, giving the tub a wide berth. The heat of his eyes followed her.

Turning back the covers, she lifted a foot to climb into bed when he spoke. "Would you mind bringing me a towel? I don't want to get water on the floor."

Grudgingly, she picked up one of the neatly folded towels. Careful to keep her eyes from straying to the murky depths of the water, she walked closer and handed it to him, stretching her arm so she did not have to draw too near. She stared at the towel in her hand, its worn, frayed edges a safer sight than the man before her and the temptation he presented.

"Thank you."

But he didn't take it.

The towel dangled from her fingers for a long, endless moment. Slowly, she raised her eyes in silent question.

"Are you certain you won't bathe?" he coaxed, his head resting against the back of the tub lazily. "The water's still warm." His dark gaze beguiled her. The heat from his eyes enveloped her right along with the steam rising from the tub.

"Will you leave the room?" she countered, lifting her nose in the air haughtily, indicating that would be the only way she would avail herself of the tub. At the single, blunt shake of his head, she snapped, "Then you know my answer."

He sighed. "Then you leave me no choice." Before she realized his intent, his fingers circled her wrist. With one hard yank she tumbled into the tub. Screeching, she landed on his lap, facing him. Water splashed and sloshed over the sides.

"Are you mad?" Meredith pushed at his slick chest and attempted to rise out of the tub, but her hands slipped off the slippery copper sides and she fell back in. Her derriere nestled snugly against that intimate part of him. She struggled. She wiggled. And his manhood stirred to life. Mortified, she stilled her movements and crossed her arms over the soaked front of her gown to glare at him. "Will you please let me up?"

He held both hands open in the air in a gesture of mock innocence. "I'm not even touching you."

"Right," she snorted indelicately. "But you aren't helping me out, are you?"

He angled his head to the side with an air of contemplation. Only the glint to his eyes belied such seriousness. "No, I'm not. I don't want a bed-mate that stinks."

"I do not stink." She splashed the water in indignation. "I bathed this very morning. And no one said you had to share a bed with me, anyway."

"Since you're already wet, you might as well bathe." He handed her the bar of soap.

She shook her head. "I'm wearing a nightgown." She regretted the words the instant they were out. A crafty gleam entered his eyes.

"A matter easily corrected."

Squeaking, she tried to evade his grasping hands as they dove below the water for the hem of her gown. She clutched his wrists, sending herself pitching forward, her mouth and nose colliding with his chest. She didn't care. The most immediate threat were the hands skimming her bare legs, grazing her calves, tickling her thighs, igniting a trail of fire right to the center of her. She panted against his neck, clawing at his hands as they locked on the hem of the nightgown. He pulled the fabric up, up, up . . .

Meredith sunk her teeth into his shoulder.

"Ouch!" He touched where she bit him. A fiery gleam entered his eyes as he looked up at her with his wolf's smile. "I didn't know you liked it rough, Meredith."

Her face burned at his husky murmur. Her

gown floated along the surface of the water like a pale lily pad. She tried to push the sodden fabric down, acutely aware of her naked limbs curled around him. Yet the fabric remained afloat.

His eyes were as dark and deep as the night sky outside their window as he grabbed her by the waist and forced her to straddle him. She sucked in a breath and her hands fluttered to his broad shoulders. His eyes glinted triumphantly as his manhood prodded her entrance. His hands slid to her hips, digging into the soft flesh, anchoring her to him, holding her prisoner in the shockingly intimate position. That easily . . . she was lost. Her hands ceased pushing. Her fingers curled into his flesh in a gesture of welcome and acceptance.

He entered her in one slick thrust. Meredith cried out, thrilled at the fullness of him. Her nails dug tiny half-moons into his shoulders. His hands clung to her waist, lifting her up and down as though she weighed nothing at all. The rhythmic sounds of the water lapping the sides of the tub and splashing onto the floor seemed to come from a distance far away. She felt his lips at her throat, her collarbone, through the wet, second skin of her gown. She closed her eyes. The prim, uninteresting Meredith ceased to exist. It was as if she floated outside herself, hovered in the air above them like a ghost, watching this wanton creature making love in a bath with a dangerous, beautiful man, hands clutching his wet, dark head to her breast.

She shuddered and saw spots behind her closed

lids. A strange, mewling cry rose from deep inside her. Ripples of white-hot sensation washed over her body. He surged inside her one final time, his fingers digging into her buttocks, drawing her down deeply on him. His groan filled the air. Sliding her arms around his neck, she sifted her hands through his wet hair and hugged him closer to her breast.

He scooped her up in his arms and stepped out of the tub. Water pelted the floor like tapping rain, and Meredith felt herself smile a small, dreamy grin. "I thought you didn't want to get the floor wet."

"I lied. Hell with the floor." He set her before him and pulled the wet nightgown up over her head. "I just wanted you within reaching distance." The sopping mass hit the floor with a smack. She trembled as he toweled her dry. But not from cold. She felt shaken by her loss of control. She had surrendered with such ease, so swiftly, without shame, reveling in the mating of their bodies.

He rubbed the towel over her nakedness as if she were a helpless child. All the while she avoided his eyes, embarrassed at her total surrender and afraid he could read more than lust in her eyes. As he dried her legs, she stared at his dark bent head, loving the simple sight of the dark hair curling at his nape. If he looked up then, he would doubtless see the love emblazoned across her face. Just as it was on her soul. The prospect terrified her.

"I'll have you warmed up in a bit," he murmured, his voice a husky growl as the towel arrived at her breasts, reminding her that—thankfully—she was not a child and he was not performing his task with the stoicism of a monk. The towel felt abrasive and rough, the friction chafing her nipples into hard points. He slowed his attention there, massaging the sensitive mounds of flesh until a low, keening sound swelled from her throat. He dropped the towel and shoved her back on the bed. She reached for him as he came over her. Cupping his face in her hands, she kissed him like a woman long denied, devouring his lips as he drove himself inside her. He pulled back to stare at her as he thrust a second time. She tried to control her ragged breathing and slow her wildly surging hips, hoping she did not appear the bungling novice in her eagerness.

He stilled over her. "You're mine." His voice was strained, an unnatural tremor running through it.

Body afire, she could only nod.

His fingers brushed the fine hair at her temple. "Say it," he commanded.

For all the quietness of his voice, a hint of desperation underlined the request. Must he hear her say it? She had pledged herself to him this very day. But if she agreed to this, to belong to him . . . in this moment, with their bodies merged, there was no going back. Once the words were out she could never protest intimacy again. Her bedroom door would stand forever open. Just as her heart.

"I'm yours."

His mouth swooped down, hard and demanding, picking up where the towel left off, continuing his amorous assault on her breasts. She tossed wildly beneath the hot, wet suction of his mouth. His hips began moving again and she clutched his buttocks with both hands, forcing him closer, faster, harder. The sting of tears threatened, and she squeezed her eyes tight, only the barest amount of wetness escaping the corners.

Still, as his mouth and body loved her so thoroughly, sadness lingered, hovering like a storm cloud. His words from earlier that day echoed in her heart. *Love was not part of the arrangement.*

Nick woke several times during the night. At first he told himself the novelty of Meredith curled beside him and his desire to have her again woke him.

But the fourth time he awoke with a gasping start, as if he did not know entirely where he was. Staring down at her sleeping form, he remembered. Dark smudges shadowed her eyes, attesting to her exhaustion. The shadows only heightened her porcelain complexion, making her appear fragile, not at all like her feisty self. She had been through a great deal in the last twenty-four hours. Unable to resist, he ran the back of his hand down her cheek. Dead to the world. Dawn washed the room in a pre-morning gray and still she slept on, oblivious to his touch or the approaching day.

He wrapped an arm around her waist. She

relaxed into his chest with a small sigh, and his heart clenched at the total trust she extended him even in sleep. He closed his eyes. Then opened them again to study her. Had he ever thought himself immune to her? Wide mouth slightly parted in sleep, lips bruised from a thorough loving, she was the most beautiful woman he had ever beheld.

Despite lack of sleep, he wasn't tired. He could watch her for hours. And the thought sent a bolt of panic straight from his heart to his head.

Until tonight he had been convinced *making love* was an expression a woman invented to make sex more significant, more than the joining of two bodies in a purely physical act, more than meaningless. But with Meredith, his past ceased to exist. Last night the rest of the world had disappeared. Last night he had learned the difference between sex and making love. With her, it was more than an expression.

He couldn't deny it any longer. His anger had long disappeared—if it had ever truly existed. Her deception was not so incomprehensible. Perhaps he had understood her motives all along but used his anger to erect a barrier, to keep himself from connecting with her. Looking at Meredith, he knew he loved her. The emotion that destroyed, that reduced one to utter vulnerability, that led to suffering and grief, had claimed his heart.

He could do only one thing.

Chapter 24

Meredith descended the carriage and faced the achingly familiar sight of Oak Run. The late afternoon sun broke through the clouds and cast down its beams as if in welcome. She looked at Nick, pleased to be home, pleased that he wanted them to come here instead of Town.

The front door flew open to reveal Maree's broad, smiling face. Until that moment, Meredith didn't realize how much she had missed her. She felt she had been gone a lifetime. Oak Run looked smaller to her eyes. Lifting her skirts, she flung herself in the ample arms of her housekeeper, disengaging herself when she heard Nick instruct the driver, "Just the lady's luggage. Leave mine. And see about switching out the horses."

Her pleasure faded and she turned back to him. "You're not staying?"

"I'll be going on as soon as the horses are changed."

She eyed the softly settling dusk. "But it's late. Won't you at least stay the night?"

At this, he said nothing. He didn't need to. That ready-to-bolt look on his face explained everything.

"When will you be back?" She hated asking, but found it impossible to feign total indifference at his departure.

He shrugged, averting his eyes. "Can't say."

Although the words weren't said, she heard them just the same. *I'm not coming back.*

Numbness crept over her as she stood on the front steps, watching the grooms switch out the horses. Nick stood silently by. Coach finally ready, he turned to face her again. She felt the challenge in her eyes, daring him to admit the truth, to admit he was leaving her and that he had no intention of coming back. He stepped forward as if to kiss her farewell.

She jerked back, too hurt, too furious, to let him touch her.

His mouth thinned into a grim line.

"You should go," she declared, tones ringing with angry defiance. "No doubt you have business to attend to in London. Nothing's keeping you here."

With one last probing look, he bounded up into the coach, hovering in the doorway for a moment. At last he settled on, "Take care of yourself."

She watched the coach disappear down the driveway, swiping at her cheeks and despising the hot spill of tears. Why should she weep? She had all she ever wanted: a secure and settled future for her family. She never set out to find love.

Why did she want it now?

"Running away never accomplishes anything."

Meredith looked up from her needlework and glared at her aunt, at once understanding her meaning. "I didn't run away. He did."

"Did he?" Aunt Eleanor asked archly, lips puckered. "So you told him you're in love with him, then?"

Since when did her aunt insist on honesty?

"Of course not," Meredith snapped. "Why should I? I'm not." At least she had not been foolhardy enough to confess that to him. Vowing to belong to him was bad enough.

"You most certainly are," Aunt Eleanor replied. "There's running away in the literal sense—which Nick has done. And there's running away emotionally—which you have done, which you always do."

"Posh," Meredith snorted, eyeing the tiny row of roses she had fashioned. Her trembling hands did not bode well for her stitches. She found herself wishing, not for the first time, that her aunt had remained in London instead of returning home the moment she heard Meredith was at Oak Run. Or more accurately, the moment her aunt heard she was at Oak Run *alone. Husbandless.* Again. Her life was miserable enough without her aunt's keen and somewhat ruthless observations.

Aunt Eleanor resumed her interrogation. "So, what are we doing here when he is in London?"

A smile twitched Meredith's lips. The first in days. She couldn't help herself. "We?"

She had found little to smile about since Nick's abandonment. Oak Run—her refuge, the one place where she felt secure, where the earth did not constantly shift beneath her feet—no longer filled the gap in her life. As long as he was gone, nothing could ever do that again.

Her aunt's next words chased the smile from her face.

"Seems like you've let another husband cast you aside to rot in the country." She shook her head and clucked her tongue in disapproval. "I just never imagined this marriage would turn out like the last one."

Meredith felt the blood drain from her face.

Her aunt took one look at her and rushed to apologize. "Dearest, I'm sorry. That was dreadfully insensitive."

"No. You are quite right," she murmured, hardening her heart and shaking her head from side to side.

Her aunt's face screwed tight in apology. "I—"

Meredith swiped a hand through the air,

silencing her. Aunt Eleanor closed her mouth with a small snap. Dropping her needlework, Meredith rose to her feet, looking out the French doors in mulling silence. The reason Edmund had abandoned her no longer mystified her. She even discovered a smidgeon of compassion for her deceased husband. The burden of a secret life could not have made for a happy existence.

But Nick?

No one pressured him to marry her.

He was a man with healthy sexual appetites for the opposite sex. Appetites that he had seemed happy to lavish on her. So what was the problem? *Why wasn't he here?* With her?

She possessed too much self-respect to hie off after him, begging for his love. After all, he abandoned her. If he felt something, anything beyond lust, then pride demanded she wait for him to come to her. She drummed her fingers over her mouth thoughtfully, gazing out the window as a firm sense of knowing grew inside her.

But he would not come.

This she knew as surely as the sun would set and rise again on the morrow.

Unless something brought him here. Someone. Her.

If she didn't act, the fate of a neglected wife would once again be her lot. Her heart clenched. Only this time it would be more painful, more excruciating, because she loved the husband in question.

"I know," Aunt Eleanor exclaimed, face alive with excitement. "You can feign another pregnancy, only this time—"

"No," Meredith cut in, her hand instinctively going to her stomach. "Absolutely not. I won't lie to Nick about that." It was too soon to tell, but her aunt's suggestion might very well be true. As much as the possibility delighted her, Meredith vowed that if it were true, she would not use their child to hold him to her.

"What are you thinking?" Aunt Eleanor asked, studying her face closely.

She scarcely paid attention to her aunt's question, too busy contemplating what it would take to bring Nick to her. If she could only see him again and look into his eyes, perhaps he would recognize all that they could have together, all that they could be. What could prompt such a proud man to drop everything and—

Seized with inspiration, she ceased tapping her lips and latched onto a single word.

Proud.

Nick was a proud man. At times insufferably so.

"Meredith?" her aunt called out as she rushed across the room. "Where are you going?"

"To pay a call."

"A call? On whom?" The bewilderment in her aunt's voice was understandable. Meredith had not so much as stuck her nose outdoors in the last fortnight, preferring to languish indoors where no one would witness her misery save for the household staff. Morose and pathetic, she had refused all callers. But no more. No more hiding. No more self-pity. Time to take matters in hand.

She paused in the doorway, a mischievous smile lighting her face. "I'm going to call on Sir Hiram."

She caught only a glimpse of her aunt's horrified expression before spinning away.

During the last week Sir Hiram acted like a carrion bird swooping in at the first scent of blood—or in her case, at the first scent of a newly abandoned bride. He had called nearly every day. She always relayed her excuses, hardly in the mood to curtail his ardent attentions. No doubt he had heard she returned from her elopement alone and wished to resume his old habits. The whole neighborhood knew, explaining the surge of callers, all inquisitive as to why the new bride lacked her groom.

Only this time she would humor Sir Hiram's attentions.

And make certain Nick knew about it.

Nick dismounted and left his horse standing in the drive, reins trailing on the ground. Solomon wouldn't go far. He was trained to stay put, never to stray. Unlike a certain wife of his. At any rate, what he had to do wouldn't take long.

Taking the steps two at a time, he ignored the brass knocker and pounded on the front door with his fist. The sound of crinkling paper in his pocket served as a reminder of Portia's letter and fanned the flames of his temper higher. If he closed his eyes, he could see the elegant, scrawling handwriting in his mind. He had the words memorized by now, emblazoned on his brain:

> *. . . Meredith writes she is busy with callers since returning to Oak Run, none as attentive as a certain Sir Hiram Rawlins who has been keeping her company in your absence with frequent walks and rides. It warms my heart to know that even as I miss my friend, she is in dear company . . .*

Dear company! Hah! He knew just what that bastard had in mind. A new bride, no groom in sight . . . Rawlins was up to his old tricks. Nick intended to alert the gentleman that Meredith had married a different sort of man this time. One that did not take kindly to another man sniffing about his wife's skirts.

A frazzled looking housekeeper, gray hair escaping beneath her white cap, opened the door. High-pitched screams that could only belong to young children instantly besieged him.

The housekeeper's eyes swept him hurriedly, taking in his fine if rumpled attire. "Yes, sir. What can I do for you?"

He removed his gloves and slapped them against his palm. "Sir Rawlins, please."

At that moment a woman's shriek added to the din.

"Mercy! That'd be the new governess. This way, sir." The housekeeper trotted ahead of him, not bothering to ask after his name or request his card. She simply waved at the drawing room door before darting away and calling over her shoulder, "Sir Rawlins will be with you shortly."

He waited in the drawing room, pacing its length with stiff strides. The cries from the other side of the house died down, and he guessed the housekeeper had gained control of the situation. He had heard a little of Rawlins's wayward children and that the unruly pack chased away potential wives. Too bad. The inept father could look elsewhere to assuage his needs and keep his paws off his wife.

"Lord Brookshire, this is a surprise. I did not know you were visiting Mer—" The man stumbled to correct himself, his eyes reflecting his wariness at this unprecedented visit. "—Lady Meredith."

Nick's strides were long and quick, his momentum aiding him in delivering a fist into Rawlins's face.

Rawlins hit the floor in a gratifying crash. Nick loomed over him, his chest lifting on an inhalation of satisfaction. Rawlins held a hand over his face and peered up at him in horror, clearly shocked to be struck down in his own drawing room. Very ungentlemanly. But Nick wasn't a gentleman. Never claimed to be.

"That's Lady Brookshire to you. And if I ever hear your name linked to my wife's again I'll be back." He jabbed his finger in the air. Rawlins flinched. "And this—" He flicked his hand to encompass Rawlin's prostrate form. "—will fade in comparison."

Sliding his gloves back on, he stepped over

Rawlins. A throng of servants had gathered in the doorway, mouths agape as they eyed their master on the carpet. They instantly parted and made way for Nick to pass.

He felt only slightly better. A certain lady still needed to be dealt with. Not, however, today. Perhaps never. He couldn't trust himself around her, especially in his present mood. His gut clenched just thinking how near she was. Even being furious with her for dancing the line of impropriety with Rawlins did not guarantee he could keep his hands off her. And it certainly did not guarantee his ability to ride out of her life a second time. Their last parting nearly killed him. The nights without her had been torment. He possessed only so much resolve. Nick feared he had used the last of it when he left her standing so resolutely on the steps of Oak Run. Those wide eyes, so accusing as they stared out from her pale face, haunted him.

He swung himself into the saddle, his lips tight as fresh determination filled his heart. With a nudge of his heels, he turned his horse for London.

Chapter 25

Meredith sat on her knees, enjoying the sensation of the afternoon sun on her bonnet-free head as she dug out weeds that had sprouted during her long absence.

"Meredith!" Aunt Eleanor called, capturing her attention.

She looked up, brushing loose tendrils from her face as she observed her aunt jerk to a stop before her, one hand pressed to her ribs as she struggled for speech over her labored breaths.

At last Aunt Eleanor managed to spit out, "Nick . . . is . . . here."

"Here?" She winced at the excited squeak to her voice, immediately trying to set her hair to rights by hastily tucking stray tendrils back into her top-knot.

"No," Aunt Eleanor clarified. "Cook was in the village buying capon for tonight when she saw Lord Brookshire pass through. He was seen taking the north road."

"The north road?" The two women exchanged looks of dismay. Given her recent letter to Portia, Meredith had a good idea where he ventured and why.

She shook her head incredulously, refusing to believe that he would not come directly to Oak Run—to her—but instead sought a confrontation with Sir Hiram.

Yet even as she shook her head in horrified denial, comprehension settled like a dead weight in her chest and she knew it to be true. Why had she not considered such a possibility when she first conceived the idea? Blast it! It had seemed a sufficient method to gain Nick's attention.

She prayed he would behave in a civilized manner. But she knew that was expecting too much. Although he did not love her, she did not doubt that his inherent maleness included feelings of possession. That very belief had motivated her into humoring Sir Hiram's attentions these last few weeks. Yet she had not anticipated Nick confronting Sir Hiram directly. *She* had encouraged Sir Hiram. The fault was hers. If her husband had issues with her relationship with Sir Hiram, then he should address them to her. She was not some dimwitted female to be held unaccountable for her actions.

Tearing off her gloves, she dashed to the stables, her boots pounding the earth with a vengeance. Admittedly, her fear for Sir Hiram was only second to her sense of personal indignation. Uncharitable of her, but it was nonetheless the case.

Her aunt squawked behind her, "Meredith, where are you going?"

"To knock someone's head in," she grumbled, never breaking stride.

Meredith fetched Petunia from her stall herself, not wasting the time it would take to call one of the grooms. She was in the process of saddling the mare when Aunt Eleanor arrived breathlessly, both hands pressed to her sides.

"Dearest, you're not wearing a riding habit," her aunt panted.

"It doesn't matter," Meredith snapped, ignoring the rest of her aunt's objections as she placed her boot in the stirrup and swung herself up.

"Meredith, your legs!"

She glanced at her bare calves and knees, exposed for all to see, and shrugged. "I haven't the time to change. And you know exactly why. I've been courting scandal for months now. Nick thrashing Sir Hiram will feed the local fervor and very well push me over the brink." She sighed, meeting her aunt's eyes hopefully. "Perhaps I'm wrong and Nick only wants to talk to the man. Surely he'll behave in a civilized fashion."

Aunt Eleanor's wide eyes blinked. "For goodness sake, of course he won't! This is Nick we're discussing. What are you waiting for?" Her aunt slapped Petunia's rump with determined vigor. Meredith almost lost hold of the reins as her horse lunged from the stables at a gallop.

Aunt Eleanor's cry warbled on the air like a shrill songbird as Meredith took off. "Do hurry! You must save us!" The rest of her cry faded to a distant whisper on the wind. "And Sir Hiram too!"

Meredith dismounted and hurried up the steps to where the front door gaped open. The throng of babbling servants was visible even before she stepped inside the foyer.

"Excuse me! Is Sir Hiram . . ." Her voice died away as the housekeeper stepped back from the throng, revealing Hiram Rawlins. Two servants carried him, one holding his feet and the other bearing him beneath the arms. His head lolled from side to side as if his neck could no longer support its weight. Mewling whimpers keened from his throat, reminding her of a newborn puppy.

Apparently she was too late.

Her hand flew to her mouth as Sir Hiram's nose, red and swollen, came into better view. She rushed forward to offer her sympathies, feeling wretched that what began as a ploy to gain her husband's attention had led to this. Sir Hiram, appearing to weave in and out of consciousness, recognized her and released an unmanly shriek, lurching wildly in the arms of the two servants bearing him as if a fire hot poker prodded his backside.

"Stay away from me!" He turned beseeching eyes on his servants. "Out! Get her out!"

The housekeeper faced her, face screwed tight with apology. "I'm sorry, my lady—"

Meredith held up a placating hand. "I understand. I have no wish to distress Sir Hiram. I'll leave." She paused at the door, glancing over her shoulder to ask, "The gentleman just here . . . how long ago did he leave?"

"Just a few moments before you arrived, my lady," the housekeeper replied.

"Thank you." Nodding, she hurried out.

If Nick were headed to Oak Run, she would have passed him. That meant only one thing. He was returning to London on the south road. And he had no intention of seeing her. His sole purpose in coming had been to trounce Sir Hiram. And not face her. Grim resolve hardened her heart. Unacceptable.

He would not get off that lightly.

Nick's satisfaction grew as the distance between him and Meredith lengthened. He had seen to the matter of Rawlins and not given into temptation. He was leaving without seeing her. No matter what his body and heart urged. He had met the challenge and risen above it. He was not weak. Not vulnerable. Not his mother.

The pounding of horse's hooves behind him

intruded on his thoughts, and he glanced over his shoulder to see Meredith charging toward him, skirts whipping about her thighs. The sight of her mocked his self-congratulatory attitude and sent a bolt of panic to his heart.

He spun his horse about and called out in a hard voice, "Go home, Meredith."

At the pace at which she galloped, she either failed to hear him or chose to ignore him. It made no difference. Any moment she would be upon him. He whirled back around and urged his horse into a gallop, caring little that he appeared to be running away, that he could be accused of cowardice. Desperate situations called for desperate measures. Even the most hardened army chose to retreat in times of need.

"Stop!" The wind carried her voice to his ears, but he didn't break speed.

Suddenly, a great force hit him in the back. He twisted around, letting go of his reins as he locked hold of her body so he would take the brunt of the fall. Because no question about it. *They were going to fall.* Hard.

They toppled to the ground in an undignified tangle of limbs. For an interminable moment he lay stunned, Meredith's not insubstantial weight sprawled on top of him as he stared dumbly at the gently swaying canopy of branches and leaves overhead, waiting for his body to alert him of any broken bones. After a few moments he ascertained nothing more than a pervading general soreness.

"Have you lost your bloody mind, woman?" he choked out.

Her head popped up and she glared at him through a tumble of fire-shot hair. The offending mass fell into his face. He batted at it, finally settling for wrapping his hand around the silken strands and holding it behind her head. The action thrust their faces closer, nose-to-nose. Dangerous proximity.

"No more than you. How dare you attack Sir Hiram—"

"Oh, I dare," he thundered. "Any man who dallies with what's mine shall get exactly what's coming. I'm not Edmund. I'll not tolerate another man's pursuit of my wife."

"Your wife," she mocked, eyes snapping green fire. "You are no more husband to me than Edmund."

"Liar," he hissed, rolling her beneath him in one fluid motion.

He couldn't control himself. Her words were a red flag in his face. His mouth slammed over hers in need. She matched that need, grabbing his face in both her hands and moaning into his mouth. The taste of her undid him. As he pulled back to tear free of his trousers, she made short work of shedding her undergarments. Reaching beneath her skirts, he grabbed her hips and pulled her against him. It had been too long, too many nights apart. He had to have her. No more dreaming about her and waking up in cold sweats in his empty bed.

There was nothing gentle or easy about it. He drove deeply into her womb. She clutched his shoulders, panting and crying out against his ear. He rode her hard, grinding her into the unforgiving earth, channeling all his fury, all his frustration, into every plunge.

He grabbed fistfuls of her hair and forced her glazed eyes to focus on his face. "You're my wife."

She bit her lip against her moans and nodded.

"Say it," he ground out, never ceasing his pounding pace.

"I'm your wife," she sobbed, rotating her pelvis to take him in even deeper.

Dropping his mouth to her neck, he bit the tendons stretched taut. He thrust one final time, his groan rumbling up from deep in his chest and echoing among the silent woods. For a long moment he couldn't move, could do no more than hold her in his arms and breathe in her intoxicating scent. Mint and honey. God, how he had missed it. Missed her.

Bodies still joined, he pulled back to glare at her, his fury more acute than before he tupped her in the road like a common whore. She must have read some of that fury because she took hold of his waistcoat with two clenched hands as if frightened he would pull away. If her desperate grip did not sufficiently convey her feelings, then her hoarse, "Nick," certainly did. The longing in her face and the pleading in her grip were unmistakable.

His only response was a curt shake of his head.

"You want me," she accused.

As though in agreement, his member twitched to life inside her. He wrenched free and rearranged his clothing before his body betrayed him again.

"I came here for one purpose. To set Rawlins straight on the matter of your availability. You shouldn't have followed me. This"—he gestured back and forth between their bodies—"just happened. I have to get back to Town."

Rising to his feet, he couldn't help eyeing her exposed limbs. Her inner thighs were red where he had chafed the sensitive skin. The sight only flamed his desire for her again.

"Cover yourself," he snapped.

She pushed her skirts down over her legs, her eyes large in her face as she stared up at him. "This didn't just *happen*. It was meant to happen. Just like you and I are meant—"

"Don't even say it. It was just sex. Good sex. Great. But that's all." He motioned to where she sat in the road. "It doesn't mean anything. Animals do it in the dirt."

Red suffused her face. "We're not animals."

He whirled around to find where his horse had wandered, ready to resume his escape.

"Nick!"

Sighing in vexation, he turned and watched her struggle to her feet. "What is it you want from me?" he shouted, arms spread wide in a gesture of defeat.

She opened and closed her mouth several times before choking out, "You. I want you. I love you."

For a brief instant a small flame of happiness lit deep inside him, in some dormant part of him long dead, but he snuffed it out before it had time to grow. He stared at her for a long moment before uttering the only words he could. "You can't."

"I do," she cried, eyes bright and glowing.

"*I can't,*" he bit out.

"You claim that I belong to you—" She paused, biting her lip before her voice cracked with the plea. "—well, let yourself belong to me!"

"I can't," he repeated, looking away from her. "You want what I can't give."

Her shoulders slumped, but she managed to accuse, "You're afraid. I would never have thought fear could rule you."

Nick turned his back on her again and walked to his horse, grazing by the side of the road, refusing to let her provoke him into further argument.

She stumbled after him, grabbing his arm. "Our marriage doesn't have to be like your parents'—our lives don't!"

Nick shrugged his arm free and swung himself up into the saddle. Knowing she watched, he resisted looking back, even when he thought he heard her release a choked sob.

Riding away, he told himself that it didn't matter that he left his heart behind.

Nick walked for hours. Until the sun dipped beneath rooftops and night settled on the city. He walked aimlessly, no direction in mind. The sounds of night emerged, thickening the air— sounds of revelry and carousing that marked the end of a day. When he passed the crumbling walls of Aldate, he could no longer pretend. He knew his destination. His feet well remembered the path to his old home.

Sailors, soldiers, and whores roamed the streets of Whitechapel arm in arm. Rough-looking men loitered in doorways, eyeing the expensive lines of his coat, sizing him up, clearly trying to decide whether he was a target worth testing. He met their gazes unflinchingly until they looked away, waiting, he knew, for easier prey.

His boots ground to a halt before the Ruby Cock. His head fell back to take in the dilapidated sign that hung from one hinge. It was like opening a door to the past. Eight years old again, his eyes drifted to the left and the dark alley that loomed there, beckoning him. *Home sweet home.*

Why had he returned to this place now, so many years later? Careful not to dig too deep for that answer, he entered the alley, his feet shuffling slowly forward. The twin walls pressed in on either side of him, smaller and tighter than memory recalled. But still just as dark. A passageway straight to hell. He followed the alley's curve until he stood before their old rented room. Light crept from the slits of the boarded-up window. He knocked, feeling strange doing so. Memories flooded him with such clarity that he felt like pushing the door open and simply walking inside.

He half expected to find his mother waiting for him, as if the last twenty-five years had never occurred.

When no one answered his knock, Nick did just that. With a push of his hand, the door swung inward. The overwhelming stench of urine and stale sex greeted him. Pressing a hand over his nose to ward off the pervading stink, he surveyed the room, smaller and more pitiable than he remembered. Almost as if he summoned her, a woman lay there, curled on her side with her back to him. His throat constricted at the sight of her long dark hair. It couldn't be.

"Mama?" His voice sounded strange and far away to his ears.

The woman rolled over. The face of a stranger stared at him. Of course it wasn't his mother. His mother was dead. Still, in his mind she was forever trapped in this room. The prostitute staring at him didn't possess a fragment of her beauty. She was an older woman. The haggard lines of her face told the depravity of a life long accustomed to the abuses of poverty.

She extended a hand as thin as a skeleton's. "For the right coin, I'll be anything you want." Her burst of coarse laughter further reminded Nick this woman wasn't his mother. But she could have been had his mother spent another fifteen years plying her trade in this slum. For the first time, Nick saw her death as a blessing. Better she had died when she did than suffer another day of this life.

Perhaps his mother's death had guaranteed him life, freeing him to pursue his own happiness. What kind of fool was he to throw away a chance at happiness when true happiness in life was so hard won? Just because his mother suffered— because the man she had loved destroyed her— didn't mean he couldn't find a measure of happiness, love. Love with Meredith.

Following this realization, something unfurled deep in his chest and he breathed easier. Only one thought emerged, buoying him even in the abject misery of his surroundings.

Meredith.

He'd been lucky enough to find her. Lucky enough to win her love. Only a damn fool would throw it away.

He whirled from the doorway, love for Meredith spurring him to run. Hopefully his stupidity hadn't chased her away. Sudden self-doubt assailed him, stopping him in his tracks. What if she didn't want him anymore? What if he had succeeded and pushed her completely out of his life? His future yawned before him, a vast bleak hole at the possibility of life without her. With a single hard shake of his head he resolved not to let that happen. He would prove his love—or spend the rest of his life trying. She didn't have a choice. He was hers whether she wanted him or not.

The need to reach Meredith consumed him. So much that he didn't notice the three burly figures coming at him from the shadows until they knocked him off his feet. Lying there, head reeling, the grisly appearance of his attackers took more definite shape. The features of one face in particular stood out, and Nick felt the absurd impulse to laugh. Trust life to toss up another hurdle the instant he came close to easing the gnawing emptiness inside him.

"What have we here? Looks like you lost your way," a thug sniggered, slapping a slat of wood in the palm of his hand.

"Hello, Skelly," Nick murmured, wiping the salty trickle of blood from his lip with the back of his hand.

"Caulfield," Skelly greeted, his gaunt face stretched wide in smile. "I've been waiting for this moment ever since that night you and your bitch humiliated me. Just didn't think you would make it so convenient."

"Bloody nob," another thug sneered. "Cocks always get them in trouble."

"Is that it?" Skelly asked. "Got tired of that bit of lace? Wanted to come slumming for a whore from the old neighborhood? You should have come to my place. I could have had one of my girls show you a real good time."

The three closed in, and Nick knew from the deadly gleam in Skelly's eyes that he was interested in more than a bit of rough play. He braced himself, instinct tightening every muscle to singing awareness. When the first blow came, he was ready, old instincts soaring to life as he deflected it and disabled the attacker with a kick to the groin. The fists of the others rained blows on his back. Turning to meet their attack, he made out a flash of silver in the gloom. The blade descended in an arch toward him. With a strange sense of detachment, he registered that someone was going to die.

Nick vowed it would not be him.

Chapter 26

Vicar Browne's voice droned like a bee in Meredith's ear. She tried to concentrate on his words, but it was pointless. Shifting uncomfortably on the hard pew, she refolded her gloved hands in her lap and relived her encounter with Nick for the hundredth time, wondering if she could have done anything differently. She had bared her heart and soul right along with her body on that road. The only thing was to beg. Or confess to him that she carried his child. The irony wasn't lost on her. To find herself with child after everything—

Nick probably wouldn't even believe her. True, he would know soon enough. The whole world would, but she wouldn't use their child as a weapon to hold him to her.

Sir Hiram's pew was inauspiciously vacant—or auspiciously—depending on how one viewed it. The church buzzed with titters and disapproving stares this morning, a testament to the fact that everyone knew Nick had thrashed Sir Hiram before immediately returning for London. Such did not bode well for her reputation. In everyone's eyes, his actions meant only one thing. He had cast aside his wife due to her improper relationship with Sir Hiram. Yet she didn't possess the heart to care. All she wanted was Nick. Not Society's approval.

Felicia Stubblefield sat looking very pleased in her pew. She arched an eyebrow in smug silence when Meredith risked a glance in her direction. It was evident who had a hand in spreading the rumors. Perhaps she would have minded and even sought to correct the misapprehension everyone was under concerning her relationship with Sir Hiram. Perhaps. If she weren't so numb. If she could muster a modicum of concern. Instead, she clung to the remaining scraps of her dignity and faced the front of the church.

Stares penetrated her, burning into her profile, drilling into her back. With everyone behaving as though she were some sort of fallen woman, Nick's long ago comments questioning the charity of her fellow churchgoers surfaced in her mind. He had been right. People were fickle. Society was fickle. Neighbors were quick to condemn.

A small part of her did not blame him for shunning these people—this life.

She was suddenly pulled from her musings. Not by any particular sound but rather the abrupt halt in Mr. Browne's voice. A quick look up revealed his startled expression focused on the back of the church. The heavy fall of footsteps thudded down the center aisle, a murmur of whispers following in their wake. Her pulse quickened and her right eye began to twitch. Still, she could not force herself to turn around.

At last, those footsteps stopped beside her pew. She waited one long, interminable moment, struggling against the fear and hope warring inside her. Finally, she risked a glance and swallowed a cry of dismay at the sight of Nick's bruised and battered face. He lowered himself beside her, pressing his fingers against her mouth, silencing her questions. His eyes burned brightly, drinking in the sight of her face, looking at her in such a way—

"Later," he whispered, and turned to the front of the church, giving a slight nod for Mr. Browne to continue.

Her mind reeled from his presence beside her. In church, of all places. She knotted her hands in her lap and didn't think it possible to remain silent for the remainder of the service. As if understanding her confusion, Nick removed one fist from her lap. She trembled as he laced his fingers with her gloved ones, calling her attention to the cuts and bruises marring his knuckles. What had happened to him? The back of his tanned hand stood out in sharp relief against her white gloves. She gazed at their clasped hands with nothing less than shock, as if they belonged to some other couple.

Mr. Browne cleared his voice and resumed his sermon.

She never heard a word.

His steady grip kept her from pulling her hand free. He knew she was dying to pelt him with questions. Yet he waited. He wanted privacy when he said everything he had to say. He would have preferred to look more presentable before joining her at Sunday service, but last night only brought home to him the fleeting nature of life. So, flaunting a black eye and split lip, he took his place in the Attingham village church for the first time in over twenty-five years.

And he didn't go up in flames.

In fact, he felt oddly content sitting in the Brookshire family pew with Meredith pressed to his side. As if he had arrived home. At last. The thought that he almost missed the chance tightened his heart. If Skelly had his way, he would be lying dead in that alley and not the other way around. And Meredith would never have known that he died loving her. As they filed out of church, she tried to tug her hand free, glancing self-consciously at the gawking speculation sent their way. He would have none of it. He fought a life and death battle to reach her. He was never letting her go. With a tender smile, he kissed the back of her hand and tucked it firmly in the crook of his arm. Her eyes widened. He chuckled.

Aunt Eleanor beamed at him in approval. "About time. Although you could have waited until you looked more like yourself, you scamp."

"And leave my wife languishing?" His thumb traced small circles against the inside of her wrist where her glove ended. She flushed a becoming pink. "I couldn't have waited that long," he said in husky tones that had even Aunt Eleanor blushing.

"Who are you?" Meredith leaned close to hiss as they stepped outside. "Where is Nick?"

"You'll not get any explanations from me," he replied with a mischievous smile. "Not yet."

Then Meredith gawked as Nick greeted Mr. Browne and praised him on his sermon.

"Er, thank you, my lord," the young vicar stammered, his thin chest puffing out and his face brightening a delighted red.

Nick moved to greet other neighbors, dragging a speechless Meredith with him. He did not even feel bothered at rubbing elbows with neighbors who stood by wordlessly when he and his mother were cast out. Not as long as Meredith's fingers stayed twined with his.

"Let's get out of here," he whispered in her ear. "We need to talk."

"We have to wait for Aunt Eleanor." She eyed him nervously, as if uncertain she wanted to go anywhere with a madman.

"Trust me," he assured her, catching Aunt Eleanor's eye and sending her a meaningful wink. "She won't mind."

"But we can't leave Aunt Eleanor. She's talking with Mr. Browne right now—"

"Isn't he coming for dinner?"

Meredith nodded warily.

"Perfect. She can ride with him. Or," Nick added wryly, "any of the other dozen people she's inviting."

"Nick, we can't—" Meredith paused as his words penetrated and exclaimed, "Oh, *she is not!*"

"I'm afraid she is." He nodded his head to where Aunt Eleanor now chatted animatedly to a large group of ladies, her words drifting to where they stood.

"I insist. You must come. The earl would love nothing more than getting better acquainted with his neighbors."

"Oh no," she groaned, closing her eyes.

He grabbed her hand and pulled her toward his horse.

"We can't both ride Solomon," she protested as he grabbed her by the waist and swung her up.

"Why not?" He swung up behind her.

"People are watching—"

"And what do they see?" His eyes locked with hers, the moss green pulling him in, warming him. "The Earl and Countess of Brookshire so in love and eager to be together that they're sharing a mount. They'll think it's romantic."

"Nonsense," she scoffed.

Nick hesitated, staring at the back of her neck. He brushed his hand against her nape and pressed his mouth to her ear. "It's the truth."

She stiffened in his arms and turned in the saddle to stare at him, saying in the barest of whispers, "Nick?"

His hand caressed her cheek. "I love you, Meredith. I've known it a long time. Stupid fool that I am, it only took me this long to accept it."

A strangled sob tore from her throat as she flung her arms around his neck and kissed him in plain sight of everyone. So much for a private audience.

When they came up for air, Nick brushed his thumb against her mouth. "Let's go work on filling that nursery you've had your heart set on."

She smiled wide, her face glowing as she replied, "We've already begun to accomplish that, my lord."

His heart stopped and he heard himself choke, "You don't mean—"

"Yes," she replied, looking uncertain as she studied him. "You are pleased?"

"Meredith," he sighed, cupping her face gently in both hands. "I don't think my heart could be any fuller." Gazing into the lush green pools of her eyes, he felt himself drowning . . . with happiness. "I love you."

She clutched his neck tighter and whispered against his mouth. "I love you."

The sound of clapping distracted them, and they pulled apart to observe Aunt Eleanor clapping madly, her turban in danger of sliding off her head as she nudged the two ladies beside her to join in. The two women obliged, and soon the entire churchyard was filled with applause. Nick doubted everyone knew the exact reason for their applause aside from the fact that Lord and Lady Brookshire were engaging in a most unseemly display in the Attingham churchyard.

But he knew the reason.

He was home.